Praise for *The Willie M*

These are lucid, fast-moving, provocative and mischievous thrillers, in the best tradition of the hero's quest, taking us on hurried journeys across the map of Scotland and Europe... to get at the truth. When politics has turned murderous, which is exactly where we are right now... the spectrum of possibility can be explored in a novel in ways impermissible to journalists.
Alan Riach, Professor Of Scottish Literature, Glasgow University

A gripping story. Scott has latched on to the aspects of 21st century Scotland that make it a perfect setting for a conspiracy thriller and cleverly constructed a plot that triggers associations with both the McCrone Report and Willie McRae's mysterious death, resonances that make it feel credibly tense.
Alastair Mabbott, The Herald

The Willie Morton series inhabits the uneasy and uncertain terrain between the agencies of a declining Britain and an emerging Scotland. Real politicians are sometimes glimpsed as you might expect from someone who recently worked for them... is rooted firmly in the recent past and strives for authenticity...provocative and thought-provoking.
Iain Sutherland, The National

Ask the awkward questions and you won't get answers. Investigative journalist Morton is blocked every which way by devious politicians and sinister spooks. Readers will like it when Morton goes on the run, like the heroes of Buchan... and love the yeasty end to the villain. Scott's point is well-made: on much that matters, we're too often told that we're not told for our own good.
Press & Journal

Gets down and dirty among the spooks and spies of Scottish politics... Morton has the unhappy knack of falling foul of some sinister spooks and agents acting on behalf of the British state... becomes a fast deadly pursuit across the beautiful landscape of the Highlands and Islands.
City Life

Fast-paced, tension-packed page-turner... hard to keep up with the twists and turns... Scott's ability to weave fact and fiction has created a thrilling tale which certainly leaves the reader with much to think about.
The Courier

* * *

ANDREW SCOTT

The author of twenty books, most under his full name of Andrew Murray Scott, including biographies of Alex Trocchi and John Graham of Claverhouse, his novel Tumulus won the Dundee Book Prize in 1999. Graduating in English and History, he was freelance journalist, media lecturer and, for ten years, a parliamentary press officer. *Suspect Loyalties* is the second in the Willie Morton Investigations series.

www.andrewmurrayscott.scot

Twitter / X: @andymurrayscott

Facebook/ScottishFictionAuthor

Suspect Loyalties

A Willie Morton Investigation

ANDREW SCOTT

– Twa Corbies Publishing –

First published in 2024 by Twa Corbies Publishing

© Andrew Scott, 2024

Twa Corbies Publishing
twacorbiespublishing@gmail.com

The moral right of the author has been asserted in
accordance with the Copyright, Designs & Patents Act 1988.

All rights reserved. No part of this publication may be reproduced or
transmitted in any form or by any means, electronic or mechanical,
including photocopy, recording, or any information storage and
retrieval system, without permission in writing from the publisher.

British Library Cataloguing-in-Publication Data
A Catalogue record for this book is available on request from the
British Library.

Typeset in Adobe Garamond Pro by Lumphanan Press
www.lumphananpress.co.uk

eBook version available on Amazon Kindle

ISBN: 978 1 7384546 0 0

CHAPTER ONE

This all started after a conversation with anonymous in Glasgow city centre. He was smartly dressed, middle-aged, quietly spoken, a decade or more older than me. Sane, by the looks of it, ordinary, normal – if there is such a thing. Raincoat, proper leather brogues on the wet pavement. It's always raining there and although I've always known it I had forgotten to bring an umbrella. But – this was the thing – he clearly knew who I was, and I was flattered, as anyone would be, given I was in the city to promote my book. My book. That makes me sound like a successful author... far from it! The man simply appeared behind me and began speaking. I couldn't make him out at first. He pointed to the Starbucks – we were practically outside it – and as I was early for my appointment at Waterstones, I shrugged and followed him inside, out of the rain. He bought us coffee and I admit then I was hoping he was going to ask me to sign a copy of the book; I had two copies in the plastic bag. There you have it. That's how we are ensnared. By our own vanity.

The coffee place was busy, noisy but it was possible to ignore all that and create an intimate space for private conversations. Anyway, we sat there, trading euphemisms about the rain, looking out at the slick pavements and umbrellas. I waited for him to explain. As a journalist you wait, that's what you do. Some of the best stories can come to you, all-of-a-piece and I hoped this might be one, though I didn't have much expectation of it. There are many ancient mariners out there with urgent tales of an albatross and I've met my share and then some. Well, I listened and made sympathetic noises in the right places and then he was gone, leaving most of his coffee behind and the crumbs of a blueberry muffin. A fine tale of conspiracy it was and I no wiser about his identity or his angle and certainly no idea he'd be dead within three weeks. What was in it for him, this mystic tale of criminal interventions and a rigged by-election? Who was he? He hadn't seemed insane, well, not visibly so and the information came out in an organic flow, not rehearsed it seemed to me. He believed in it. There was an intensity about him and clearly he wanted me to do something about it. He'd not selected me particularly, he said. He'd not been stalking me but knew of my investigative work in the *Scottish Standard* and seeing me on the street, thought I was just the man to look into it all. Sort of flattering I suppose. And seeing him prepare to leave, quite abruptly, after I'd had time to only ask a couple of questions, not enough to get to the bottom of it, I asked him again: 'who are you, I can't do anything without evidence…' he turned back and muttered: 'I think you might be able to work that out. But in the meantime, think of me as a well-wisher, someone as elusive…' he paused, 'as a ptarmigan,' and was gone. A ptarmigan? I looked around the café, everyone fully absorbed in their own bubble, outside the rain still coming down. I knew he'd turned right and was probably heading that way along Sauchiehall Street. I wondered if I should had gone after him, or followed him, or snapped a photo of him with my phone, but, frankly, was it worth it, for what had he given me, really? Hearsay, at best. A preposterous tale and completely unverifiable. And I had my appointment at Waterstones. I took out a pen and jotted down what he'd said on the back of the receipt slip he'd left lying on the table, the two names he'd given me. Then I looked at the front of the receipt. Cash, he'd paid in cash; no way of tracing him, even if I'd wanted to. I left Starbucks and still thinking about it, walked quickly to Waterstones.

Bookshops are pleasurable interiors, pervaded by the smells of coffee and home baking, as you linger in the hushed serious realms of exciting new fiction, wonderful new worlds waiting for you to arrive and cut the ribbon. I glanced around covertly but could not see my book, *Death of An Activist*. I didn't expect it to be on display, having been published eighteen months ago, but my publisher, Bob Cameron of Rannoch Books, had emailed me to suggest I visit to sign some copies for them, a special request apparently and he had also told me to "play it by ear" and try to get some promotion, perhaps a book signing event. I was a bit wary, Bob being prone to flights of exaggeration. The quarterly royalty cheques for the worthy tome had reduced from more than a hundred quid to barely twenty, although the book had been a big seller in the first two months of its run. Edward, the manager was in the stock room, I was told by a distractingly sweet bookseller at the main till. Shouldn't be long.

I meandered around the carousels of non-fiction, searching for my book without making it look obvious. There was very little of Scottish interest, I noticed, few books that I would consider buying, mostly twee or parochial guff and of course lots of (yawn) bipedal tartan crime. In the 'new fiction' section, I studied the blurb on the back of the new William Boyd hardback: *Ordinary Thunderstorms*, described as "a compelling fugitive chase through the dark side of modern-day London" which looked interesting though I could wait until it was in paperback. I had most of Boyd's works although I don't read much fiction.

'Are you Mr Morton?'

I turned to see a stooping bald young man in a baggy green wool sweater and heavy spectacles. His name badge read: Edward Fuglewitz, Manager.

'Hello.'

He frowned. 'What can I do for you?' I noticed his slashed skinny jeans and clumpy workman's boots tied with multi-coloured laces.

'My publisher told me to... um... he made an appointment, I believe.'

He smiled sadly. 'Appointment?'

'Rannoch Books, Bob Cameron.'

'None the wiser, I'm afraid. What was it about?'

'My book.'

He sighed. 'I'd assumed that. What is the title of the novel?'

'Not a novel. Non-fiction. *Death of An Activist.*'

'Sounds vaguely familiar,' he said, although the tone of his voice betrayed his complete lack of interest. 'I'm sure we have it. I'll just ask one of our assistants... Julie... what was it for...'

So I told him that I was under the impression I had to sign some copies for a special order. He looked dubious at this, as if it was something he'd never ever heard of, and though a copy of the book was found, one copy, no orders had been placed for signed copies or any copies. Julie the bookseller, a middle-aged academic-looking woman was more sympathetic, said she was sure it had done well, suggested, perhaps to spare my embarrassment that it had sold out, which we both knew was unlikely and neither jumped to suggest reordering it, even though I did actually suggest it. There was some kind of vague promise. Embarrassing. It came to nothing, this great trip to the bookshop in Glasgow and then I walked back to Queen Street and got on the train home, cursing Bob Cameron and Rannoch Books and my bad luck, my authorial dignity somewhat deflated.

Through the rain-streaked windows, I gazed out at the hinterland and tried to take positives from it; my book was stocked in Waterstones in Glasgow. They might re-order more stock, even a second copy. I took out the Starbucks receipt and thought again of my anonymous informant, that rare bird, Mr Ptarmigan. I'd accepted what he'd told me about the co-incidence of seeing me, that he wasn't a stalker. I remembered the series of events that had led to me writing the book; the murder of Angus McBain by a 'maverick' member of the Scottish Nuclear Installations Protection squad. It'd been a while since I'd thought about Daniel McGinley and still the memory could make me shiver. I didn't want that kind of nonsense again, the fear of agents of state stalking me with evil intent. And what the man had told me fitted into that shadow world of secrets and conspiracies, inhabited by patriots and traitors, lunatics and spooks. But McGinley was dead; I had killed him and escaped charges because it was self-defence. I was a free man and there was nothing to fear except fear itself, which is worse, a lot worse…

William James Morton got off the train at Waverley, a tall, burly man of thirty-six, craggy-featured, the collar of his dark raincoat up around his straggling fair hair, a professional journalist and former rugby player for his old school, George Watson's. It was nearly knocking-off time at the *Scottish Standard,* and he had the momentary thought of going there and having a word with his pal, the news editor Hugh Leadbetter, but thought better of it. Better to walk home though he fancied a swift pint and considering various howffs in the vicinity, decided on The Vaults. It was nearby, practically on the route home.

The Vaults is the kind of grimy, tucked-away pub, halfway down steep flights of stone steps in dim light between the High Street and Cockburn Street that only members of the cognoscenti are aware of. *Abandon hope all ye who enter here*, Morton often quoted on stooping in the unobtrusive entrance. It was a low shebeen frequented by veterans of one type or another: hacks and flacks and uncivil servants, loudmouths, shakers, fakers and mickey-takers of all description, even on occasion a woman or two. And there, unexpectedly, was his old school chum, Archie MacDonald, in his solicitor's get-up and briefcase, straight from the courts, ordering a pint.

'Good grief, it's the man himself!' Archie chortled, in that cod-public school accent he affected.

'Hello Archie,' Morton frowned. 'Not your kind of drinking hole this, eh?'

'Quite,' Archie said with feeling, loosening his collar. 'Hellhole of a place.' He chuckled. 'One's seniors would never find me here! Pint?'

'Please.'

When Archie got served, they moved over to a wooden bench near the door and sat down, pints in hand. The place wasn't yet as busy at it would be in half an hour or so. 'T'trouble at rumour mill?' Morton asked in his best Yorkshire accent.

Archie looked glum. He was putting on weight, Morton noticed, and losing his hair too, from the stresses of parenthood, overwork and under-exercise. He'd been a good wing-half in his day. Now he had two young children and a socially ambitious wife. He waggled the briefcase. 'One's client has just been sent down by the beaks despite my best efforts. I have a feeling one's seniors at Halbron, Finlay & MacDonald will not be chuffed.'

'Hmn. And how are the kids?'

'Well as can be expected. And Marion too. You're still outwith the bonds of matrimony?'

'Never again, my friend. Although last time I heard from Sally, she was dropping ominous hints about coming back to Edinburgh.'

'Thought she was safely ensconced at Canary Wharf? She's with the *Mirror*, yes?'

'I suppose so. Yes, she is, but I think property prices down there are through the roof.'

'Well, same here. Do your best to scare her off. Singleton status seems to suit you.'

'Aye, *you'll no be getting ony mair divorce fees oot o me, Mac-Donald!*' Morton growled and they laughed.

The solicitor took a deep draught of his pint. 'Anyway, Willie, better be getting back to barracks to dump these, shut up shop and then home.'

Morton commiserated. 'I'm just off the Glasgow train. Waste of time. Some business about my book.'

'Oh, the great tome? How's that doing.'

'Well, it isn't. Not any longer. Had its day,' he pulled a face. 'Rather like me.'

'Never! Think yourself lucky, old chap, you got a book out of it. All that nasty business about McBain, that brute McGinley.'

'I had a chap come up to me in the street in Glasgow today,' Morton told him. 'Quite a tale he told, and I have a feeling, a terrible feeling I'm going to be heading back into those murky depths... again. If I take it up.'

MacDonald nodded sympathetically. 'As your solicitor I

would heartily recommend you don't but I'm aware that my advice is not often heeded in such matters by my clients.'

'Does the name Roger Carnoway mean anything to you?'

'Ooh!' Archie shivered. 'Lord Carnoway of Froy. You'd do well to avoid that brute. Have no dealings with him. Keep well clear. The man is an assassin, figuratively and metaphorically, though perhaps not in person. I give you this advice for free, no fee involved. Well, must go, old chap. As they say, see you in court.'

'I hope not Archie. I do hope not.'

'But if it comes to it, Willie, my fees are, as always, reasonable.'

'Huh!'

CHAPTER TWO

Next morning, Willie Morton was slow to rise although the central heating had come on, and the bedroom was warm. Reluctantly he pushed aside the duvet and got into his dressing gown and wandered through into the small kitchen, put on the strip lights. He made himself a coffee and took it through to the living room, pulled the curtains apart in the bay window and stood looking out at the fragile pink and grey winter dawn of early January.

Through a gap in the screens, he could see down at street level cars parked on both sides of Shandon Place and part of the white roof of his own, parked near the junction with Merchiston Grove. His mind was filled with depressing thoughts about finance, or lack of it. The two-bedroom flat was too expensive. He was going to have to sell and move to somewhere cheaper, smaller. The car was an expensive luxury. He would have to find a way to pay his mounting debts. He just wasn't making enough as a freelance since he'd lost the job as Scottish stringer with *Politics Today* and had been turned down for the staff job of political reporter vacated when Danny Stark moved to the *Guardian*. Hugh Leadbetter had secretly backed him, but he suspected the malevolent hand of Alan Bailey, the senior news editor. The job had gone to a woman, a recent graduate. There wasn't much chance of another staff job at the *Standard* anytime soon. She was making a good fist of it, to be fair. He was thirty-six and needed a decent occupation, that's what it amounted to. He could get rid of the landline, bicycle, two old laptops and the car, that'd save some money. He never used the car anyway. He wondered how much he could get for it, the white VW Beetle that had been Sally's originally. He had an idea they were collectors' items. It'd have to go. He had his name on a list for a housing association flat in Heriot Street though they'd told him there could be a long wait for a vacancy.

He sat at the breakfast bar in the kitchen waiting for the toaster and thought about that abortive trip to Waterstones in Sauchiehall Street and why he hadn't been more assertive. He was going to have to email his publisher and explain what had happened. Why hadn't he been more pushy? He had done a few book events when the book first came out, though only one in Glasgow, at John Smiths up at the University, but surely there was still some interest? And that man in Starbucks... a lot of hogwash. Unverifiable certainly, although he intended to Google the two names: Neil Shankwell and Roger Carnoway when he had the time. He wasn't even sure he'd run it past Hugh because he knew what he'd say. What he needed was to recover his mojo, find some new ideas, work at it, more elbow-grease, as his dad would say.

Dressing in black jeans, clean blue shirt and warm grey merino wool cardigan, he shaved and washed. Pulled on socks, his sturdy brogues and heavy rainproof parka, gloves. He locked the door behind him. Descending the stone stairs in the dim light of the close, he anticipated the positivity of a decent walk. The front door to the street, to his annoyance, had been left open and there was a small drift of brown leaves inside. He pulled the outer door behind him, briefly glanced over at the bridge, hearing a train in the viaduct and set off at a fast pace up the hill, towards the bulk of Craiglockart Primary School. All traces of the ice had melted days before, but it was still windy and wet and cold. He was going to head in by the canal path to Lochrin Basin then cut across to Lauriston Place and through the university, a forty-minute walk.

Was it remotely likely, he asked himself, that a political party, in government at Westminster, would have any truck with rigging a by-election in Scotland just to stop their opponents from building momentum? Frowning, he remembered the Glasgow East by-election of July the previous year. The new minority SNP government had taken one of Labour's safest seats with a huge swing. Then just weeks later, the Labour MP for Glenforgan had died. As he walked along beneath the trees, flotillas of mallards scurried off into the water. A narrowboat serenely glided past him, *Neptune's Hero*, the name in red letters outlined in gold on the green painted sides.

Glenforgan was much more promising territory for the SNP than Glasgow East and from the first, the media had no doubt it too would fall to them. They had a good candidate already in place, their leader on the local council. Done deal according to the media. For Prime Minister Gordon Brown was the 'bottler' whose sulky dithering on an early election date had provoked widespread ridicule, low opinion poll ratings, Cabinet resignations and a lingering internal war between Brownies and Blairites. Morton sidestepped to avoid a racing cyclist as he approached the narrow path under the Viewforth Street bridge.

While the global financial crisis more recently had allowed Brown to claw back some credit and modestly claim to have "saved the world", the Tories had only one Scottish MP to lose, while each of Labour's forty-one MPs was nervous about rising SNP momentum. They needed Scottish votes at Westminster to have any chance of holding off the resurgent Tories in England and having 'generously' granted Scottish devolution in the nineteen-nineties did not want to be held to ransom by that overweening oily Salmond acting as a kingmaker, intent on moving the agenda on for independence.

He crossed the Leamington Lift Bridge and cut through Tollcross to the double pedestrian crossing, deafened by screaming ambulance alarms and flashing blue lights. The sound trailed off as he reached the Art College and Heriot Place. This was where the housing co-op was based, with his name on a waiting list. Rain had started but it was only light as he rehearsed what he planned to say to Hugh about his retainer, while continuing past Sandy Bell's down into the Cowgate. He had to try to get more income. He might be able to get shiftwork sub-editing. He hated subbing, he hated nightshift but would have to swallow his pride.

Most visitors and staff of the *Scottish Standard* enter by the main doors on South Bridge but for those who prefer there is a side entrance to the building in a nondescript wall in the Cowgate. This is operated by a five-digit code which was changed every week. Morton often used this entrance and enjoyed the notion that he was a man of mystery, a spook of some sort. He loved the idea he could get in and out unobtrusively from the grimy, deserted Cowgate in the time it took to press five digits on an entry pad.

The narrow corridor led him by various admin and storage rooms into the noisy pressroom where all the desks were. Above was a high panel of whitewashed windows streaked and grimy that barely emitted any daylight even in the summer. Each desk had its own lights and there were strip lights in the ceiling but it was a dingy, shambolic, untidy vaguely-industrial workplace. Morton knew that the paper had made steady if unshowy success since the bloody days of its formation as a workers' co-op based in George IV Bridge and had desperately needed new premises. Some of the staff had survived a failed merger bid for two national titles and the mass redundancies and were nervous of unnecessary further investment in their own printing operation and despatch if the *Standard* was to fly higher. It was two years since the move to South Bridge; larger premises, more staff, more ambition, more successful too.

Leadbetter's cramped office was one of several at the far end of the pressroom. It had a small window looking down at the bottom of Blair Street and a six-storey student hostel in the Cowgate. Most of the room was taken up by a large, old-fashioned desk and swivel chair and piles of newspapers. He knew that the editor used to stand at the window, which he would open, and smoke cigars 'outside' there, in flagrant contravention of smoking laws. Leadbetter had been supportive of Morton's career, so such quirks had to be tolerated. He saw that the office was empty, looked at his watch and realised the editorial meeting must have overrun. Alan Bailey, the senior news editor, was looking at him. 'Bow-tie Bailey' was an odd relic of the carnage that had beset the world of Scottish journalism over the past decade and many suspected him of being a nark of some sort, there was that about him, an odd insouciance or confidence and he'd survived on his wits from senior job on one title to another, defying gravity somehow.

Bailey seemed to smirk at him in passing. 'Meeting's just broken up.'

Morton nodded. It had been Bailey's intervention that had stopped him getting the staff job. That's what the smirk meant. Then he heard doors open and Leadbetter's guffaw preceding him along the corridor.

'Here's trouble!' the editor, a big-bearded bear of a man, grunted, bowling towards him. 'How did your book event go?'

Morton tutted. 'Not great.'

'Didnae like ye in Glesgie? Shame. Right, what can I do for you, my son? Come on in.' He stopped in the doorway. 'Ah, I see the maid's been.'

'How can you tell?' Morton deadpanned. 'Oh, the ashtray's been emptied.'

'Whit ashtray, Willie, eh? Somebody been smoking in here? I'll have their guts for garters!'

He plumped himself behind his desk as Morton perched on a stack of papers opposite him in front of the window. The weak light cast his shadow on the insipid limey-green wall behind the desk.

'Story?' Leadbetter asked, leaning back. The chair creaked. 'You ken I'm willing, and able, to take more stuff from you? I'll give you some leads if I can. Might even pay you.'

'I know, and I might have something, but first… Bow-tie just smirked at me. Says everything. It was him who…'

Leadbetter rummaged in his beard reflectively. 'I believe it was. I put in my tuppence worth.'

'I was thinking… how about I take on some sub-editing shifts. Just to get me sorted, to tide me over the next few months.' He looked up. 'I need the money, frankly.'

'Aw jeez, really, man? That's nightshifts. A waste of talent. Investigative features is what ye're good at and I had high hopes… ach, Willie, really, it's come to this? I didnae think things were this bad. Wait – ye've a story idea, naw?'

Morton nodded. 'Aye, well, maybe… the usual unlikely shot in the dark… probably will come to nothing more than sheer speculation and gossip…' He briefly outlined the information he had been given in Glasgow the previous day.

Leadbetter's eyes bulged incredulously. 'Ach, rubbish, man... whit? They'd sue us for everything we've got. A government involved in rigging a by-election. How? Why? Naw, drop that one, Willie. Look, I can get you subbing shifts if things are really that bad. Maybe two or three weeks if ye're up to it. We're always a bit strapped there. It's slave labour of course, but ye ken that. Anything else I can dae ye for?'

Morton thought quickly. 'Um... I'm thinking of an interview-type piece with Ailsa McKinnon of Labour's Scottish Executive on Mandelson coming back as a fixer.'

Leadbetter sneezed into his hand and frowned. 'Rather treading on Rami's toes? McKinnon of the GMB? Has she agreed?' He wiped his hand with a tissue.

'Yes,' Morton lied. He'd phoned her and it was possible, though not certain.

'What's her beef?' He tossed the tissue into the wastebasket.

'Can't stand Mandy. She's a die-hard Brownie.'

'Aye, well, but you'd better speak to Rami first, explain it as an interview offered to you. Maybe Rami can add an op-ed on the side? You don't want to give the impression of sour grapes.'

'Okay. Let me know when I start the subbing, cheers for that, Hugh.'

'Nae bother. Keep me informed.'

Morton moved to the press room and sat down at the spare desk allocated to freelancers. He Googled the two names. There wasn't much on Neil Shankwell, several hits in the US, Brazil and Sydney, one in Glenforgan with links to a local newspaper story about the council and the GMB trade union. Okay... But the other name, Archie's brute, Roger Carnoway was none other than Lord Carnoway of Froy, a member of the highest legal circles, insider in the British establishment, elite member of the Supreme Court and of the Loyal Obsequious Company of Queen's Bowmen. There was a rather camp picture of him in green livery and bow and arrow with feathered hat alongside Princess Anne. Well, Morton scratched his chin, thinking it was hard to see what connection, if any, there could be between the two names. He jotted the information briefly in his notebook and left the *Standard* by the front entrance on South Bridge into the raw salty wind. Walking briskly across the Royal Mile, he crossed the wide chasm above Waverley Station on the viaduct. He had considered – and discarded – the notion of heading over to Great Frederick Street to see Bob Cameron at Rannoch Books. He couldn't face it. He continued to Leith Street heading north into Broughton Street and the basement offices of the GMB trade union.

CHAPTER THREE

Ailsa McKinnon was the only person in the office, she said, buzzing him into the small subterranean front reception area that doubled as a storage space for cardboard boxes. He stood and waited, in the dim light from the street, six feet above the window, hearing sounds of a telephone conversation from one of the small rooms, not quite loud enough for him to hear what was being said. He gathered it was a personal call. McKinnon was a rising star of Scottish Labour, a hardline union militant whose ascendancy was very recent, dating from the reluctant hand-over of power from Blair to Brown. She had a fearsome reputation as a scourge of Blairites and Tories and a record as an organiser of winning pay claims for workers in the public sector by threatening strikes. Finally, he heard the phone being put down.

'Right, Willie,' she said, coming into the room, 'what's it about, now? I tellt ye ah wis busy. As ye can see we're short-handed.' She stood with arms folded, sleeves of the red and white GMB sweatshirt rolled up to the elbows. He noted the trademark black leggings tucked into green Doc Marten boots.

'Of course,' he said. 'You said you might…'

McKinnon grinned. 'Ah, ah did, so ah did. C'mon through.'

The small but tidy office was packed to the ceiling with shelves of foolscap box folders and thick wads of documentation. There were some GMB posters, a framed print of someone familiar; he thought it might be Jimmy Maxton, speaking on Glasgow Green to a sea of cloth caps.

McKinnon sat behind the desk, neatly piled with folders, books and a portable radio, bakelite old-fashioned phone, pens. 'Right, chum, what was it ye wanted again? Ye're wi the *Standard*, yeah?'

'That's it. You said you might do an interview on how things are going.'

'Hmn,' she frowned. 'For the *Standard*? I usually only talk to the *Record*, or the *Guardian*, of course. Anyway, what does "things" mean?'

'Whatever you want it to mean. The Glenforgan by election victory, Mandelson back in the cabinet…'

'Prince o fuckin Darkness! Don't tempt me!'

'Iron Broon saving the world… whatever.'

'Aye, well, he did better than the media thought, that's for sure.'

Morton took out his dictaphone and pressed the 'on' switch and sat it on the desk. McKinnon looked at it and at him and snorted. 'Christ, beam me up tae CNN!'

Morton smirked. 'As a Brownie you must be pretty pleased with the way things went at Glenforgan? An unexpected victory.'

'No really. The voters there had the guid sense tae realise the double-whammy coming their way from the SNP council's home-care charges and other daft notions. They wanted tae send a clear message tae smug Salmond that Scotland jist cannae go it alone, no at a time o global crisis. They realise what Gordon has done at the G20 summit tae stabilise the economy.'

'Yes, your Glenforgan campaign concentrated on local issues; negative scaremongering about the local council,'

Morton said, frowning. 'You can't surely count it as an endorsement of Brown's leadership?'

'Of course it is! Look at the polls. He's up.'

Morton inhaled deeply. 'Well... still looks like you'll lose when the general election comes around. And the full impact of the recession is yet to hit the voters. And what do you say to the idea that the small upturn in the polls is due to Mandelson coming on board and Blunkett, rather than Brown's leadership?'

McKinnon laughed. 'I see what you're getting at. When we're down in the polls it's all Gordon's fault but when we win, it's not Gordon's victory! Can't have it both ways.'

'You were personally involved in the by-election?'

'Oh aye, I did a heck o a lot of door-chapping. I always thought we'd win. We'd the better candidate.'

'Why then the delay for three months in calling the election? The MP died in August. I heard you had a struggle to find someone to stand.'

'Nonsense. Malcolm Cook was always first choice.'

'He spent the whole campaign claiming he wasn't a politician!'

'He didn't mean... he meant he was a conviction politician no a bloody careerist. He stood because he felt he could beat the nats, and they needed to be beaten.'

'Okay, so if the result is a ringing endorsement of Brown, does that mean that the internal coup against him is dead?'

'Internal coup? Ye've obviously got better information than me. I'm only on the Scottish Executive!' She laughed and Morton found he was enjoying the sparring, a kind of polite wrestling match but he needed something more for a story.

He tried another angle. 'I mean following the resignation of Purnell, the Work and Pensions Secretary, the disastrous Euro

Elections result in June, the fact that Mandelson "dripped pure poison" about Brown to Osborne, just a couple of weeks before he got called back to serve in Brown's government, the rumour that he told David Miliband a month ago Labour could not win an election with Brown in charge…'

'Ah well, he just has!'

'The general election they meant. And Blair too… behind a huge build-up of ministers and backbenchers who believe Brown will have to go. Not least, Tessa Jowell telling him last week to consider his position.'

'Tessa Jowell…' McKinnon grinned. 'No even a minister anymore.'

'So you believe Brown can lead Labour to victory in England?'

'What's the alternative? We've been through eighteen years of the Tories.'

'And ten years of Blair.'

McKinnon pulled a face. 'Don't remind me. Ten wasted years. Foreign wars and anti-trade union legislation, palling up with Bush. WMD for fucksake! Gordon is different. He's on our side.'

'He backed the Iraq war. And everything that Blair did. Come on, Ailsa, even wee Dougie Alexander, your election co-ordinator, thought you'd lost Glenforgan. He was given a special briefing for the media because he was out in Bahrain, based on extensive exit polls taken by Labour agents at several big polling stations right up to the close of poll, for goodness' sake.'

McKinnon shrugged. 'So what, we won. Maybe I'm more in touch with the grassroots?' She grinned. 'And my parents live in the constituency. Malcolm Cook is a fine MP.'

'Okay, were you involved in Glasgow East in the summer?'

'I'm always involved, me. Yes. I was there a few times.'

'So how did you lose that so disastrously and yet hold on to Glenforgan? What do you think is the reason? It must have been the same activists, the same teams. What went wrong there that went right this time?'

'I don't know. We won, we lost. That's politics. Look, eh, Willie, I've got work to do. All I can say is the GMB plays its part, we had lots of members active in both campaigns.'

'By the way,' he said, closing his notebook, 'does the name Neil Shankwell mean anything to you?'

'Nuh. Who he?'

Morton watched her face closely. 'Isn't he a GMB steward in Glenforgan?'

She looked away, just for a second. 'Oh, yes,' she said, 'Neil, of course. What of him?'

'He works for Fife Council in Glenforgan.'

'Does he? He's a steward somewhere there, I think. I don't know all our guys personally, you know.' She smiled. 'Big organisation.'

'But, Ailsa, you have family in Glenforgan and as you said you're more in touch with the grassroots there. Well, this guy…'

McKinnon laughed. 'Yeah, yeah. Not sure what you're wanting me to say. Anyway, I need to cut this short and get some work done. Hopefully you've got what you need?'

'Well, okay,' he said, reluctantly. 'Might have to use the interview as part of a wider piece that I'm doing with my colleague Rami El-Jaffari.'

'Whatever, right, cheers Willie, can you make your own way out? Bye.'

Morton walked briskly to the end of Princes Street and caught a bus that toiled westwards and down the Dalry road into Gorgie. He was thinking about the importance of by-elections in political history. They were seen as pivot points, useful dramas cited by the media as crucial evidence that power and momentum was shifting from one side to another, even when turnout was very low. Often their effects were exaggerated and hyped up and so later were seen as meaningless, a sign of voters' petulance or a moment in time of temporary mass insanity. It had been clear for several years that power was shifting away from the Labour leviathan in Scotland, slowly but remorselessly. The Iraq War had played a big part as had the perception that to get into government and win elections Blair had assumed the Tory mantle, that Labour in government had become the Tories, that there was no difference between them, the Punch and Judy Show as his dad called it. Morton's dad had been an independence supporter since the war years. Maybe he'd chat about it on Sunday when he visited his parents? If he could drag the old man indoors out of the potting shed, that is. He smiled, thinking fondly of him. He got off the bus in the Slateford Road and hurried home. Back in his kitchen, he prepared some lunch and a cup of coffee and switched on the radio. The third item on the BBC Scotland News astonished him: *An independent investigation is being carried out after marked electoral registers for the Glenforgan by-election were lost by the courts...*' Morton had nearly dropped his coffee mug as he stood up and went over to turn up the volume. '*The registers, the only record of who voted on 26th November... must be kept for a year... nationalist MSP Janet Kirkwood said the blunder was "beyond belief." The Scottish Courts Service confirmed an external investigation would be carried out into the incident. Scottish Labour backed calls for a probe into "why an SNP government managed to lose confidential personal data."*

Morton stood at the breakfast bar with his cup of coffee, feeling intense irritation that he had not known about this earlier when he spoke to Leadbetter and interviewed McKinnon. Well, well, what did it mean? Would Neil Shankwell know anything about it?'

CHAPTER FOUR

Two days later, the independent investigation concluded that the marked electoral registers for the by-election at Glenforgan, kept in bin bags in the basement of the Sheriff Court, had been thrown out with the rubbish sometime between the end of November and early January. Morton smiled wryly. The true value of democracy! Human error and management failure were to blame, according to the Inquiry, quickly carried out by former Crown Office deputy chief executive Tom Stonehouse. There was no malicious intent but he recommended stronger security measures in future. The SNP were predictably outraged, Labour blamed it on SNP incompetence: the Scottish Court Service was a Scottish government department, but no-one suggested, publicly at least, that it was anything other than an unfortunate accident.

Morton and Rami El-Jaffari had been busy in the intervening period, contributing to several news features in the *Standard* on the investigation and the wider political reactions. They had compared the impact of the by election victory on the embattled Brown's prospects in a general election to the first public setback for the Salmond minority government. Sources within Labour had said there was such 'euphoria' in Number 10 about the unexpected Glenforgan result that the Prime Minister had briefly considered calling the early general election he had 'bottled' the previous year. The SNP had lost but had longer-term momentum. Both parties had been able to claim some credit but the Tories, in third place, stood to lose their single remaining Scottish seat if the result was replicated more widely at a general election. Morton had been able to use some of the interview material from Ailsa McKinnon and some of his theories about by-elections as 'over-hyped' pivotal moments. At least that was some income, though he was scheduled to start sub-editing nightshifts next week.

He called in to the office early on Friday morning to speak to Rami about the possibility of a new piece on the outcome of the investigation. She was at her desk, talking on the phone, dark hair in braids with silver and purple beads throughout. He waited till she was finished. She swung herself round on her chair to face him, eyes dark and humorous through purple spectacles.

'Piece looks okay,' she said, jotting something down on a pad, chunky rings on every finger. 'I thought about an update in the light of the Inquiry's conclusions today, but Hugh says the News team will cover that. There doesn't look like much more we can do at the moment.'

'I might do a little digging,' he told her quietly.

'Oh, yes?' she rolled her eyes at him and smiled. 'Do tell.'

He tapped his nose and grinned. 'Later.' He coughed. 'Might be nothing in it.'

'Keep me informed, Willie,' she said, swinging back to her screen, beads clinking.

It was a short downhill stroll via the Royal Mile to the Kilderkin on the Canongate. The bistro was practically empty at 11am., a few patrons on coffee or half-pints. He ordered a Peroni and sat up at the window, feet on the metal bar, watching the street, his coat draped over the adjacent seat back. A few minutes later, he spotted the tall, spare figure of

Janet Kirkwood MSP, in a dark coat, white scarf and sheepskin mittens, blonde hair visible beneath an oversized white tammy. He watched her leaving the parliament by the Queensberry side entrance, stepping across the road towards him.

He had met her once before during the Open Day garden party at Holyrood prior to the opening of the third session of the parliament in 2007. His father knew her. Although tipped for ministerial office in the minority SNP administration, she had instead been made chair of the Finance Committee, perhaps because she had been an accountant prior to election.

'Janet, thanks for coming,' he said, standing up. 'What would you like to drink?'

'Latte, please,' she said, divesting herself of her coat, scarf and hat.

'Anything with that? Croissant?'

The politician smiled sweetly, rearranging her hair. 'Ah, go on then.'

When they had had settled and shared some small talk, Morton began to question her about the by-election. 'As the local MSP you must have been pretty heavily involved on the ground, I suppose?'

'Oh yes, I acted as mentor to Jamie, along with Graeme Sim from our Comms team. You'll know him?'

'A wee bit. How seriously do you take this story of missing registers? I mean, I've seen your comments, but privately, do you think…?'

Kirkwood toyed with the silver Celtic knot medallion that hung around her neck on a slender chain above the white blouse and grey woollen tailored jacket. She exhaled slowly. 'Don't quote me, but no. I have to say it's unlikely. I mean, dirty tricks… you wouldn't put past them, but rigging an election… can't see it really. I mean how could it be done? We were at the count; we took voting samples.'

Morton waited. Took a sip of his Peroni. 'Well, it's just… I had some information given me, suggesting it had been rigged.'

'Really?'

'A few days ago. Before news of the missing ballot papers and registers became known. I thought it was nonsense at the time, of course, but now, well, I'm starting to wonder.'

'And where did the information come from?'

'Oh, well, I… can't reveal that at the moment. Does the name Neil Shankwell mean anything to you?'

Kirkwood frowned. 'What… the GMB steward, yes. I know him. Did he give you the information?'

'No. But my source mentioned him.'

'Curious. He's a Labour man of course, works in the council admin department, I think.' She reflected. 'Maybe in the electoral registration office… you don't think…?'

Morton sipped his beer. 'What about Lord Carnoway?

Kirkwood laughed. 'Hardly. The Tory magnate? One of the bewigged elite. Back in the day though, when I was first involved in elections, he was just a humble millionaire, stood for the Tories somewhere, never elected though. I've never met him and frankly am unlikely ever to do so, even if I wanted – which I don't! What's his connection to Shankwell, or Glenforgan?'

'Indeed,' Morton murmured. 'That's what I'm trying to find out. But basically, Janet, as we've said in the *Standard*…'

'I read it, Willie, faithfully. I read it every day!'

'Everyone seems to accept everything's been above board, just the swings and roundabout of normal elections, the fickle electorate?'

Kirkwood chuckled. 'Well, I wouldn't subscribe to that

notion, Willie. "Fickle electorate?" After all, we are now in government and gradually overtaking Labour.'

Morton nodded. 'And they must know this, the steady loss of influence, the seemingly remorseless rise of support for independence, both maybe caused, or exacerbated, by the expenses scandal. I think that's fuelled your rising poll figures. The disgusting spectacle of Westminster MPs' snouts in the trough. I mean, quite apart from Labour's manifest implosion as a failing government at Westminster. Everyone knows Brown has no chance of holding on in a general election.' He studied her face. 'They know this, Janet… and you think they will just accept it? Do nothing except normal electoral activity? That they won't try anything… dodgy?'

'Ha ha, well, they are dodgy enough, already!'

Once Kirkwood had left, to return for Ministerial Questions in the Chamber, Morton rang the phone number of the Scottish Court Service and asked to speak to the chief executive who had commissioned the Inquiry. He couldn't get through to her. The assistant told him she "wasn't accepting calls" and that he should email his queries and gave him the email address. He read Tom Stonehouse's report in full. They had been unable to precisely determine when and how the documents were lost. They included ballot papers, counterfoils and marked registers and some had been kept in bin bags, other material in properly labelled boxes and stored in the basement with broken furniture. Contractors had been given access to move court documents in crates – so they could not say for certain who was involved or when the material had been disposed of between the last week in November and early January. The whole thing sounded to Morton downright sloppy. Anyone could have gained access to the basement.

Election material had been treated rather casually to say the least.

He left the Kilderkin and was walking up the Canongate when he spotted Paul Symons across the street. He dodged through the traffic. 'How ya doin, Paul?'

The lanky aide stopped to look at him, took out his earbuds, eased the shoulder strap of his heavy rucksack. 'Willie. Yup, all is good. You goin my way?'

'Yes, back to the office. You on an early lunch?'

'Finished for the day. They only pay me the equivalent of three days a week in the parly,' Symons explained, 'the rest of the time, I'm in the constituency office.'

'I'd forgotten. Anyway, how's things in the Brownies?'

Symons adjusted his heavy specs and snorted. 'Pretty dire.'

'What? Even with the Glenforgan result? Thought you'd be cock-a-hoop?'

'Ipsos has the Tories fourteen points ahead of us. Brown, Darling, Balls and Alexander are at each other's throats, while the Dark Lord holds their coats with Blair giving him instructions in his earphones!'

'Were you at the by-election?'

'No. I didn't go.'

Morton laughed at his crestfallen expression. 'Would it be true to say you're a tad disillusioned?'

'Don't quote me, Willie, please!'

Back in the *Standard* office, he used the computer on the spare desk and began researching Fife Council. It took him only a minute to find a picture of Neil Shankwell on the council website. He was Deputy Returning Officer! *What?* And Ailsa McKinnon had not met him? Pull the other one! What was going on? Hugh was out so he'd dig a little further before speaking to him.

CHAPTER FIVE

But Morton had more immediate problems of his own. His ex-wife, Sally Hemple, had decided to return to Edinburgh for 'a day or two' and he'd rashly agreed to meet up with her at the station. She'd booked into the Balmoral. Of course, she had. He'd not had any contact with her for nearly six months, although he was aware of her on TV every now and then on that ghastly gameshow where everybody seemed drunk and deeply in love with themselves. He never read her columns because he never went near the two disreputable muck-raking tabloids she worked for. She was still in her Kensal Rise maisonette he supposed. They'd lived in Leith for most of their brief marriage until 2003. Four years ago, their divorce had been made final. He glanced at his watch. He had enough time to stroll down there, and most likely the London train would be late anyway. He sat at the desk and considered. How did it all tie up? The informant Ptarmigan had suggested the election was rigged, days before the shock news that the marked-up election registers were missing and were thus uncheckable. What did that mean? Presumably the result declared on the night could not now be verified, but had the ballot papers themselves been lost? He looked again at the original news report. It only referred to marked registers. The new press release from the Inquiry referred to registers but the BBC online report referred to: 'a number of documents relating to the by-election, including ballot papers and counterfoils…' The report concluded: 'The investigation also found ballot paper accounts, rejected papers and verification sheets were missing.' Morton puzzled over this wording. Ballot papers, yes, but what were ballot paper accounts? Or was there simply a missing comma? Should it have read *ballot papers, accounts, rejected papers…*? There was an ambivalence of the language, an irritating lack of precision. He glanced again at his watch. Time to go. He logged off the computer and drew on his raincoat and left the building.

Waverley Station was a favourite haunt of his boyhood days and his father; an engineer had often taken him there simply to watch the trains. He loved trains and the romance of train travel, bought into all that, although the train he was waiting for was bringing his ex-wife whom he didn't really want to see. He knew there'd be some sort of gloating over her success and his lack of it. She was shallow, superficial, they were chalk and cheese. Beer and champagne spritzer, meringue and mince pie… The last time he'd seen her she still had that cropped spiky platinum hairdo that reminded him of Dudley D. Watkins' Oor Wullie. Not that he would mention that. The train was nearly fifteen minutes late but when it finally nosed into the station, he knew to look for her in First Class. That was another thing. He'd never consider travelling anything other than economy, even if he could afford it, on principle.

Finally, he saw her getting off, a petite figure in a short skirt, suede jacket and high-fashion heels having already co-opted a man to assist her down from the train onto the platform and help with her lumbering suitcase. The man obviously thought he was in with a chance, but she had dismissed him with a wave before Morton arrived, noting with interest the platinum crop was gone. She'd let her hair grow and it was the shade of light brown he remembered from when they first met, him at the *Edinburgh Evening News*, her newly taken on to cover teenage fashion at the *Daily Record*. A lifetime ago.

'You made it.'

'Hello Willie. It's good to be back in Auld Reekie!'

'Could you not have found a bigger suitcase?'

She skewered him with a look. 'Still the sarcasm? It's got wheels. You wheel it.'

'Ah yes, we've been told about these newfangled contraptions…'

'Huh!'

'There's a lift to the Balmoral over there,' he told her, towing the case along.' Takes you straight in.'

She clacked along the platform beside him, a head lower than him. 'That's handy, and we'll be in time for afternoon tea.'

Morton turned and crooked his little finger. 'I've been practising all morning!'

'Oh you. Anyway, I'm looking forward to a real catch-up.'

'It's just a holiday, is it? You've not been sacked?'

'Willie, be serious.'

'No, I'm acutely aware how much carnage there's been in the tabloid world.'

'Well, that's true, but I've been very fortunate. And I've diversified. I do lots of other things, lot of TV and that kind of stuff.'

'Yes. *Woman Talk*. I've seen a few of those and that gameshow thing.'

Sally Hemple laughed. 'So not your thing, Willie!'

The elevator took them slowly up into a rear reception area of the famous Balmoral Hotel with sunny windows between elaborate columns and lilac-coloured drapes giving a view of the former *Scotsman* building beyond the railway station, and the rising silhouette of the castle in the west.

'Nice!' Morton commented, tugging the suitcase towards the main reception area. He'd never been inside the place before, it was well above his paygrade, the sort of place where toffs, successful gangsters and rap artists could be found. There were white pillars and columns everywhere, holding up foliage, statues in alcoves, framed paintings; very rococo he thought, or Georgian. He had no idea really about design. He saw a sign to a whisky-tasting room and smiled, liked the sound of that.

As Sally checked in and a porter took her and the case up to her room, he waited on a chaise longue in the central atrium, where light poured in illuminating polished brass and muted fabric drapes and in the stained glass behind the grand staircase, he saw small lion rampant motifs. He was suitably impressed.

They took afternoon tea in a grand room where the tiny sandwiches and cakes sat invitingly on silver tiered stands and the rosy colour of tea pouring from a silver-plated teapot was caught in the light as waiters and waitresses hovered discreetly. It was muted, discreet, background noise rarely above a vague murmur.

'How are your dad and mum, Willie?'

'They're keeping fine. Yours?'

'Oh yes. They're in Majorca now, of course.'

'I remember.'

'I'm going to be seeing Muriel, remember her?'

'Yes, what's she doing now?'

'Got married, three kids, lives in Davidson's Mains. And Tessa Thorne.'

'She's with the *Sun*, isn't she?'

Sally laughed. 'She's Scottish editor, Willie, as I'm sure you're aware. She's always on the box. A survivor, rather like me, I suppose. We talk on the phone now and then. I haven't seen her for an age. And a few others you won't know. Anyway, how about you? Working on anything big at the moment?'

He cleared his throat discreetly. 'Few things. Resisting the offers to take up a staff position,' he said. 'Prefer freelancing.' He grinned. 'It's all I know.'

'And you're good at it, I hear. And you work with this new political reporter, Rami…?'

Morton blushed. 'Um, yes, Rami El-Jaffari. We're doing joint by-lines now and again.' He wondered if she was trying to catch him out in a lie. Had she been speaking to somebody? And if so, why? Did she know he'd missed out on that opportunity?

'Still living in Shandon Place?'

'Yes, well, it's a few streets away from mum and dad. Handy. I'm thinking of moving soon, actually. And you're in Kensal Rise?'

Sally smirked. 'I still have that place, but mostly I stay at Oliver's in Westferry. Handy for work. Two stops on the DLR.'

'Oliver? You're seeing someone?'

She smiled faintly. 'A while now. He's a corporate executive with Reach PLC, divorced, no kids, we're planning to get a place together somewhere central maybe and sell our own places.'

'Wow! Big moves. Good for you.' Morton was thinking of the eye-watering sums that would be involved. He wouldn't want that kind of lifestyle even if he could have it, too much risk, too much debt.

'And you're not seeing anyone at the moment?'

'Too busy being me,' he grinned deprecatingly. 'It's a full-time job.'

'Don't put yourself down,' Sally reproved. 'You still look

good for your age. I mean, fit, remarkably slim. I'm surprised you're not dating.'

'I didn't say I wasn't dating,' Morton said smartly, 'just that I'm not seeing anyone at the moment.'

'More tea?' she asked, pouring herself another cup. 'You haven't had a cake.'

Morton laughed. 'Not really a cake person. Another cup would be nice.'

Sally reached up to pluck a dainty pink and yellow confection off the stand. 'Oh well, if you won't, I'll have to… Anyway, apart from the *Standard*, what other work do you do?'

Morton felt under pressure to impress. He sighed. 'I'm still Scottish stringer for *Politics Today* although that's beginning to fail, I think.' He wondered if she knew that had already gone. He shrugged. 'Heavy competition from *Current Agenda*, *Total Politics* and up here, *Holyrood* magazine. How long it'll last, I don't know. I'm putting out feelers to some of the foreign news agencies. And my book is still out there of course. Had to go over to Glasgow early in the week to sign copies.'

'That's been out a while now. Still selling?'

'Tailing off a bit now,' he admitted.

'So it's a struggle making ends meet?' Sally suggested sympathetically.

'Well… it always is. I mean, for everybody.'

'I blame Gordon Brown.'

'Yeah, he's the one to blame! The Great Sulk.'

'Least he's not a braying donkey like Blair!'

'I thought you'd approve of B.liar?'

Sally hesitated. 'We did, but… it's those teeth, that manic grin. I think he's actually insane.'

'Oh, let's change the subject… shoptalk!'

From the front entrance of the Balmoral, Morton crossed the main road and headed quickly into Broughton Street and down the steps to the GMB offices and pressed the entry phone. He was buzzed into the chaotic front office, where several staff were emptying cardboard boxes, counting wads of leaflets into plastic bags.

'Come to lend a hand?' a burly man in denim shirt asked.

Morton laughed. 'Ailsa in?'

'I'm here,' she called, from the back office, 'but busy. Who is it?'

Morton pushed through. She was in teeshirt and denim dungarees, black hair coiffed into a bandanna, from which a few locks escaped, flushed and hot from physical exertion.

'Oh, it's you again. Good grief! What now?'

'Sorry to bother you again. Is it possible to have a wee word?'

'Phoo! Really? We're up to our armpits here, Willie. Is it that important?'

'Won't take a moment. In private, though.'

'Oh aye?' she winked, hands on hips. 'Come through to the staffroom.'

It was a glorified cupboard with a single narrow window looking over an unkempt, shaded backyard, four seats filling most of the floor space, a steel sink under the window with a small table large enough for a kettle on a melamine tray and four mugs. There was no room to stand, so they sat opposite each other, about two feet apart.

'I'd offer you tea, but… anyway what's so important?'

'Neil Shankwell.'

'What about him?'

'You didn't tell me he was Deputy Electoral Returning Officer… and nor did I know then that the marked-up registers had gone missing!'

'Oh… but I didn't know that. I mean about the registers.'

'You said you knew him. He was one of your stewards, but you didn't tell me….'

'I vaguely knew he was in the electoral registration department, Willie, but you didn't ask me where he worked. I told you he was a GMB steward. That was the most relevant thing to me.'

'You can see how it looks,' Morton said. 'It's starting to look quite fishy.'

'I don't see that. Anyway, what's this to do with me? Or Neil, even? And… I understand it's all been investigated. It was human error. Happens.' McKinnon grinned. 'And don't I know it? That's what we've been doing all morning, replacing material that had a bloody misprint in it.' She leaned back and the chair creaked. 'So you're working up some conspiracy theory that the result was rigged? Surely not?' She laughed abruptly.

Morton frowned. 'I wouldn't go as far as that. But… this is a miserable room, isn't it? Very small.'

Ailsa McKinnon laughed. 'Aye, isn't it?'

Morton heard himself say: 'Would you fancy a drink sometime?'

Ailsa jolted upright. 'Are you kidding me? So ye can pump me some more?' Then she creased into laughter. 'Oops that didn't quite…'

Morton blushed. 'Um, no, no, just…'

'Aye, alright, Willie, that'd be nice. Have to be Thursday or later, busy week.' She stood up and they were very close. He followed her out of the tiny room into the congested office.

'I'll give you a call, then.'

'Aye, right. Do that.'

Outside on the pavement, he realised it hadn't quite gone

the way he had expected. And he'd asked her out. He hadn't meant to, but he was attracted to her, or was it just a reaction to something Sally had said? He couldn't believe Ailsa would be involved in something dodgy. There was something idealistic about her, she had strong principles. He knew he should never mix work and social life, but the words had just come out, without thought. Ah well, it was done. And after all, she hadn't really concealed anything. Neither of them had known then there was anything to conceal.

CHAPTER SIX

What had to happen next was that Morton was going to get into his car and see if the engine still worked, then drive over to Glenforgan and find something... anything to make into a story. He could easily get lines from Janet Kirkwood if he could come up with something new from Neil Shankwell even just to clarify precisely what had been lost. All the ballot papers, or only some? Could the marked-up registers be somehow recreated so that the result could be verified? He hoped he could get something to justify the trip.

He got up early with the sky still peachy-grey, strolled to the car parked around the corner by the park in Ogilvie Terrace and it started first time. He hadn't been inside the Beetle for a fortnight. Usually, he used it to shop at The Gyle but elsewhere parking was a problem. He hoped he could get the same space when he returned but there was no guarantee. For sure, he ought to sell it. He enjoyed the functionality of it, and always took pleasure in driving, as a source of empowerment, a reminder that he had options, possibilities, resources. It had been Sally's of course, and it was strange that she hadn't asked whether he still had it. He wondered what she was doing. Probably chinwagging with her old cronies. Then he thought about Ailsa McKinnon. She wasn't as proletarian as she made out. He happened to know she came from a middle-class home in the Stirling area. How did he know that? He knew his dad would approve of her. He hadn't been too keen on Sally, thought she was a 'flittertygibbet' – one of his words. His mother had got quite close to her, which had made their separation harder to bear.

He reached the approach to the Forth Bridge and as he climbed, the sun filled his wing mirrors briefly. It was a nice if cold winter's day. He regretted the lack of a radio, of companionable voices in the car, as he glanced down through the bridge structure at the houses of North Queensferry. He would reach Glenforgan inside twenty minutes if the traffic was light. He tried to concentrate, gather his thoughts and focus on the questions he wanted to ask Shankwell if he could get to speak to him. After all, it was a public matter and there were concerns that needed to be raised. The rest of the media seemed to have backed off, reassured by the statement from the Scottish Court Service. That was his next possibility if Shankwell wouldn't see him. He'd have to get some petrol on the way home.

Although Glenforgan was a sizeable town of about forty thousand, and had given its name to the constituency, it was a largely rural area, encompassing eight smaller towns and a villages within a few miles of each other. Morton had Googled and discovered there were no less than thirty-four polling stations dotted around the constituency. There had been over thirty-five thousand votes cast in the by-election, a turnout of fifty-four percent of the electorate. He wondered if that made it easier or more difficult for the political parties to campaign. He could imagine loyalties, issues and sensitivities widely differing from one local area to another, the complicated logistics of canvassing and leafletting and holding public meetings. He'd ask Shankwell that too. Did it make running a by-election easier or more difficult?

Morton had been in the town a few times but usually

only passing through and observed it with keen interest as he approached. He began to detect the familiar signs of run-down shopping precincts, vacant office space, closed-down shop units, a proliferation of charity shops. He drove the car into a multi-level carpark and found a space on level six. He stood looking over the concrete parapet at the tarmac grounds of a large modern secondary school, some trees and beyond, the main shopping centre, a cinema, church spire, furniture warehouse and a large red sandstone building that looked like a public library. On the street level, he walked by intuition towards the High Street and in a pleasant square, lined by trees and wooden benches, was the council HQ, what might have been called in the old days, the town hall. It was a generously proportioned sandstone building of three storeys with an ugly modern extension and on the roof, as if to explain the architectural confusion, flew a saltire and a union flag. The main entrance was around the side, in the middle of the concrete and glass extension. A large board directed the visitor to a plethora of departments but there was no direct access to any of them. Two middle-aged receptionists sat behind a glass hatch chatting to each other while a few miserable supplicants waited, seated on red plastic chairs attached into rows of ten. To Morton it resembled A&E and the two people waiting looked like they needed treatment or attention of some sort, but they waited stoically. He stood looking over the sea of red plastic and the receptionists watched him. Finally, he walked over to the hatches.

'Can I see someone from Electoral Registration Department, Neil Shankwell?'

'Got an appointment?'

'No. Look, I'm media.' He showed them his NUJ card. They both peered at it.

'You want the Press Office?'

'No. Neil Shankwell.'

The older lady smiled faintly. 'You'll need to go through the Press Office. I'll ring Alison and they'll come down.'

Morton sighed. 'Okay.' He stood at the side, hands in pockets. A woman in a denim skirt and anorak came in and glanced at him, then led one of the supplicants away. Social worker, he wondered. He studied the notices on the wall. Fife Police, Glenforgan Community Council, Surgery notices for Janet Kirkwood MSP and Malcolm Cook, the newly elected MP, and local councillors. He took down the phone number for an SNP councillor, Ian Brown, whose poster showed a bearded man of about his own age. There was a framed panel of photographs of the chief officers of the council too and he spotted Neil Shankwell, under the Electoral Registration Officer, Ron Marshall. He noticed Shankwell was 'Acting Deputy ERO' and presumed he had since been promoted. He'd ask about that.

Alison Bridger looked to be in her twenties, a professional, dressed like an executive. She asked to see his press card and he followed her to the lift. She wasn't into small talk, and he decided to follow suit. On floor three, she showed him into the Press Office, a large light room with a view of the tops of the trees and the library building across the street.

'This is my colleague, Seamus,' she said, pointing to the overweight young man working on the laptop on one of two desks on the other side of the room. 'Would you like to sit... Now how can I help?'

'I'd like to speak to Neil Shankwell, the Acting Deputy ERO,' he said. 'Is that possible?'

She frowned, rubbing her palms together. 'He's the Deputy now. You want to speak to him rather than the ERO, Ron Marshall? Is it about registration or... a particular issue? If it's about the by-election, I'd have to redirect you to the Scottish Courts Service, they've conducted…'

'Yes, I know. But this is a specific issue only Mr Shankwell can deal with.'

'Not about the by-election?'

'Well, yes, it is, but…'

Bridger smiled. 'Because of the investigation of the missing material, all press issues are now dealt with by the SCS.' She relaxed a little. 'You must know how councils work? Staff sign a declaration of confidentiality and in the first instance bring to this Press Office any matter that should be released to the public. Otherwise, if there was no policy in place, everything that happened, even confidential, personal issues, would end up in the public domain. In no one's interests. You must see. That would be chaos.'

'Thank you for that advice,' Morton said, smiling, 'now can I see Mr Shankwell, and if there is anything for the public to know about, I'm sure he'll bring it to you first.'

Bridger coloured. 'Look, Mr Morton, I'm not trying to be obstructive, but that's our policy.'

'But staff are not prisoners here, are they? They can come and go and speak…?'

'Of course, the policy only covers speaking to the press. Honestly, you'd do better talking to the chief executive of the Scottish Court Service.'

Morton tried again. 'At elections, the ERO speak directly to the media, don't they? They don't go via the Press Office.'

'At elections.'

'Okay, so if it was about a registration matter, could I speak to Shankwell then?'

'No. Someone from the Department would come down and speak to you, then give you the necessary form.'

'I see.' Morton sighed. 'When was Mr Shankwell promoted to Deputy, if you can tell me that?'

For the first time, the press officer laughed. '*I can* tell you that,' she said, 'if you'll give me a minute.' She went over to her computer and tapped a few keys. 'Two months ago. Do you need the exact date?'

'No, thank you, but could you also tell me when he became Acting Deputy?'

'What? I can't see what relevance… anyway, here it is. He was acting up from… just a fortnight before the by-election.'

'Right and he'd been in the ERO since when?'

'That was also when he joined the ERO. Before that he was in Cleansing and Roads.'

'So,' Morton frowned, 'I don't understand. He was appointed to the ERO as Acting Deputy in mid-November and just days later, was promoted?'

'That's right. It was days.'

'Is that unusual?'

'I wouldn't have thought so. Probably happens all the time.'

'Thank you,' Morton said, rising. 'I'll take your advice and try the Courts Service.' He smiled. 'Thanks for your help,'

'Pleasure. I'll see you to the lift if you'd like to make your own way out.'

He stood in the lift and his finger hovered on the button for Main Reception/Ground Floor, then vengefully he pressed Floor 2 as the doors began to close.

The main thing, he knew, was to look confident, as if he was in the right place. If challenged, he could always say he was lost or looking for the toilet. He walked along the corridor, glancing at the information on the doors. At the far end, as the corridor turned, he saw he was at the back of the building and there was a sign 'Electoral Registration'. He peered through the glass window in the door. It was a small office and no-one visible in it. He pushed in and looked around. Two heavy wooden doors with signs and on one of them was *N. Shankwell, Deputy ERO*. Taking a deep breath, he went forward and knocked.

'Come in.'

He turned the handle and went in.

'Mr Shankwell?'

'Yes. And you are…?'

The seated man facing him was large and heavy, as he had known he would be, his prominent fleshy nose, unfortunate broken red skin on his cheeks and forehead, the fraying hair sticking up, giving him a permanently startled look.

'My name is Morton. I wonder if you can clarify a few points for me?'

'Who are you? What is it you want?'

'I'm a journalist.'

'Then what the hell are you doing here?' Shankwell was on his feet, staring at him. 'How did you get in?'

'I spoke to the Press Office, Alison…' just for a moment he couldn't remember her surname. 'And I need a few moments…'

'What is this? You've no right to be here.'

'It's a public matter I need to speak to you about the by-election material. Are all the ballot papers lost? Or only some?'

Shankwell was coming around his desk, threateningly, fists raised, spluttering in anger. 'You… you… get out!'

'I've been informed that the by-election was rigged,' Morton said, backing away. 'What would be your comment on that? What? Are you going to *hit* me? Come ahead!'

'I'm no going to hit you, ye daft bugger, if ye get oot ma office!'

'Calm down man,' Morton said, holding his arms out in front of him. 'Why are you so angry? No-one would seriously believe a by-election could be rigged. But the statement put out by the Scottish Courts Service is vague.'

Shankwell reached behind his desk and picked up his phone. Morton watched him dial and begin to speak. 'Intruder… in my office…'

'I'm going,' he said. 'No need to bother… but I'll get to the bottom of it. You seem very defensive. As if you've got something to hide.'

Shankwell put the phone down and sneered. 'Something to hide? You can fuck off! Your name's Morton is it? I'll remember that. I'll have you sorted out.'

'What did you say?' Morton turned, appalled, as the security man came into the room. 'Did you hear what he said?'

Security, a bloated, puffy faced man in a blue uniform, took hold of his arm. Morton noted he was long past retirement age and had a hearing aid. 'Come on, sir, time to go.'

'You probably didn't,' Morton concluded. 'Okay, okay, I'm leaving.'

Morton was escorted in silence to the lift and out through the main entrance, watched by the astonished receptionists and the few supplicants in the red plastic chairs, back out into the cold but pleasant square. He felt a little sorry for the security man, poor old geezer. 'Thank you,' he said, 'for your kind assistance.'

'No bother sir,' the man smiled sadly, adding: 'I did hear what he said, and it's scandalous the way that man talked to you. They think they're the unco guid and we're just their serfs. Have a nice day, sir, mind how you go.'

CHAPTER SEVEN

Strolling along the High Street, a little unnerved by the encounter, Morton keyed the number for Councillor Brown into his Blackberry. He got straight through and explained who he was and that he had spoken to Janet Kirkwood.

'Okay? What can I do for you?'

'I'm here in Glenforgan…'

'There's a pub called the Red Lion in Market Street… see you there. Give me twenty minutes.'

He found the pub, on the corner of Market Street and the High Street, a friendly-looking place, unpretentious, a little in need of refurbishment. There was a pleasant smell of home-cooked food and he saw a menu chalked on a slate by the bar when he went to order. Regretfully, scanning the half-dozen real ales they had on tap, he asked for orange juice and lemonade and sat down on crimson upholstery, leaning back against the wall in an alcove. There were a few other patrons, and some couples eating. He felt hungry.

He noticed the councillor when he came in, recognising him from the photo in the council offices, even though he was in overalls and a brown leather jacket. He waved.

'How's the man?' Brown asked cheerily, though they had never met.'

'I'm fine. Can I get you a pint?'

'Aye, please. Thrappledouser,' he said draping his leather jacket on a nearby seat.

'I was thinking about having some lunch,' Morton said.

'Good idea. They do a braw steak pie. I'm going with the chicken tikka.'

'On me,' Morton said.

'Oh no. Can't have that. Bribery... whit? Pay our own.'

'Okay, but... as you wish.'

When they were settled, with their drinks, in the alcove, the councillor stretched his legs out and Morton saw the heavy boots had streaks of what seemed like rust on the exposed steel toecaps.

Brown laughed cheerily; moustache wet with froth. 'Aye, this is my local. I run a wee garage doon the street. Anyway, ye saw Janet, so how can I help ye?'

Morton told him about his investigations and his altercation with Shankwell. 'Do you know him?'

'I've had the pleasure,' Brown admitted. 'Not one of my pals though. As ye probably know, he's a Labour man. That's not a problem, but he wasn't very helpful when I had an issue with postal votes. It was a surprise to see him at the election count.'

'He was only moved to the ERO a fortnight before polling day.'

Brown put down his pint and looked at him. 'I understand so. And as far as I know, Ron Marshall put him in charge of the postal votes. Ye know how that works?'

'Chicken tikka?' the young barman approached, holding a tray.

'That's me,' Brown said.

'Vaguely,' Morton muttered, taking charge of an enormous platter of steak pie and chips.

'Anything else you require? Sauces?'

'We're fine, thanks, Jed,' Brown told him. 'People can register for a postal vote up to a few days before polling, then they post their papers to the ERO right up to the close of poll. Or they could drop them into any polling station. Postal voting starts weeks before polling day.'

'I knew that. And that the postal votes are opened and the registers marked-up as they come in, then, presumably, they are taken to the count?'

'Aye, where they are then put into the correct polling station box for the voter's address and counted just like ordinary votes. A lot more people nowadays vote by post. Much more convenient.'

They ate for a while. A few more customers came in, the start of the lunchtime rush. The steak pie was excellent, plenty of gravy and succulent chunks of beef. 'This is good,' he commented, chewing.

'Aye, good honest fare, and plenty of it. And the owners are fine folk, fine SNP voters!'

Morton laughed. 'I love the way you put those two statements together.'

Brown snorted. 'Didn't mean it quite that way. All my constituents are fine folk, whichever way they vote.'

'Of course. Listen, Ian,' Morton said, leaning forwards and speaking quietly, 'I had a man come up to me in Glasgow telling me the by-election was *rigged*. And that was days before the shenanigans with the missing marked-up registers became known. Then I find a Labour man just happens to have been parachuted into the ERO two weeks before a crucial poll – who gets very aggressive when I ask him a question about the ballot papers… and everyone and their granny believes the result is a foregone conclusion, then it goes the other way.'

Brown stopped eating and sighed. '*Rigged*? No. Does Janet think that?'

'Well, I don't think so. I can't believe it myself, but…'

'A bit far-fetched. I mean, we were at the count. We didn't see anything funny.'

'What about the postal votes? How many came in before polling day? Could there be enough to affect the result?'

'No. They get counted but face down so that they can read the elector number that's on the back and mark it off on the register. The parties send a representative to watch the process. You can't really get any meaningful sample of how it's going, although we do try. And of course, there's a law against passing information to anyone else from the postal ballot verification that might influence the election.'

'Right. So they get marked off the register as having voted, postal votes are then kept somewhere in the ERO until polling day…'

'I know what you're going to say… could the ballot slips be altered in some way inside the ERO?'

'Yes, I'm thinking the ones with pencil marks could be rubbed out and changed.'

'Christ! What a thought.'

'I mean, it's a small office, I only saw four desks. The staff must take lunch breaks.'

'That would be pretty damn obvious though. I mean every one of the postals voting one way?'

'But who would look at them, after, presumably they'd been separated and bundled into envelopes for the different polling districts? And that could be done by one man. How many are we talking, total number of postal votes?'

Brown frowned, chewing. 'Um, maybe nearly thirty percent of the total, say nine, ten thousand.'

'Ah, that's a lot. And what was the margin of victory?'

'Three thousand, three hundred and eight.'

Morton sat back and pushed his plate away. After a minute or two, he said: 'Well that'd do it.'

Brown took a long pull at his beer, put down the pint and wiped his lips with a paper napkin. 'Nah, Willie, I just cannae see how one man could fake enough ballot papers to ensure they would win. For a start, he couldn't possibly have known how many he needed to fake. It would look funny at the count because the postal votes get added in to each polling district at a certain time, and someone would notice. Ron Marshall or some of the other staff would be suspicious. Too risky for… whoever it was.'

'Well, but he might have been clever enough to keep it a mix, with Labour just on top but not by too much?'

'Phew! Some theory. And are you going to be publishing this in the *Standard*?'

'Not until I get some hard evidence.'

'Hmn, well, that might be difficult. You should go back to your source. Who was he? Does he have any proof?' He frowned. 'Is it somebody I might ken?'

'No, Morton said. 'He seemed sane but I'm none the wiser who he is. A man with a grouse certainly. Maybe an old turkey looking for a Christmas voucher…' He laughed abruptly. 'He called himself a wellwisher, a rare bird. As rare, he said, as a ptarmigan.'

'That is rare, endangered even. I'm for another pint. Another juice?'

Morton winced. 'No, thanks.'

He was trying to think how it could be done, how a by-election could be rigged. Having seen Shankwell close to, and having experienced his belligerence, he was starting to think some kind of fiddle could have happened. Maybe some postal ballots had been altered? How could that be proved, either way? When Brown came back to the table, he sat back and let him take a good swallow, then he tried again.

'Okay, Ian, if you don't mind, what was it like on polling day? I mean there was an expectation of victory for Jamie Sharp, but what about the Labour lot?'

'Aye, they didn't look so happy. I had a chat with some of the councillors. They thought they had been well gubbed. One was happy to tell me their choice of candidate was to blame and several blamed the negativity of their campaign. No, I didn't see any who expected to win, except maybe that arse Raymond Mearns, but he's... a bit of a fanatic.'

'Raymond Mearns?' Morton frowned. 'Who is he?'

'He's not from round here.' Brown shrugged. 'A Labour staffer somewhere, I think, or some kind of official. Him and another guy I've never seen before. I don't think they stayed long. Mearns gave the impression that the local Labour lot are idiots. Has a sort of superior air, as if he's the man in charge. I didn't really pay him any attention. I had other things on my mind, what with the polling box samples.'

Morton tried to focus on the nub of the matter. 'Yes, as the count proceeded, how did you feel with the way it was going? I mean was it obvious you were going to lose, or was it more up and down in certain areas... what was your feeling?'

Brown's eyes narrowed as he sat back. 'Well, since you ask, it was a little odd. We were a little way behind everywhere, even in our best areas.' He frowned, rubbed at the hair over his ear. 'It was puzzling, a very sort of even result, the same everywhere. In my polling districts, in every box we were narrowly behind, but not in front, not in even one. Thinking about it, that is very strange. We've been doing ballot box sampling assiduously; I mean since the nineteen-eighties. No other party does it as much as we do, so even when we lose elections, we know that we always win certain boxes, but not that night.'

Morton stared at him, feeling his spine tingling. 'That's... what you've just told me... is the strangest thing yet. Ian, do you think there is a chance that it *was* rigged?'

The councillor scratched at his beard. 'Ah, now, well, I just don't know. You've got me thinking, for sure. But how can we find out?'

Morton stood up. 'I'll get to the bottom of it. Might need to speak to you again, but thanks for now.'

CHAPTER EIGHT

Raymond Mearns enjoyed the smooth onward progress of the Virgin fast service as the train swept quickly across the York plain, smilingly convinced that the journey was enhanced by being in the First-Class carriage. A better class of people, discreet, polite and it had more legroom, more space, fresher air and servile minions to offer you free refreshment. He must have been smiling or looking untroubled and that had prompted the woman opposite, reading the Margaret Atwood novel to speak to him. She was classy, early middle-aged, probably quite wealthy – he allowed himself to speculate. And so maybe she had thought him classy too? Perhaps enigmatic. He wondered what she thought of him, wondered if she was a little impressed by him. Something must have prompted her to speak. He'd told her he was a civil servant – which was not wrong. But don't ask me what I do, he'd joked. That had intrigued her. He'd enjoyed the conversation, brief as it was, basking in her regard, in being in her eyes at least, for a while, a somebody. He'd told her he was based in London, which was partly true and certainly he was heading down to meet his colleague, although she'd irritated him by her insistence that he 'sounded Scottish'. He was half-Scottish he'd told her, but it had put him into a pique and the conversation waned. She was not that classy really; except she lived in Surrey.

He preferred to enjoy the landscape as is flashed fleetingly by. He was looking forward to his meeting, partly because he had done well and would bathe in the esteem of his colleagues and partly because he liked the new identity which being in London conferred on him. He glanced upwards; his red leather holdall on the rack was perfect for a two-night stay at Claridges. He hadn't told the woman but perhaps she stayed there often herself. To him it was a mark of his success. And the expensive suit, the loafers from Church. Dressing well made you feel well. Made you feel you had arrived. He glanced at the black face of his Tissot Classic chronograph. That made him feel professional too, though it had only cost a hundred quid. Still an hour to Euston. Should he order a glass of wine? He decided not, didn't want to doze the rest of the way. On the table in front of him, his zip-up folder with the typed-up report to present to them. He'd emailed the summary of course and that was why they'd asked him to come down, because of the stunning success of what he had achieved. Usually, he came down once a year, but they wanted to absorb all the details and get his advice on how to replicate the success of it. He felt a sweeping wave of satisfaction. His parents had grudgingly come to accept that he had made his own life and was successful. He had given them plenty of evidence of that but still they overlooked how hard he worked, didn't understand it. Which was their loss. Now they knew that it was the success of his work which meant he barely saw them, back in their embarrassing council house in Craigend. How many years since he'd visited? At least five. That was better for them and certainly for him. Their attitudes and half-baked questions had eroded his confidence but now he was flying high. The smart female attendant was doing a beverage round. Coffee, he decided, and a biscuit, not wine. Didn't want to make any stains on his new tie. The Atwood reader was falling asleep, her head lolling above the pages and he could see the edge of the line of face-cream under her ear. Not classy at all, he shuddered, Surrey notwithstanding.

Mearns dismounted onto the platform at Euston, breathing deeply and trying to walk taller than his five feet eight inches, in his suit and raincoat and good shoes, gripping his holdall. It occurred to him he might have requested a company car to take him to the hotel but as it was early afternoon, the tube would be relatively tolerable for only a few stops. He looked about him with enthusiasm, taking in the usual chaotic scenes, homeless people, passengers queueing for the Glasgow train; he could tell many were Scottish. They had an obvious down-at-heel look about them, a rural look, bucolic… whatever, he could tell at ten paces if someone was Scottish, and he wasn't often wrong. But he didn't like the idea that he too looked Scottish and avoided looking at them. He had bigger fish to fry. He was a success, a man with imagination and the ability to make things happen. The tube was quiet and he made the changes without having to consult his A-Z.

The doormen at Claridges greeted him like an old friend although it was only the second time he had stayed there. He disliked being fawned over and yet… He ordered afternoon tea and dinner. A porter took him up in the elevator to his room, which was a balcony suite, with a wonderful view over Davies Street and in the distance, the London Eye imperceptibly revolving. It was all so easy. You glided from place to place, your smooth passage lubricated by money, whose provenance was of no concern to anybody.

After unpacking, he went for a stroll along Brook Street as far as Hyde Park Corner then enjoyed leisurely afternoon tea in the wonderful Art Deco Foyer & Reading Room. He had taken a book with him: Antony Beevor's *Stalingrad*, which he'd been dipping into for months without getting it finished and sat on in front of the fire. But no-one spoke to him. He was mildly disappointed that his stay here would not elevate him into a leisured camaraderie of classy people. There was another guest making a fuss and being made a fuss of; a black rapper apparently, the typical baldie with gold chains around his neck and covered in tattoos. Who? He'd scoffed at the waitress. Was everyone supposed to bow down to the cretin? And the staff were fawning over him, as if they were so proud to have him staying here, this vulgar braggadocio. He went up to his room for a little nap. They'd call him for dinner.

On the Sunday morning after breakfast, Morton dressed warmly and left his flat, walking over to his parents, from Shandon Place up Ashley Terrace, over the railway bridge, along Spylaw Road and into Merchiston Crescent. It was a fifteen-minute walk along leafy lanes and, although very familiar to him from the years of Sunday visits, he looked about him with interest. There was always something new to see, and always the anticipation of the deep joy of his parents' company and the conversations they would have. Stuart Erskine Morton was eighty-six but very active, tall and spare and wry. His mother Margaret was sixty-seven. She was his dad's second wife and had retired from the civil service two years ago. Sometimes her younger sister Libby came along on Sunday. The house was substantial, typical of Merchiston Crescent, detached, built of solid granite, with a sizeable garden, greenhouse and some trees. It was a stone's throw from his old school, George Watson's and he liked the Sunday visits partly because of the sense of continuity it gave him with his past: his parents, his school, his earlier life. He had not yet lost any of it, it was all still intact. That grounded him.

When he turned up the drive he looked back and took in the skyline, the Merchiston Tower of Napier University and beyond the church spire on the hill. It was a nice locale. His mother was in the kitchen baking, still in her night attire and dressing gown, making fruit scones. He kissed her and went into the back garden to find his father.

'Ask him he wants his coffee yet,' she called after him.

His dad in brownish flannels and a red v-neck pullover, was digging out the root of a bottlebrush, bending and struggling with it.

'Good grief, dad! Let me help you.'

'Ah William.' He straightened up. 'You're right. My back hurts.' He snorted. 'Okay, you have a go. Try not to cut into the roots. I don't think I'll be able to move it this year. You need to confine the roots over a whole year before you can move it. Tricky devils, bottlebrush.'

Morton had a go with the spade but he wasn't very experienced.

'No, no, son. You're cutting into the roots! You'll kill the fella.'

'Let's take a break, dad. Mum asked if you're ready for a coffee.'

Morton senior rolled up his pullover sleeve to look at his watch. 'Little early. Anyway, what have you been up to? Let's have a seat. It's a lovely day.'

'Out here? It's five degrees, dad!'

'I feel warm.'

'You'll die of hypothermia, dad, come on, inside.'

'Ach, it's not that bad.'

Most people meeting Stuart Morton for the first time and seeing the grand house would naturally assume he voted Tory, but nothing could be further from the truth. When he was demobbed after the war, as a sergeant in the 51st Highland Division who had served in the desert and in Sicily, he had developed a strong resentment for what he called 'the officer class' and the arrogant rulers of a colonial Britain. His wartime marriage having ended in divorce in 1946, he retrained as an engineer and poured himself into his new career and building a Scotland free from the hierarchical restrictions of a post-imperial mind-set. He would have remained a driven career man had he not encountered Margaret Tait in the late 1960s. She was nineteen years his junior and it had been a wonderfully successful and enduring marriage giving him a blessed childhood free from stress and anxiety. Neither were conventional in thought or deed, fervent supporters of Scottish independence, freethinkers and scornful of cant and hypocrisy in all its forms. He told his father of his investigations into the possible rigging of a by-election arising from the tense political situation. Stuart Morton, who had been predisposed to like Gordon Brown, in the dim days of his shining expectancy prior to election as an MP, had become a severe critic of the 'son of the manse' and his dithering and sulking and backbiting.

'He hasn't got long, in my estimation,' he told his son. 'The English voters initially approved of him, as a solid, respectful and thoughtful leader, though he has proved anything but. They thought he might be another John Smith. They liked that one. He might have won Labour a general election in England, had he not died. He had that country doctor style, perhaps reminding them of Dr Cameron's bedside manner.'

Morton smiled. 'There's another Cameron waiting in the wings. Fourteen points ahead of Broon.'

His father shook his head and tutted. 'Such promise he had, at an early age. But where did it go? Yon Salmond now, he has the same promise and talent. Student politics, tipped for success just like Brown but he's making something of it. One going up,' he concluded, waving his hand on a curve, 'and one going down. It's like they represent the two different choices we might take: attempting change yet again via London or making our own change up here.'

Morton thought about the neatness of that remark. It was true. Personalising things was fraught with problems but both men wanted significant change in Scotland and saw different routes to it. Like Cosgrove and Redmond, or Collins and De Valera. But change was organic, could not be contained and personalities could ride on its onrush only for a while. History would write itself and Brown and Salmond would be written in the narrative in a manner perhaps somehow beyond their own predictions.

Later, his aunt Libby arrived, in her Fiat and things got livelier as they sat down to a lunch of roast beef and all the trimmings in the rarely-used dining room with the garden view. She was prone to outrageous statements on everything, as if trying to provoke people, though sometimes he wondered if she believed in anything at all. She was planning a big hill-walking trip in the Italian Dolomites with three cronies.

CHAPTER NINE

Raymond Mearns ordered a taxi to take him from Claridges to Great Smith Street. It was the only way to ensure he arrived in good order and on time for his meeting. He enjoyed a leisurely breakfast then had more coffee in the library reading the newspapers, watching the comings and goings in the foyer. It was a sunny day outside but looked cold as he stepped into Brook Street and the doorman held the taxi door open for him. They set off down Bond Street heading for St James' Park. When the taxi turned off Victoria Street, in front of Westminster Abbey in Great Smith Street, he waited till he saw the Education Department looming up on the right, leaned forward and tapped the flexiglass. 'This will do here, thanks.'

'Okay, squire.'

Mearns clambered out onto the pavement and moved towards the government building as the taxi reversed and returned to the junction. When it was out of sight, he turned, quickly crossed the road and entered Little Smith Street, continuing right into the narrower Tufton Street. It was a shadowed red-brick chasm of three and four storeys, barely wide-enough for two cars to pass each other without going up on the narrow pavements on either side, with no parking in the street allowed. Apart from the discreet, black-painted premises of J. Wippell & Co Ltd., an upmarket clothier, on the other side of the street, there was no indication of the activities conducted in the street, no sign of residents or pedestrians. 18A was a brown polished door adjacent to a steel roll-shutter gate, slightly indented behind a projecting red-brick wall. This meant that Mearns, standing in front of it, effectively disappeared to the view of anyone coming down the street. Above the door, the inevitable CCTV camera and a pattern of windows of one-way glass. There was nothing on the door to indicate whether it was an office, residential apartment or the rear door of an establishment. Pedestrians were rare and few would notice the discreetly positioned steel button between the door jamb and the frame of the steel shutters that rang a bell in the interior. On the other side of the shutter door, black iron railings mounted in a low brick wall guarded the narrow void in front of one-way glass in the basement. Looking down to the junction with Great Peter Street further on which seemed bright with natural light, the broody dimness of this section of Tufton Street was emphasised. Mearns pressed the button. He was at the heart of the secret establishment, in the centre of a sprawling, anonymous, inscrutable, omnipotent warren of offices between Millbank and the Home Office on Marsham Street, where all the power cliques were based, including Smith Street and Cowley Street, home of think-tanks, right-wing institutes and political parties that played their part, behind the scenes in stiffening the resolve and resilience of the British state. He had felt that throbbing power from the first and it made his trips to his controller all the more gratifying. He was part of it, a member of the Great British Team. His real paymasters he knew (he had found out) were the slightly more prosaic Scotland Office, but he could fantasise he was in speaking distance of something ineffably grander and more historic than the nature of the unheralded work he did for them.

The door clicked and began to open. Mearns shuffled inside, and as it began to close behind him, walked along the limey-yellow corridor, passing several doors, which he knew were locked, to an open door at the end of the corridor. Despite the grandeur of the location, the interior was subfusc, nondescript, no paintings, or any corporate information, simply beige carpet and lime-yellow walls. In the end room, where his briefings took place, it was the same, with a few basic items of furniture; a brown leatherette three-seat sofa, a chair, a small wooden desk and a window whose inner surface was covered completely in an opaque thick plastic. Some light came through, but it was impossible to see anything through it. Modern strip lights harshened the space and these were prone to flickering. There was no ambience or comfort, except for the warmth of radiators. It was like a room in a low-budget hotel. He suspected the premises were not manned and only used for meetings. But the work they did here was important, he and Trenchard and occasionally Collins. He knew there was a third man, Brewster but rarely saw him. He sat on the sofa to wait for Oliver Trenchard and felt a slight sense of let-down. First-class train, Claridges and then this dismal cell. It was as if he was not fully integrated into the team. He knew he *was*, and Trenchard had explained it all to him in detail at the beginning; the importance of 'sound-proofing' and secrecy but it meant that he could never quite be sure how highly his work was valued. It was a one-way relationship except that his controller would occasionally drop a mention such as 'the others think very highly of your work' or 'the rest of the team thought you did that piece of work especially well'. He wondered about 'the others' and what they really thought of him. Did they even know his name? Not that he was going to complain. He had it easy, able to do his agreed work with minimal interference, the pay was excellent, more than any other job he had had. He heard the handle being turned and Trenchard came in smiling. He was quite an old man, Mearns believed but this may have been because he was slow and deliberate in everything he did and his thick eyebrows and baggy woollen cardigans, his dark tweed suits. He was like an old man.

'Ah, Raymond, you're already here? Apologies for the slight delay.' He unbuttoned his coat and hung it on the peg at the back of the door.

Mearns sat up. 'That's alright.' He wondered where he had come from and the cause of the delay. Once he had been told he had just 'come from the committee' but Trenchard, almost as if acknowledging his mistake, then reminded him of the confidential agreement he had signed.

'Now, we'll just get started,' Trenchard said, taking a folder out of his briefcase and placing it on the small table. He sat on the other end of the sofa and rubbed his hands together. 'Cold out, isn't it? Well, it's good to see you, Raymond and I'm very glad to have the chance to see you in person,' he crossed his legs smiling and blinking, 'and to have the chance to congratulate you again on the excellent piece of work you've completed. First-class.'

'Thank you,' Mearns said, relaxing a little in the sofa. There was never any offer or tea or coffee. Their meetings or briefings as Trenchard preferred to call them, were entirely businesslike, focussed on the work, no chit-chat, no anecdotes, gossip or intrusions. He had learned to accept it. Everything else was handled entirely by messages left and received within the VPN portal, all admin and any queries in relation to his salary or tax issues.

'Of course, Raymond. And thank you for your excellent report which we've studied and absorbed in full. It sets an excellent precedent for timely interventions on future occasions, and we have learned some useful things.' Trenchard reached to the side to retrieve his folder. 'This briefing will quickly recap some of those and we can explore certain key points then.' He looked up at the white digital clock above his coat hanging on the peg. 'Two colleagues will join us for discussion of strategy on some new work.'

'Right.' Mearns frowned. This was unusual, though he expected it to be Collins and Brewster, nothing to get excited about, not Miss Moneypenny. 'New work,' he said. 'That sounds good.'

'Oh yes, Raymond. We're keen to utilise your abilities, your local knowledge to the maximum and while what you have done is excellent, we feel there are other ways we can deploy you.'

'Fine.'

Trenchard deeply inhaled and patted his folder. 'But first... let's catch-up. The preparations you put in place were meticulous and everything worked out as expected. What did raise comment was that you broke cover... you attended in person... on polling day. Wasn't that a little unnecessary? Taking a bit of a risk?'

Mearns sat up straight, putting his hands on his knees. 'No risk. I found it necessary... the only way I could absolutely ensure everything went perfectly and no suspicion had been aroused was to be present. I wanted to know for sure that everything tallied-up exactly.'

Trenchard nodded, smiling. 'And it did. Did you have any doubts that it would?'

'No doubts, not exactly... but there were a few variables. As it turned out it didn't quite tally-up. There was a discrepancy, very small, after the first verification. So they did a partial recount, counting the box totals again. Took them nearly half an hour and it was still three short but at that point they decided against a full recount and all the party representatives agreed. It was a negligible number and couldn't affect the result, so they declared the new total and went on to the actual count for each candidate.'

Trenchard nodded. 'I see, well these things happen.'

'It was always likely something unexpected would crop up, but only three – from thirty-five thousand – is not bad going. Could be attributed to spoilt papers wrongly left in the main bundles, two papers stuck together, or simply human error.'

'Okay,' Trenchard nodded, 'so you feel that attending in person gives us greater certainty that all was well?'

'That's it. Having that kind of detail confirms it.'

'The press release put out this week caused the expected reactions,' Trenchard observed, 'but on a reduced scale than even we predicted. All parties have fully accepted the result and even the most belligerent of them has no inkling of your work. The outrage expressed has been muted, which is perhaps an indication of the accuracy of your work, how perfectly judged it was. And the variance, though significant, was in the end quite small?'

Mearns grinned. 'Turned out to be 8.75%.'

Trenchard sniffed. 'Is that figure in your report? I had thought it was smaller.'

'It is in the report.'

'Apologies, I must have missed it. How long did it take you to work that out?'

'A day, thanks to the counting machine.' Mearns grinned. 'Much faster than the counting agents, even though there were fifty of them.' As he said it, he wondered why he always felt the need to embellish, to add complete lies, just to make himself feel good, to feel superior. And there was no way Trenchard would ever find out. He'd never even seen a counting machine. Why had he said that?

'In the warehouse in Renfrew? And the shredding process? Is that complete?'

'Sadly, no.' He exhaled and sighed. 'The incinerator has not yet been fixed. They've promised that within a fortnight.'

'Let's hope so. And they are in secure containment now?'

'Oh yes, very. I made quite sure. Not in the warehouse though. That was compromised.'

Trenchard opened his mouth as if to speak but thought better of it. 'Good. By the way, we've added more useful supporting documentation for the premises; asset manifests, staffing and tax records through our agencies, mainly DTI and HMRC and the running costs, security and so on, are being operated remotely.' He glanced up at the clock. 'Better move on – just to let you know also that the 'tidying-up' phase starts in the next few days. This will include a parliamentary committee debate, apparently triggered by the investigation into the 'lost' ballot papers and this will be described as a full discussion and airing of those issues…' he pulled a mournful face. Mearns laughed.

'That's good to hear. Closing the stable door after the horse has bolted.'

'Very true, Raymond. Yes, there will be an agreement – it has already been brokered – between the members of the committee to instruct the authorities to 'reproduce' the marked-up registers so that the election can be checked – an impossibility of course because all that will be checked in reality is the total number who voted – not the way they voted. That would contradict the secrecy of the ballot. Anyway, Raymond, after that charade is over, the by-election and any queries over the result will be at an end.'

He opened his folder and briefly added some words onto the top sheet, using a ballpoint he had abstracted from the breast pocket of his jacket, humming slightly to himself, which Mearns had seen him do on every previous briefing. He had assumed that it was a slight correction of something already written down, or typed, but by design or accident, Trenchard always held the folder at such an angle that he could not read the top sheet. There was no sound in the room except that sound, of the plastic nib of ballpoint on paper and in the background the omnipresent rumble of aircraft stacking over central London awaiting permission to land at Heathrow.

Finally, Trenchard looked up and put his pen away, closed the folder and put it back in his briefcase. 'All done,' he said, lightly. 'I think we'll be joined shortly by our colleagues. It'll be a brief session, Raymond, no more than thirty minutes, just a brief outline of some planned activity and some suggestions for your involvement. No need to take notes, we'll send you a digital record later.'

Mearns involuntarily looked at his watch. 'Sounds interesting.' He was thinking that he would be back in time for lunch at Claridges.

Mearns was glad to get out of the building half an hour later, his head full of new ideas and suggestions. It had been full on, questions hurled at him, as if they were checking him but Collins and Usman – not Brewster at all – had been picking his brains, as they called it, so it was quite gratifying. He hailed a passing cab on Great Peter Street and anticipated a good lunch.

The other three men remained behind in the room, discussing the finer points of some of the details of the projects they had put to Mearns. Trenchard told them of the time when he had left the building first and Mearns had surreptitiously followed him.

'I didn't know about it at the time though. It was picked up later on CCTV.'

Collins was mystified. 'An odd thing for him to do?'

'Very,' Trenchard said, sniffing. 'Not like him at all. We've never discussed it or mentioned it. He has no idea at all.'

'Why did he do it?'

'Well, we believe he was simply curious to find out where I was based. Although he agreed – agrees – with that and all the protocols. It was his vanity that forced him to discover which department was paying his wages, we believe. Nothing more sinister than that.'

'Strange. And did he?' Usman asked.

'As far as he is concerned, he did,' Trenchard explained. 'It so happened that I had an appointment that afternoon at the Scotland Office, so he assumes…'

Collins laughed. 'He's a dark horse. Still, who isn't!'

CHAPTER TEN

At around ten past seven on a cold January morning, thirty-seven-year-old Willie Morton in tracksuit and trainers bounced down the stone steps into Shandon Place, jogging on the pavement uphill to the bridge over the canal and into Colinton Road and the brand-new sports centre in the grounds of his old school. Its recent opening, much heralded in the media, by Chris Hoy, recently knighted by the Queen for winning three cycling golds in last year's Beijing Olympics, had inspired him to get fit. Hoy had been in the year above him at school. That added a masochistic flavour to the pleasure on a frosty cold morning as the sun made its appearance over the roofs of the Royal Edinburgh Hospital and Morningside beyond. For if Hoy could be gonged for simply doing a bit of pedalling, surely he could yet be a success by breaking a really-big public interest story? He dreamed of coming upon a story of fraud at the highest levels of the establishment, or uncovering the misdeeds of the rich and notorious, or taking down the self-made criminal gang lords, people traffickers, sniffing out corruption in echelons inhabited by untouchables of one sort of another. He'd done some good stuff for the *Standard* on an affair between a senior staff member and a married MSP which had compromised the integrity of the nascent Scottish parliament. As the Scottish stringer in London for the Scottish Radio Group in 1996, he'd produced an influential feature on loansharking among asylum seekers in the Red Road flats in Glasgow and before that for the *Edinburgh Evening News* on housing subsidy fraud and corruption in the Scottish Premier League over transfer fees but that big career-defining story still eluded him. He pondered these thoughts as he pounded the pavements on the six-minute jog to The Galleon Sports Hub, pushing open the swing door. The digital clock showed 7:19. He felt himself heating up as he made his way to the changing rooms, one of the first there, though he heard splashing from the pool area. He stripped off his tracksuit and changed to indoor trainers from his locker and made his way to the smaller of the three gyms which he preferred and began his thirty-minute routine, treadmill, bike, rowing machine and a few fixed-weights work on squat thrusts. He returned to the locker and, in trunks, did twenty fast lengths of the twenty-metre pool. Around 8.15 he was walking back through the foyer where sometimes he grabbed a coffee from the machine but more usually walked home for breakfast. He didn't do it every day, perhaps three times a week but it set him up for the day, made him feel virtuous, kept his bowels regular and helped him to sleep too.

Later, he power-walked to the *Standard* office, still pondering career-defining possibilities, worrying about his income or lack of it. Looking around him as he walked, he noticed the temperature had risen by a few degrees; his breath no longer hung around his mouth in a white cloud, as it had that morning. He was two weeks into the fitness routine, and he did feel more energetic, fitter. He saw a man pushing a golf cart along Fountainbridge and wondered if he should take up golf. Many of his contemporaries were heavily involved. It was a good enough sport although it had become a new religion. He had played a few times in his senior years at school, with borrowed clubs, enough to realise how frustrating it could be. Sane otherwise normal men devoted their lives to it, in the days when they weren't at Tynecastle roaring on the Hearts, or Murrayfield mumbling the words to 'Flower Of Scotland' as the Scottish pack succumbed heroically yet again in the eightieth minute.

Rami El-Jaffari was at her desk, he could see from the door. And as he approached, she swung her chair round. 'How's the investigation going, big guy?' she asked with her wry twisted smile, one dark eyebrow arched above the faintly pink lenses of her purple-framed spectacles.

Willie sniffed. 'Since you ask, I have learned some interesting things but not enough yet for a story.' He gave her a brief rundown of his encounter with Shankwell, concisely quoting what Shankwell had said and emphasising the crude manner in which he had said it.

The political reporter blinked up at him, brown eyes magnified by the lenses. 'Nasty man. Very defensive. And it's odd that, his sudden promotion two weeks before polling day. I was there, of course, but I had no contact with any of the staff, except briefly with the ERO Mr Marshall. He seemed a nice man.'

Morton shifted from one foot to the other. 'Could be co-incidence,' he said. 'Of course, none of that can be used – yet.' He had no intention of letting slip the name that Councillor Brown had mentioned to him, not until he'd checked it out, nor even his conversation with Brown. 'And what are you up to, Rami?'

She swivelled round to her screen. 'Follow up story. There's a debate in Westminster today, Public Bill Committee, brought by the Secretary of State for Scotland, Ann McGrath, looking into the loss of the papers. I think they're trying to pin the blame on the SNP or at least the Scottish Courts Service.'

'Well, good luck with that,' Morton said, drily.

'Yes, so I'll check for the online Hansard report for quotes – usually appears three or four hours after the debate. No doubt they'll be keen to head off any public suspicion about the result. There are no SNP MPs on the committee of course.'

Morton grunted. 'Aye well... okay, Rami, I've got a couple of things to check out, so I'll be around for a while.'

At the spare desk with his back to her, he typed 'Raymond Mearns' into a web search engine, firstly Google, then switched to Yahoo. There were the usual hundred thousand irrelevant hits worldwide that were mostly dead-ends or people living elsewhere in the world. There were some hits in the Greater Glasgow area or Strathclyde. He switched back to Google and tried Google Advance, searching both text and images; nothing stood out. It was quite likely, if not certain that Mearns had a digital footprint of some sort but he needed more specific information, a location, or a photo to get any further. Morton knew the quickest and best searches were to look someone up on Facebook. Four out of five people in Scotland have a Facebook account. There were eighteen men called Raymond Mearns whose location was in Scotland and who were or looked to be between twenty and sixty. His eyes began to swim with peering at tiny text onscreen and his stomach was rumbling. He looked at his watch. Lunchtime. He picked up the landline at the desk but couldn't remember the number for Holyrood, so he had to go through the switchboard and asked for Paul Symons. As he waited, he wondered if Sean Kermally would be there, in the FM's office. Paul Symon answered.

'Hi Paul, couldn't remember if this was one of your days...'

'Oh, it's you, Willie? Aye, one of my days. What's cooking? Did you go see that guy in Glenforgan?'

'Yes. Paul, I was going to drop over for a wee bite, I'll pay, if you sign me in. If you're free?'

'Ah, yeah, can do. Make it one-ish?'

'Cheers, see you.' He put down the phone and wrote an SMS text to Sean Kermally. He closed down the computer, said cheerio to Rami and strolled out into the wan sunshine of South Bridge heading down hill for the Canongate.

By the time, Morton had gone through security and collected his Visitors Pass at the front desk, Paul Symons was waiting for him, casting a long shadow in the gloomy stone-flagged foyer.

'So, not too busy,' Morton smiled. 'Anyway, my stomach's rumbling. Lead on MacDuff.'

The sun was filling the Garden Lobby in a shower of a million golden dust motes as they entered the parliamentary refectory and joined the small queue. Morton selected some ham and pea soup and sandwiches and paid for both of them, showing the woman on the till his Visitor's Pass number. He was a regular visitor to the parliament but had never got around to asking about a media pass; it was technically possible Hugh could have enabled him to get a pass on behalf of the *Standard* even though he was only a freelance, but a lot of hassle.

They found seats beside a gaggle of young American interns, mostly from Utah, judging from their appearance. He remembered something about an SNP MSP for one of the Aberdeen constituencies having a Mormon connection and that had led to a lot of internships but he couldn't remember the details. While eating his soup, he filled in Symons on his Glenforgan visit.

'Bit of a stinker,' was Symons only comment. 'I've never met him though, therefore I can't help you. There's a lot of hard old Labourites out there with views dating back to the days of the dinosaurs. Not just our party though.'

'Of course. And how are you getting on with Georgina?' Georgina Harkness was the Labour MSP for Rutherglen and Cambuslang, formerly junior minister for health in the McConnell government until May 2007.

Symons looked out of the window at the greenery beyond, the lower slopes of Holyrood Park. 'Well, you know, it's got a lot less intense now. Even constituency work has reduced. It's difficult for politicians to keep pushing forward when you're not in government. For me, as a humble assistant, it's pretty much the same level of work I used to do five days, now spread over three. There's a lot of despondency about.'

'You've probably got Gordon Broon to thank for that,' Morton suggested, holding his pastrami on sourdough sandwich in both hands. 'He seems determined to take the party down with him. Anyway, as I'm paying, I was going to ask you something.'

Symons grinned, a toothy smile lighting up his wan, white face. 'Here it comes... I knew you would.'

'Wanted to run a name by you, that someone mentioned. Supposedly a Labour man. He was at the by-election count.'

'Fire away, Willie.'

'Raymond Mearns.'

Symons put down his sandwich and reflected. 'Presumably no relation to old Howe of the Mearns?'

Morton frowned, then he got it. 'Very humorous. Grassic-Gibbon reference? Seriously now, does the name mean anything to you?'

'Hmn, there is something vaguely familiar, seen his name

somewhere. Did he defect to UKIP? Or was he booted out, of Labour, I mean?'

Morton shrugged. 'Well, you tell me? I didn't find much on yon internet. There were a few hits in Glasgow and Strathclyde but too many Facebook profiles.'

'I think he was from the west of Scotland somewhere, but that's just a vague feeling. What you need is a picture. Didn't you say he was at the count in Glenforgan?'

'So I believe. Representing Labour in some capacity, some kind of official position. So it's unlikely he was booted out, or joined UKIP. I get the impression he's about my age, early to mid-thirties.'

'Your guess is as good as mine,' Symons shrugged. 'Oops, there's Georgina looking for me. I have stuff to do, sorry, Willie, will have to dash. We'll talk again, yeah?'

'Of course, Paul, and thanks.' Morton smiled at the sight of his friend scuttling out into the Garden lobby in the wake of his formidable red-haired boss. The Scottish Parliament had empowered women and she was one, he knew, though one swallow does not a summer make.

CHAPTER ELEVEN

It had been quite a while since Willie Morton had been out and about, suited and booted, of an evening, in company with a young woman. He was nervous about it, took longer than usual in the shower, deliberated in the back bedroom in front of the mirror over what to wear. Normally, when he went out, which was almost invariably to the pub, he'd wear his leather jacket and jeans with a smart shirt and good shoes but he felt the need to smarten himself up a bit. He initially put on the mauve shirt, changed it for the black, decided against wearing a tie. The thing was to look casually smart, rather than deliberately smart. He was thirty-seven. A difficult age, he told himself solemnly. Trapped between generations. The thought made him laugh out loud. He could hear his dad's scorn: Come off it, William. Get a grip! He put on his Italian suit. That was how he thought of it. He'd bought it in a charity shop for £25 because of the label inside: *Caraceni Via Monte Napoleon, Milan*. It was a light grey 100% wool, shiny, almost silver under a certain light and the lining, which he thought was silk, was probably hand-stitched. His father had approved and his mother had been very hands-on, patting the lapels, adjusting his tie. She told him it was a good suit because there were no care labels inside and the four buttons on each sleeve seemed to be a non-plastic material, perhaps real horn. He felt good in it. It gave him confidence. He looked out the window at the night sky, the streetlights and heard a train at nearby Slateford Junction. It looked cold out. He'd need his overcoat. He looked at his watch: 7:10. Time to get the bus. He took a last glance at himself in the hall mirror. Okay.

He'd arranged to meet Ailsa at Corleones', a popular pizza and pasta place on Hanover Street. He stepped off the bus in Princes Street and walked up to the glass-fronted premises, one side of which operated as a takeaway. The music was the usual muzak, not as he had hoped, the theme from the Godfather. The restaurant was much less busy, only one or two tables occupied. He could see at a glance Ailsa hadn't yet arrived though he was a few minutes behind time, so he took a table in the middle of the place from where he could watch the door and ordered a Peroni. He felt a little ill at ease on his own. It was the kind of place people mostly popped in to after work or before going to the cinema or theatre and he wondered if it was the quiet period before evening diners arrived en-masse.

Ailsa had suddenly appeared while he was perusing his Blackberry. He looked up and got a shock to see her there in a long dark wool coat, black hair up in a ponytail, full makeup on, eyeliner too. He stood up. 'Ailsa, let me take your coat.'

'Very gallant,' she said, twirling out of the coat. He saw her smart shiny dress and couldn't help himself commenting. 'I wondered if you'd be in the dungarees…'

'Not for clubbing,' she laughed.

'Well, you look… different.'

'It's a start!'

'Well, I… it's difficult to… I like the way you have your hair.'

'A compliment? Steady on! I like the suit. You made an effort.'

'I haven't been out on a Friday night for quite a while. I

mean, other than just in a pub with pals. What would you like to drink?' he asked as a waiter approached.

'It's the cocktail hour. I'll have a cosmopolitan.'

'And another of these,' Morton instructed. 'Well, here we are.'

Ailsa smiled. 'I was surprised you asked me out.'

'Me too.' He pulled a face. 'I hope you don't think I asked you for any other reason than I thought it might be nice.'

'It was unplanned? That's a surprise. I thought two visits to my office in a week was evidence of a campaign of some sort. Only kidding!'

Morton pulled a wry face. 'I think it was just the smallness of that backroom, the proximity… I felt under pressure somehow.' He laughed. 'I mean, it just came over me, the words I mean. I don't regret it.'

'I'm glad to hear it. And you're not married? Not going out with anyone? Young, free and single? That's a surprise. How old are you?'

Morton snorted. 'Woah! I *am* single, don't know about those other two things. Been divorced for four years now. My age?' He inhaled noisily. 'That's on a need-to-know basis. Anyway, you?'

'Never been married. Was in a long-term thing but that ended a couple of months ago. He was a politician. And before you ask, no, not a Blairite! Ah, divergent paths just. I've been very busy getting the new office established, campaigning, you know…'

'I think you're probably a good bit younger than me.'

'Fishing? Need-to-know basis…'

Morton relaxed and sat back. 'Okay, look, I'm thirty-seven.'

'Christ, that *is* old!'

'Fucksake. Sorry.'

'Three-oh.'

'Really. You look younger. Young for a union boss anyway.'

Ailsa laughed. 'Some men find it intimidating. Others just patronise. The "wee lassie" type of thing.'

'I'll bet. That looks glamorous,' he said as the waiter brought their drinks.

'Just vodka and cranberry juice, with a slice of lime and a dash of Cointreau.'

'Looks sophisticated.'

'Huh. Most cocktails are very simple but I suppose not many men go for them.'

'Probably just a male laziness thing. Anyway, should we order?'

Later, as the restaurant began to fill up and after a perfectly reasonable carbonara, followed by panna cotta with chocolate sauce and raspberries, they had exhausted their level of small-talk and moved on to politics, specifically, the subject of the prime minister, Gordon Brown. While he imagined the PM as a kind of Auld-Nick figure from *Tam O'Shanter*, glowering and sulking in his 'winnock-burner in the east', Ailsa had real admiration for him.

'I know him quite well. We've met a dozen times or more. He's absolutely charming and easy company.'

'Hmn,' Morton mused. 'And at least he's not grinning inanely all the time like Blair. Possibly that's one of his strongest plus points.'

'Oh yes – that he's not Tony Blair.'

'But here's the thing, Ailsa, he supported all of Blair's projects, WMD the 'sexed-up' dossier, the Iraq War, his cosying-up to Bush. So, in what way is he different?'

'He had to. Collective responsibility. He was stitched up. But now, he's moving in a better direction.'

'Oh? Is that why he's summoned Mandy back as a fixer? It's sad to see, really. Once he was the great white hope of the left, the darling of Scottish Labour, but in government he went along with it, or was stitched-up, whatever, he lent his credibility, his intellectual integrity to the snake oil charmer. It's not just him. What has happened to all the great ideas, all the powerful intellectuals, the visionaries of the Scottish Labour movement in the seventies?'

'Crikey, bit before my time.'

He guffawed. 'And mine, but I have read about it. I even have a copy of *The Red Paper on Scotland* that Brown edited while he was Rector of Edinburgh University in 1975. Extraordinary seam of talent in it. Not all of it Labour of course. Tom Nairn and others, Vince Cable, Jim Sillars, no less. I got it in a secondhand bookshop. Think it was about fifty p. But back then Scottish Labour was at the centre of things and although only a minority were interested in a Scottish Parliament, or Assembly as it was referred to then, they had all the intellectual firepower, the vision-thing, as George W Bush senior called it. The boys who were destined for great things. And Brown was the leader of it, the major figure.'

'Well, maybe he still is. He's the PM!' McKinnon snorted.

'Yes, but a beleaguered figure now. Doomed. The black beast trapped in its lair, crashing in freefall down the polls. What has gone wrong? I mean, compared to Alex Salmond, who's like a yin to his yang, a polar opposite twin, though they have a lot in common.'

'Both white males, middle-class, heterosexual, if that's what you mean. Male, stale and pale. And Salmond's so smug, isn't he? Like a Cheshire cat. Always so chuffed with himself.'

'Is he any more smug than Broon? Here's a question for you, Ailsa. Which of them do the English voters hate the most?'

'Well,' she paused, sniffed, considered, 'that's a question and a half.'

'Anyway, what I was going to ask you is how Labour stands in Scotland now. Are they all behind Brown? Do they think he can win an election in England?'

'The unions are solid but you're right, there's a lot of fear that England will reject him. Especially now we've lost power at Holyrood.'

'That's another thing. Why is your Labour team at Holyrood all the second-raters? Why doesn't Brown come back and stand here? He'd be a shoo-in to beat Salmond for First Minister. All their big hitters are stuck in Westminster. They haven't adapted to the idea of the Scottish Parliament, it's like they see it as glorified council chamber, and MSPs are of lesser importance than being an MP in London. This is why Labour is losing support in Scotland. Well, one of the reasons.'

'But the nationalists exploit grievances with Westminster to divert attention from their own lack of talent, anyway… let's get out of here. And let's stop talking shop!'

They laughed at their seriousness. The bill when it came was divided between them and they laughed about that as well. It was dark, cold and windy when they got outside. Princes Street was busy. Morton wondered if he should take her hand but decided it was premature. He was enjoying her company and was going to let her lead. He didn't know if she was looking for commitment or just a night out. Was he a pal, or a potential lover? Was she his girlfriend? Would they make an arrangement to see each other again, or was this a one-off?

'Come on Willie, keep up!'

'Right, where are we off?'

'Clubbing. That was, is, the plan. What's your favourite club?'

He stopped at the pedestrian crossing and looked at her. 'No idea. Haven't set foot in a club. Well, not for years. What would you recommend?'

'Okay. There's Erotica, Bongo, the Honeycomb, the Establishment, in Semple Street…'

'No, not that one. The Establishment just doesn't sound like me…'

'It's an ironic name, Willie. But my favourite at the moment is in the Cowgate. Faith. That's a nice place.'

'Oh, I've seen it. Former church? Near where I work.'

'Well, that's a good start. Come on.' She grasped his arm and pulled him across Princes Street into the Mound.

It was noisy and dark, reddish dark. Ambience he supposed they'd call it. They managed to get soft seats in a sofa in a corner hard by a whitewashed stone wall under a stained-glass window. They were several rounds of drinks further on into the evening and he was hot and sweaty. She'd had him up dancing to music that he supposed was 'hip-hop' or rapping or something, massive thumping bass and incomprehensible snarling vocals. For some reason he'd become loquacious and all about Sally! Couldn't stop himself. She'd told him about her childhood which had been difficult and her first involvement in politics at school then working in a factory and becoming a steward and he'd told her of his difficulties trying to make his way as a freelance and then the subject of his ex-wife got mentioned somehow and he went on and on about her. It was hard to hear anyway, hard to keep up a conversation. He went to the toilet, a place of dark green mouldy walls and puddles of urine on the floor tiles. He stood at a pedestal, one forearm holding himself off the wall. He had to sober up. Stop talking about bloody Sally! Find out what she thought about him. Was this a date, or not?

She wasn't sitting in the sofa when he got back. He looked around the crowds, blearily, wondering if she had gone to the toilet too. He felt a responsibility for her. Then he saw her on the dancefloor, beckoning him. He joined her.

'Thought I'd buggered off?' she teased.

'What? Sorry...'

'You're not really enjoying this, are you?'

'I'm doing my best,' he countered. 'I'm not a natural dancer. More of an elite athlete!'

'Ho-har! Well, look, it's nearly one. Let's go. I could do with some fresh air.'

'Good idea!'

He was glad to get out though it was cold in the Cowgate and nearly deserted, a few couples and groups of males straggling about. The wind quickly found all the damp parts around the neck and under the oxters where sweat lingered. It sobered him up but his ears were ringing and his throat was sore. He felt old.

'I work up there,' he pointed as they walked along the narrow, deserted underpass under streetlights. He saw the unobtrusive rear entrance to the *Standard* office with its keypad entry. He could go in there and speak to the nightshift, sit at the freelancer's desk. It would be funny to be there at this time of night. The pavements were obstructed in places with bins, or boxes of rubbish and in some parts the old cobbles could be seen as they passed under the iron filigree work of the viaduct beneath South Bridge.

'I know you do, Willie. What are you working on now?'

He exhaled, suddenly weary. He didn't feel in the mood to

go over all his anxieties about work, his money problems, his nagging feeling that he needed to find a better career. 'Well! I'm still looking into the Glenforgan story,' he told her reluctantly. 'This guy Raymond Mearns and Neil Shankwell, your steward.'

'He isn't a steward anymore. He was.'

'Look,' he paused, hands deep in his coat pockets, 'Ailsa, I know I said I wouldn't ask you stuff... I'm sorry, but you saw Mearns at the count you said. Is he... about my age? What does he look like?'

'Very ordinary. I didn't speak to him. I don't know him. I'm not aware that he's really anything to do with Labour but there he was... with a rosette so he must be. What do I know? I noticed the person he was with, was, incidentally, a former GMB member too, as it happens. I remember one of my regional officers represented him at a tribunal somewhere. He was made redundant, no, wait,' she reflected. 'He was sacked I think... something to do with sexual harassment... that I do remember, in Glasgow, I think.'

'Don't suppose you remember his name?'

'Yes. Darren Barr.'

Morton stopped, ran a hand across his forehead. 'Right. Listen, I could murder a cup of coffee now, sober me up a bit. Any ideas?'

'Willie! That's a clumsy line. I'm surprised at you. You mean mine or yours?'

'Nooo-oo, honest. I live in Gorgie, I don't even know where you live. No, I meant...'

'Relax. I know a place. Open all night. It's just along here...'

'Then I'll walk you home, assuming that's not East Lothian. Where do you live anyway?'

'I share a flat in Marchmont. But I'll get a taxi.'

'That isn't too far out of my way home.'

'It's a cold night, Willie. Don't fancy walking. I was thinking we could meet up on Sunday if you are free.'

'Yeah. I could be,' he said. He had no plans but the suddenness of it took him by surprise. 'That's a nice idea. What do you want to do? Film, maybe?'

'Aye, we could, or maybe just have a stroll about. Lunch in Leith, I don't know.'

'Leith?' Morton repeated faintly, though he stopped himself in time as he was about to mention Sally's name yet again and their first married home. 'I used to live there. In a flat in Prince Regent Street near Leith Theatre.'

She clasped his arm. 'Or somewhere else, anywhere. The world's our oyster. Just a walk somewhere. Get some fresh air. Here's the coffee place. Small but perfectly formed. All human life is here.'

He looked at the doorway and the lights. It was very small. 'I didn't even know it was here.'

CHAPTER TWELVE

When the train pulled in to Glasgow Central, Raymond Mearns got off, mingling with passengers, stepping confidently out onto Union Street, car keys in one hand, wheeling his suitcase with the other. It had been a successful trip, a boost to his self-esteem, particularly the stay at Claridges, but now it was time to go to work. A pale afternoon sunshine lengthened the shadows on the busy street as he strode the hundred yards to the multi-storey carpark. The Range Rover Freelander was on the fourth floor. He put his suitcase in the boot and soon was driving west along the M8 as the streetlights came on. It was twenty minutes' drive to the small Meadowside industrial estate north of Renfrew, composed of low, aluminium-clad industrial units; premises of electrical contractors, a plumbing supplies unit, a small wholefoods distributor and several empty units. Beyond the end of the cul-de-sac was a line of trees, visible in the light of a lonely streetlight and beyond that the Clyde and the lights across the river. Streetlights were few and some had been vandalised and not replaced. Few people came here after normal working hours. It was a bit creepy; the kind of area people would avoid after dark and there were no direct roads to it, few people would stumble upon it by accident. It was not a place dog-walkers would frequent.

He stopped at the gate of the last unit on the left. It would seem to visitors as disused as its neighbours behind the high wire mesh fence though lacking any For Sale or To Let signs. This was one of several premises to which he had access. He got out of the car and applied several keys to the padlock and swung the gate open. He drove in and closed it behind him, reattaching the padlock and locking it. He glanced up and down the street but there was no-one, no activity apart from the sound of jets taking off and landing nearby so he got back in the car and drove carefully around the building over weeds sprouting through the tarmac to the rear and parked the car. It was a paved courtyard that had previously been a dispatch yard for the business that had formerly operated from the premises, some years before. It had a high brick wall on three sides and behind was the wood and beyond that, at some distance, the lights of Yoker across the river.

Mearns unlocked the glass doors and took his suitcase inside. The former dispatch unit had been converted to living quarters and contained a kitchen-diner, a lounge and a small bedroom. There was a TV, a telephone and a broadband connection. It was one of three addresses he could access. Where he came when he had work in hand that required complete privacy. He didn't mind the isolation. From the small freezer he took out a ready-meal, barely glancing at the frosted label and put it in the microwave. He took off his shoes and his jacket and began to spread his papers on the table. He had some planning but first had to make some calls. As the microwave pinged, he cradled the phone between his shoulder and left ear and deftly slid lasagne onto a plate.

Oliver Trenchard had always a tendency to regret the rapidly changing world because changes, he felt, were generally not for the better. Certainly, in his life, he felt that he was on a downward slope, descending rapidly towards retirement and insignificance. His earliest memories of the rolling downs of Southwold and little villages of Suffolk, the absolute certainty of family life, endless warm summers, the camaraderie of school cricket were the brightest. And then Oxford, golden days beneath the dreaming spires. Punting on the river in the fading glow of the evening sun. Part of a set, he had shown promise, was clubbable. And early had planned a political career. But circumstances had conspired to throw him off course. And later he had settled into the daily routine in the Home Office as a middle ranking clerical worker, rising slowly through the ranks to his present level. He had married, to the surprise of his contemporaries, in his late thirties. And he and Audrey had been blissfully happy. Reading books together, country walks. Genteel holidays abroad.

But after less than twenty years Audrey had died and since then Oliver had lived alone in the garden flat in Camden. His life had shrunk to fit the final five years of his working career: all his efforts devoted to keeping up appearances, the mask of respectability, maintaining his calm exterior as befitting his position. Living his life to please Audrey, doing the things she would have wished him to do. It often seemed to him in his introspective moments as if he was becoming ever more insignificant with each passing year. Sidetracked, certainly, he felt, even perhaps overlooked. It was a surprise to be called upstairs on that particular day, and to find himself alone with Sir Edward Bullough, the principal officer, on the fifth floor, whose windows overlooked the sea of trees of St James' Park.

Sir Edward was a high-flyer who had parachuted in from the Foreign Office, trailing gossip in his wake of glamorous assignments, postings overseas. He had a blue dead-eyed stare that unnerved his underlings, something that so far, Trenchard had only heard about. Now he began to experience it and looked down at his shoes. He sat in the proffered chair by the window screens.

'Trenchard,' Sir Edward said, pronouncing each syllable with relish. 'We've never met?'

'No.'

'And yet you've been with the department...' he glanced down at the briefing note on the desk... 'with the department for twenty-four years?'

'Twenty-five.' He noted the impeccable coiffeur and the unmistakable aroma of... aftershave, or perfumed oil. Was Sir Edward's hair slightly coloured, tinted? He forced himself to cease such irrelevant musings and concentrate. 'In a month's time,' he added.

'Quite so. Well, Trenchard. We want you to lead a new unit that's going to be set up, funded jointly between the Home Office and the Scotland Office. It'll be a small team – a unique opportunity to really make a difference. There's two rooms allocated and you'll have staff – a small team. How do you feel about making such a move? Or perhaps you feel you'd rather not?'

'No – it sounds interesting,' Trenchard said.

Bullough was nodding complacently. 'It will have unique lines of oversight. In fact, you will be working more or less on your own. The funding,' he paused, with a sly smile under his clipped moustache, 'the funding will be very hush-hush, and it won't appear anywhere. You'll have *carte blanche*, Trenchard. Think of that.'

'Carte blanche?' Trenchard repeated. It sounded to him highly unlikely – as fanciful as a carton of ice cream which was equally as likely. He frowned, trying to keep calm beneath that steely gaze. 'And what will be the focus of the unit's work?'

Sir Edward leaned back, smiling pleasantly, fingers coming

together into a pyramid. 'Broadly, interventions.' Seeing Trenchard's puzzled look, he added. 'It will have a very specific focus in politics in Scotland. You will be creating opportunities and deploying resources to highlight the benefits for Scotland of the union with England.'

'I see, yes,' Trenchard said, nodding. 'I understand.'

Sir Edward leaned forward. 'But what exactly you will be doing, initially at least, is bringing people together to set up groups and organisations to take forward the work north of the border. You will be a kind of liaison unit working behind the scenes to link groups together.' He waved his hand generously. 'Apply funding where it is needed, Trenchard. Create something greater than the sum of its parts. Some of the groups – perhaps think-tanks – will be quasi-academic. Others will be more media focused.'

Bullough smiled expansively. 'Of course, some of this work has been ongoing for a while, as you might expect. A lot of it, in fact. But you will work on expanding it into a critical mass. Intensifying it, making it more…' he beamed, '…successful. You will have significant funding – all of it completely protected from public scrutiny. Your own empire, in fact!'

Trenchard had a sudden vision of himself ennobled, an emperor in robes with a golden sceptre. He smiled, then coughed to cover it.

'You will – Oliver – fight the good fight on behalf of us all.' Trenchard was jolted by the sudden use of his Christian name, but his superior was in full flow.

'Without significant intervention now, the union will be on a slippery slope. The sovereignty of our nation needs to be defended against saboteurs, dissidents, and those political actors who would wrench us apart. Yes, indeed. Now they're in government, there is a very real risk the nats in Scotland can make headway. Which must not be allowed to happen. So, Trenchard, what are your initial thoughts?'

'It sounds good,' Trenchard said warily, wondering how much of it was hyperbole, a small carton of ice-cream. 'Will I have any say in the staffing?'

A shadow passed over the Principal Officer's eyes. 'Well... possibly. I'll see what I can do. Have you someone in mind?'

'Hutchison – grade seven. He's from Scotland. That might help.'

'It might indeed. I'll look into it. So am I to assume that if offered the post you would accept?'

'I will,' Trenchard said confidently.

'Good, good. Well done. Good man. I'll email the details to you and your section head. He'll assist you with the logistics. Good man, thank you, Trenchard and good luck.'

It had all gone smoothly. Within a month he was installed at a equally creaky oak desk in two rooms on the second floor of the interior of Home Office building C behind Marsham Street. He was happy enough there, within walking distance of his old haunts and Whitehall. There were two panelled wooden windows that often stuck but could be opened slightly with effort to let in the sparse inner light from the courtyard beyond, particularly in the afternoon and the two rooms had an interconnecting door. Anyone passing along the general corridor of the second floor would see the obscure title 'Interventions Section B' stencilled on the door, with *Lead Officer: O. J. Trenchard*, though there was little foot traffic. It was almost equidistant between lift 1 and lift 3 on the north-western corner. Ten minutes' walk from his office to the Red Lion, including a first sip of a gin and tonic. The move had been accompanied by a promotion and a modest increase in salary. His over-riding feelings were that he had been selected for this important new work. He had been noticed. And it was important work. The Labour government was on its last legs, the Brown Cabinet falling apart, the advent of a minority nationalist regime in Holyrood led by Salmond had increased the general anxiety that the centre could not hold. The paranoia was palpable in Whitehall and he had been brought in to steady the good ship of state. Even though it was a small, even a dingy office on an obscure second floor corridor he could make an impact and justify his selection. It was not too far a stretch to imagine the successful conclusion of his unusual task might lead to a gong in the future, the fervent hope of every civil servant; the ultimate justification. It was an opportunity to combat the rising tide of disaffection and disillusionment with Britain and Britishness.

Within the first month, Trenchard's small team had successfully launched a pro-union think-tank, 'This Island Nation' with a large and prestigious advisory board mainly comprised of attention-grabbing historians, academics and crystal-ball-gazing economists including one from Scotland, with a sprinkling of Tory, Lib Dem and Labour politicians and members of the House of Lords. The launch had made waves in the media, trumpeted by some channels and newspapers as the long overdue heavyweight defence of the shared values and heritage of Great Britain. The think-tank was administered by a paid team of media professionals churning out press releases to the receptive media rebutting the daily iniquities of the nationalist regime at Holyrood and the inevitably false and divisive arguments used by pro-independence supporters. Trenchard's team had managed to persuade a reputable company of economic advisers, Atkinson Morley, to commence opinion polling on Scottish attitudes to 'inform the debate'. These were often useful outliers that showed support for the SNP and independence slipping while other mainstream polls may show the reverse. It was useful to muddy the waters and to allow pro-union spokesman apparent backing for their arguments, to suggest there was 'a disparity of opinion' at all times even if the mainstream polls sometimes seemed unanimous.

Trenchard had further gratification in that his staffing suggestion had been taken up and Julian Hutchison, who had many Scottish media connections, kept up a veritable barrage of programme ideas for celebration of British heritage and common effort in World War Two and these were often successfully received, particularly if a little associated seed funding could be offered to make the programme, or series, a reality. The benefits of the union, the wonders of each of the four nations, national pride, the appeal to shared history were now by far the most common elements of programming on the main TV and radio networks in Scotland. And the success of this had led to a sub-unit of retained feature writers working on the same theme led by a freelance, former *Daily Mail* staffer, Nigel Evans, who had become media consultant for Interventions Section B.

By hiving off all the media work, Trenchard was able to refocus on his intervention projects: four men in a small office, whose efforts though largely unattributable, beyond scrutiny, were starting to make things happen. After their early successes, they had begun to devise ever more audacious direct interventions by scooping up a number of useful activists at grassroots level and getting them to do things in their own areas, and that was when he had first got to know Raymond Mearns and others like him.

Morton found Darren Barr easy to track down. He had featured extensively in the media, firstly in the small print of news-in-brief stories of a disciplinary hearing for sexual harassment that had been transferred to Airdrie Sheriff Court. The case had attracted salacious commentary. The victim had waived her right to anonymity and so had been pictured in several tabloids with a small inset photo of Barr, who was definitely less photogenic. Morton stared at the small, grainy picture. It showed a type; a flabby-looking young man with a contemporary haircut, floppy on top, shaved at the back and sides, a stubble beard sprawling over several chins and, just, visible, a white teeshirt. He was probably around thirty, Morton reckoned. Ailsa had been right about the Glasgow connection but one of the reports of the court case noted that he was now living in Glenwood. Morton learned that he had been given a suspended sentence of eight months. He looked up Glenwood and saw that it was a housing scheme on the outskirts of Glenforgan. Was that another coincidence? No time like the present, he thought, driving north towards the Forth Road Bridge.

In the library in the main street of Glenforgan, he approached the General Reference desk and asked for a copy of the electoral roll. The middle-aged woman with green streaks in her blonde-brown hair hesitated slightly before handing him a copy – or perhaps he was just imagining it? He leafed through the Glenwood ward, finger sliding down the streets. It took him less than five minutes. There were several Barrs but only one Darren Barr and he lived alone. He found a map covering the Glenwood scheme in a shelf of Ordnance Survey maps and did a quick sketch of the scheme's layout. Then he was back in the car, heading west. He ran through various scenarios, considering what was best to put Barr at his ease and make him talk. He didn't want to appear to be a policeman or a reporter. Barr had probably developed a hatred of people asking questions but there was no other way. What he wanted to know was about his political connections, his reason to be at the count and his association with Raymond Mearns. If there had been something untoward at the by-election then Barr and Mearns would know about it. Given that it was a racing cert that Barr would be defensive if not physically aggressive, perhaps the only way to get something from him was to catch him by surprise and try to provoke a revealing reaction.

As soon as he turned into the street, he realised that it would be difficult to catch him by surprise. The tenement windows looked outwards, a military line of windows, and Barr lived in the middle of the street on the ground floor. He would be clocked as soon as he began to walk along. It was the kind of down-at-heel place where a stranger meant trouble, meant suspension of benefits or police charges or bailiffs posting warrants. He noted there were two flats on every floor and no outer doors on the close. The council properties were pre-modernisation and most of the open space was overgrown and litter strewn. He parked around the corner, attracting the attention of a barking German Shepherd – or Alsatian – behind a low wooden wall. It looked like a psycho, like it hadn't been fed for days and he saw froth between its rows of teeth. It was still barking as he turned into Barr's street.

There were no name plates on the identical, black-painted doors of the left and right ground floor flats. If he got the wrong one Barr would be out his back door and away, or behind his front door listening. There was no chance of surprising him. As soon as he knocked on the left door, he suspected it was wrong. A face of a very old wizened grey man peered out. Morton leaned in and spoke quietly: 'Barr?'

'Eh? Na.' The man's white finger pointed silently to the door opposite, and he was gone.

Morton waited in the silence, looking out at the street. He could hear the big dog barking at someone else. Imagine living next door to that? He contemplated the metal letterbox and wondered if it would creak if he lifted it to look through. He tapped the door frame and waited. No answer. He tapped again louder. Nothing. Not in. He leaned down and lifted the letterbox. Musty smell, unwashed clothes but no sounds, no movement. Barr was out. He went round to the back green. First, he checked the walls. There was no telephone cable into the house from the BT pole in a neighbour's backgreen. There was a disused and rusty satellite dish on the wall, but the cables had been severed. He peered into the bedroom. It looked a mess, there was an unmade bed and sheets piled on the floor. And a huge union flag pinned to the wall. Rangers fan? He moved to look into the kitchen, registering the sound of a front door closing somewhere and was immediately aware of a light bulb being switched on inside. Barr was back.

Mearns had arranged to meet the other two members of his team at the warehouse but planned to get there ahead of them. Keenan and Mouncey had been recruited by Trenchard and operated in Glasgow, but he could co-opt them for tasks as required. They were hired muscle as far as he was concerned and his main thought was how to keep the details of his operations to himself, even though in theory they all worked on the same side. He couldn't be sure they weren't spying on him for Trenchard. Nor did he have an understanding of what exactly they did when they weren't working with him, or where they lived. It was quite possible they were spies of one type or another. He didn't like them, but needed assistance now and then and they did what was asked. Keenan looked like a policeman, but denied that he was, or had been, while

Mouncey was a bit more forthcoming. He had worked for years in London and hoped to return there eventually. He was older, almost pension-age. Another mystery he considered, as he turned off the A741 Paisley Road, was how they knew each other, how they always turned up together. Mearns didn't like that, felt ganged-up on. He took precautions to hide the key aspects of what he was doing, just in case. There was no sign of their vehicle outside the warehouse as he turned his Freelander into the marked parking space.

It was an old brick two storey Victorian place, a mill or a factory of some kind or carpet warehouse, and they only used the ground floor part of it. He had only once ventured up onto the first floor, the haunt of pigeons and possibly rats. Some of the windows were broken. Another grim feature was the earth floor and the poor light. It was perfect for hiding vehicles as there were no windows on the ground floor. The entrance was unobtrusive at the front, a simple unmarked door with several locks but there was a double-doored exit around the side. Mearns glanced left and right down the street before tackling the locks and let himself in. He switched on the lights across the entire space, illuminating the three white-panelled vans parked haphazardly on the earth floor. He walked to the nearest van and examined the padlock on the roller shutter at the rear. It was unlocked. He unhooked it and heaved up the roller shutter a few feet. He looked inside. The black plastic bin bags were lined up as he had last seen them. He pulled himself up into the van and experimentally tried to lift the nearest one. It wasn't too heavy, perhaps thirty or forty kilos. What was inside was only paper, after all.

Morton knocked again and heard movement. The black door opened. Darren Barr, looking exactly like his picture in the paper, stood there, mouth open and flapping. He was big, tall and heavy, like Morton, but out of condition, with a big gut, thick limbs. There was a healed scar on his right cheek.

'Yeah? What is it?'

'I'm looking for your help, Mr Barr,' Morton started.

Distaste spread over Barr's face. 'My *help*? Fuck off, you.'

'I'm trying to get in touch with Raymond Mearns. I work for the GMB.'

'The *what*?'

'The union.'

'Right. Mearnsie? I've no seen him for months.'

Morton knew that was a lie. 'I was going to speak to him at Glenforgan but…' He watched Barr's face as he said that word.

'Why did ye no?'

Morton snorted. 'It was a busy night. We had things to sort out.'

'Well, ah've no seen him since.' He began to close the door, frowning. 'How does the GMB no ken?'

'Why would we? He's not a member.' He wondered if he'd be contradicted, but no, Barr let it pass. Maybe he wasn't a member?

'Ye could try… Labour HQ.'

'You know he was expelled.'

'I didnae ken that. Look, ah'm busy the now, eh, so piss aff!'

'You were with him on the night.'

'So were hunners ither fowk.'

'Wearin big Labour rosettes.'

'Ah wisnae.' Morton thought: *You liar*!

'Ye don't get into an election count if ye don't have ID, Darren. You were there. I saw you.'

'Ah don't have tae speak to you.'

'Come on. All I need's an address.'

Barr snorted. 'See the hameless unit. They'll sort ye oot.'

Morton frowned. 'Do you work for him?'

'What's it to you?'

Morton tried another tack. 'Okay, look,' he sighed, 'he owes me money.'

Barr laughed and seemed to relax a little. 'Join the club. Look, he contacts me for jobs and it's cash in hand. I don't know where he lives. There's a wee office in Glasgow he used to use. It's in Duke Street, eh. Used to be a Labour office but last I saw it was used by thae nutters New Britain Party or something, that rich tosser, Michael Ramage. You could ask there. That's all I ken. Anyway, he owes me for last time and I wisnae paid. So if ye see him, tell him, eh?'

'So what did you do for him?'

'What? Fuck off.'

Morton reached into his jacket pocket. 'I would pay for that kind of information.'

Barr seemed to consider this but rejected it. 'He'd find out and I'd no get my money.'

'How would he find out?' But the door was shut and Morton had no option but to walk away, thinking over what he'd been told, until his thoughts were fragmented by the demented barking of the Alsatian – or German Shepherd, as he walked to his car. Barr was involved, somehow or other. He knew something.

CHAPTER THIRTEEN

Morton tried to switch into leisure mode as he walked along the promenade from Portobello to Joppa with Ailsa. It was a breezy Sunday morning, blue sky competing with swirling banks of cloud and even sporadic bursts of a fine rain that disappeared before you could get the umbrella up. The sand looked churned up and muddy and some of it had blown up onto the concrete and lay in little barkhans and wet crusts along the path.

To get out of the rain they went into a bright vegan café on the junction with Musselburgh Road. Despite his intentions not to discuss work, he began telling her about his meeting with Barr. 'He has a huge union flag in his bedroom,' he said, illustrating the size of it with both hands. He laughed. 'Huge. I wonder what that's about?'

Ailsa did a double take. 'His *bedroom*?'

Morton coloured. 'No this was... I saw through the window when he wasn't in... before he came back. Probably just a Rangers fan, although he did mention the New Britain Party and Michael Ramage.'

'Oh God! Them,' Ailsa exclaimed, a look of distaste on her face. 'They're building up support. In the north of England particularly. We've lost members to them. They've latched on to a sort of xenophobia, a populist anti-EU feeling that draws support across the working class and Tory supporters too.

Ramage is an acolyte of Goldsmith. Lots of millionaires are behind it.'

'So maybe he's in it? But he had a Labour rosette on at the by-election?'

'Yes, or maybe I just imagined that? He was with Mearns, and I believe they both had rosettes or stickers. I couldn't swear to it, though and they were in the background, not really with us.'

'But how otherwise would Mearns and Barr get in to the count? How would they get through security? If they had rosettes could they just breeze in?

'No, Willie, security's tight. The election agents for the candidates provide a list of what's called counting agents. Each candidate gets up to about thirty, I think it is. So if your name is on the list, you just turn up, but you have to show ID to get in.'

Morton pursed his lips. 'At a by-election I guess lots of activists want to go to the count but if there are only thirty places... some wouldn't get in? Would be good to get a look at that list. Any chance of that? And would it have their addresses on it?'

Ailsa stirred her hot chocolate. 'I'm not sure. Probably. The list would need to be handed into the ERO days before the count. But you might get folk on the list who can't make it on the day – illness or accidents – and so someone else would just substitute for them. That happens. It's a bit informal. I don't think the lists are kept afterwards. Or maybe the agent keeps them, but I doubt it. There's probably no requirement to do so.'

'Barr mentioned an office they're supposed to be using in Glasgow. Which apparently,' he sniffed, 'used to be a Labour office.'

'Well, I don't know about that, Willie. I've no idea why a Labour office would close and turn into an NBP one. If it has.'

'Maybe this Mearns guy is a link somehow with… I don't know. His name keeps cropping up.'

'As I've told you, I don't really know anything about him. Barr I was aware of, as a former member, and the sexual harassment case, but Mearns means nothing to me. Just a guy on the fringes.'

On Monday morning Morton got up early and pocketed the car keys. The white VW Beetle hadn't been used for nearly a week and sat forlornly alongside the fencings of the park in Harrison Gardens, its roof littered with leaves and bits of twig. Although he always had doubts, it started first-time, without the need for pulling on the choke and soon, with sidelights on, he was puttering along amongst heavy traffic at Calder Junction, heading for Junction 1 and the M8, heading towards the weak sunrise, Radio Scotland on, listening to the news on 'GMS'. As he drove west, a wind got up, spattering the windscreen with squalling bursts of rain. It was cold for the time of year, no obvious signs of spring. He quite enjoyed the long trip, a rare pleasure these days. He even began to feel guilty about his previous treacherous thoughts of selling the car.

Morton found a parking space close to a building site just off Cathedral Street near Strathclyde University and walked down onto Duke Street. It was a long way to the address he had, nearly at Dennistoun in fact, on a junction with a small cul-de-sac. The ground floor premises were locked up, an iron bar padlocked across the red door. The streetlight in front of it showed the red paint was peeling and was much graffiti-ed. The single window had a metal grille cemented into place. A poster for the New Britain Party behind it showed blond Aryan youths waving a union flag. There were no other pedestrians, except for a couple of people across the road waiting at a bus stop. Morton peered through the scummy window grille. He could make out cardboard boxes and piled furniture. On the shallow shelf below the window, he saw a pile of unopened mail. Someone was probably visiting the premises, he realised, to check the mail. But otherwise, it was a dead end. He sighed. Well at least Darren Barr hadn't lied. The office did exist, though whether it had anything to do with Raymond Mearns was pure conjecture. He couldn't very well sit and wait until someone came along. He took a quick snap of the office frontage from the pavement. Long journey for very little he decided and began to walk back to the car.

Fifty yards back, the way he had come, he saw a run-down pub near a gap site. The Albion Arms. He hadn't noticed it on the way out. Light spilled from the glass in the upper part of the wooden door, but the sandstone walls looked sodden and some mortar was literally dissolving and falling away. He felt hungry and wondered if they did hot food. Steak pie and chips... probably they wouldn't do more than a bag of crisps. It occurred to him he might be able to ask a local about the office if he got the chance. Maybe he'd book into a hotel and stay the night. Although it was only mid-afternoon, it was already quite gloomy.

There were three customers in the bar, old men sitting by themselves, though he could see a larger group through a doorway in the Snug. The barman waited. Morton hesitated.

'Pint of 80 shilling. Any chance of something to eat?'

The barman leaned forward and pulled the pint. He looked up. 'Hoat mince pie?'

Morton sighed. 'Okay. Make it two. And a packet of crisps.'

The barman smiled. 'Hungry man? Wantin broon sauce? Or tomata?'

Morton grinned. 'One of each.'

The old man on the bar stool looked over. 'Livin dangerous, eh?'

Morton took his pint. 'Aye, ambition is a terrible thing.'

He took the pint over to where he could watch the huge TV on its metal bracket on the wall. A game show of some kind, mercifully with the sound turned very low. The modern equivalent of wallpaper. He looked at his watch. Nearly six-thirty. Maybe there'd be some news. He glanced through the doorway into the Snug where it looked like half a dozen men were having a meeting of some sort but he was struck by the fact that one of them, the one doing most of the talking was smartly-dressed in a suit and dark raincoat while the others looked like drug-dealers. When Morton saw them looking curiously at him, he quickly turned away. The people on the game show were winding up, getting very excited; one of them had won a plastic hairbrush. Numpties!

When the pies came, soggy grey pastry casings with the classic round hole at the top, he got stuck in, instantly burning his mouth. It had been microwaved long enough to melt plastic. He used the knife to cut them open on the plate and let the steam out and swallowed mouthfuls of beer. 'Any napkins?' he asked.

'I'll bring some over,' the barman said, 'they're hot by the way.'

'Now you tell me,' Morton joked.

'Burn yourself?' the man in the suit asked, standing over him. 'That microwave is lethal.'

'Yeah,' Morton said. 'I found that out.'

'Another?' the man asked, nodding at the bar. He had an English accent, Morton thought, or maybe just posh Scots that reminded him of many of his former classmates at George Watson's. Professionally English Scotsmen.

'Well… alright. Thank you. Eighty shilling.'

'Tam, my good man,' the man said at the bar. 'Another round and a pint of ale for our injured friend.'

There was no doubt in Morton's mind that his benefactor was, or had been, a military man and reminded him more than a little of the late Daniel McGinley. The quick hail-fellow-well-met bonhomie, the short hair, upright physique, just the bearing of the man. On the surface, amiable, convivial but underneath, well, what lurked there? Ruthlessness and a single-minded determination to take control. And perhaps too, a propensity for violence? He carefully ate one section of the pie. But McGinley was dead and that was all in the past.

'Pint, as ordered,' the man said now, carefully placing it in front of Morton.

'Thank you,' Morton said, noting the steel cufflinks, the folded back shirt cuffs, the steel watch strap, hairs on the back of the hand. He extricated some gristle from his mouth and placed it on his plate. He looked up. 'Decent of you.'

The man smiled down at him. 'You must either be very hungry or a glutton for punishment? Two of Tam's notorious pies?'

Morton laughed abruptly. 'Well… maybe.'

'Why don't you join us… once you've eaten?'

Morton looked round, frowning.

The man leaned in and offered his hand. 'Alan Melville,' he said.

Morton cleared his throat, 'right…sorry…' his hands greasy. 'Willie Morton.'

'I'll introduce you to the boys, Willie.' He shrugged. 'Up to you… if you prefer…' He went back into the snug.

Morton considered, as he slowly ate the cooling and rather bland food. Why did the man want to introduce him to the group? Was it a group of gay men? From what he could see they looked like very ordinary working-class blokes. If it was a men's group, Melville seemed out of place. Perhaps he was a probation officer and the others were ex-cons? But that didn't seem right either. They seemed to be talking about politics but they were not over loud, as if aware of not attracting attention, so if that was true, why introduce a complete stranger to the group?

He looked at his watch. Just after seven. The games show had given way to a tense and gritty serial drama set in a London pub. Threatening looks and a scuffle breaking out in the street. He had never consciously seen it before though he knew millions were addicted to it. What now? It was too late to drive home. He'd find somewhere to stay the night and drop by the closed-down office in the morning. Or he could ask about it at the library which was just around the corner. He finished his pint. It occurred to him to buy Melville a pint though he didn't want a third one himself. He stood up and went into the snug.

'Ah hello, Mr Morton,' Melville stood up. 'Come to join us?'

'Well, I was going to head off,' Morton admitted, looking round at the faces of the group. There were one of two half-smiles but this did not look like a group he wanted to join, whatever it was. 'But I'll get you a drink before I go.'

'Oh no need, no need. Why don't you sit down for a moment or two. We were just putting the world to rights. Isn't that right, boys? We were just discussing the state of our economy. Where do you stand Morton? Are you one of us? Do you want to save your country from the socialists and foreigners?'

Morton scoffed. 'What?'

'The country is going to the dogs,' Melville said, jovially. 'What it needs is a good old boot up the backside.'

'So you are a political group?'

'We are the New Britain Party,' he said proudly. 'You must have heard of our leader, Michael Ramage? He's offering us a brand-new start, escape from the EEC. It's time for a radical new direction,' he concluded.

Morton grinned and waved. 'Speaking of which... no offence but I must go. Goodbye.'

CHAPTER FOURTEEN

It was getting colder, the evening air failing like invisible ice on the back of hands and cheeks. Morton hoofed it back along Duke Street looking for an inexpensive hotel. He needed something to eat, a hot shower. He knew he should simply drive back to Edinburgh where he could have those things for free. He couldn't possibly justify the expense of a hotel room for the night. It had been a fool's errand. What had he discovered? That Barr had given him the correct address for a closed Labour office now apparently in use by the NBP, which had some connection with Raymond Mearns. He was no further forward in his investigation. He needed to speak to Mearns, but first he would have to find him.

It was a long way to where he had left the car, and it was starting to rain, or sleet, coming intermittently in wet squalls. Just before the High Street, Morton spotted a Premier Inn with an underground car park attached and was simultaneously overwhelmed by an urge to eat hot food and have some warm indoor comfort. He went into the reception foyer and booked a room for the night. Within five minutes, he was scuttling back out to retrieve the car.

Once he had parked in the hotel's underground park, the lift brought him up to the foyer from where he could see the bar through glass doors. He knew the restaurant would close in half an hour and did not want to have to go out again into the cold and wet looking for somewhere to eat. He went into the bar and ordered food and a drink and on instinct glanced round to his right. The man seated there next to him on the bar stool, looking at him with a slight quizzical smile, was Alan Melville. He had got rid of the suit and raincoat and wore a burgundy-coloured sweater over an open-necked shirt and looked amiable, even avuncular, but it *was* him.

'We meet again,' Melville said. 'Coincidence, I suppose?'

Morton frowned. 'I thought you were having a meeting?'

'We did.' He smirked. 'Our meetings are generally short and to the point.'

'Which is…?' Morton said.

Melville snorted. 'Join me, if you're eating? I've ordered too.'

There was no way out of it. Morton thought he might learn something. He'd ask him about Mearns. He wasn't happy at being seen in the company of a racist but sometimes you had to sup with the devil, or his minions, to get to the truth. At any event, he seemed different, more relaxed than he had been in the pub among the knuckle-draggers. Hard to believe it was the same man. Melville must have left the pub just minutes after him in a vehicle and passed him on the road. It was a bit of a coincidence.

Morton spilled a few drops of water into the tumbler of Glenfiddich, watched approvingly by the racist or ex-military man… or whatever he was. He signed the chit to his room number, careful to ensure that Melville couldn't see the number.

'I'll talk about anything,' he said, 'except politics. We're going to have to disagree there.'

Melville laughed. 'No problem, old chum. Glad of the break.'

'You're obviously ex-military,' he said. 'First thing I noticed about you.'

'I'll take that as a compliment if I may. And correct. I have served. Done my time.'

'And gave it up?'

'I wasn't kicked out, if that's what you meant? These things have a natural life span.'

'And is what you're doing now fulltime?'

Melville smirked. 'I thought we weren't going to talk about politics?'

'Okay. I just have a natural curiosity about whether the NBP can afford to pay people to organise.'

'No, they can't. Not yet.' Melville shrugged. 'We will eventually, progress is very rapid. Well, in certain areas it is.'

'Not Glasgow though, I'd have thought.'

'We have support here, but it's fragmented. Ach, what am I doing... we said we wouldn't talk about it.'

'My fault. It just seemed to me as if you were an organiser. The others...'

He laughed. 'Oh, I know what you're going to say. The others looked like scruff. You're not wrong. Our appeal is felt strongly in certain sections of society. Here, fans of a certain football club... you know... that support the Queen, the union flag... not keen on foreigners...'

'Well, obviously, the Orange Lodgers, as I call them...'

'But not just them, also the type who get awfully stirred up about Muslims, and Jews and people of an African or Indian persuasion.'

'People of an African... *persuasion*?'

'You know what I'm getting at. Let's not argue, Morton. Look, here's our food coming.'

The waiter attended to them and when he left, with his tray and white towel on his forearm, Morton peppered his pasta sauce and tried to work out how Alan Melville fitted into the picture. He would ask him about Darren Barr – he could imagine him as one of the knuckle-draggers – and Raymond Mearns, he might even slip the name of Lord Carnoway in somehow.

'And what's your racket anyway?' Melville asked, forking chips.

Morton reluctantly told him: 'I work for a newspaper. The *Standard*.'

'The nationalist one?'

'Morton laughed. 'It is pro-independence but it's not nationalist. The two things are not necessarily the same.'

'If you say so. So what were you doing in the *Albion*?'

Morton swallowed a forkful of penne. 'Checking out an old Labour party office… that I was told is now used by the NBP.'

'Oh, yes, we use it, mainly as a store and a mail address. Needs a lot of work before it can be opened to the public. So you're interested in doing a story on us?'

'Well, maybe. If there is a story. Like how did a Labour office suddenly become an NBP one? Did someone defect?'

Melville raised an eyebrow. 'A grotty old office… not exactly prime real estate.'

'Darren Barr was the person who told me about it.'

'Who? Don't think I know him.'

'He was a Labour man and now seems to be in the NBP, or a supporter anyway.'

'Maybe he is. I don't know them all. I only see the ones who… interested in coming along to a meeting. So you thought this Barr chap had something to do with us getting the office? That's not how it works. Glasgow City Council would put you right on that.'

'There's also Raymond Mearns.'

'Mearns, yes, he's somebody I have heard of. But he's not one of us, the NBP, I mean.'

'How do you know the name then?'

'Well, funny you should ask that, Morton. It was in connection with my employers…'

'Your *employers*?' Morton repeated and sat back. 'Not the NBP?'

'Good grief, no. What I do for the NBP is only a small part of my job.' A smile spread across his face. 'Thank goodness. I mean, fair play to Michael Ramage, he's on the right track, but I have an actual job too.'

'Tell me about it, if you don't mind.'

'I don't mind,' he shrugged. 'I'm happy to. Obviously, I can't go into detail. Well, when I was discharged after a long career in the services – I was made up to the rank of Major – I tried various things but couldn't settle, then a former CO of mine invited me in to see him. He'd heard I was having trouble and put me in touch with – well, I can't give you the name of the outfit, but – let's just say it's London-based. Turns out it's the perfect job for me, a bit of travel, I'm up here in Scotland too, which is perfect for my family.' He grimaced. 'Not that I ever visit my ex-wife, but the kiddies… anyway, to answer your question, I'm a kind of liaison officer for a large organisation. That's it, really.'

Morton shrugged. 'Not giving much away, are you?'

Melville seemed amused. 'You are a journalist. My employers would take a dim view of me speaking to a journalist, least of all one working for a nationalist paper.' He finished his pint. 'Secrecy is the name of the game for them. Even secrecy when there's no need for it.'

Morton chewed the last morsel of ciabatta. 'Give me a clue about the "large organisation" at least. That can't hurt.'

'Well, let's see. It's London-based.'

'You said that already.'

'It's work is exclusively in Scotland. It works alongside government but is not a government department.'

Morton frowned. 'MI5?'

'Nope!'

'Special Branch?'

'Good grief, Morton! You over-estimate my skillset! MI5, Special Branch? I can understand why you might think that because of my services background, but my role is a lot humbler, I can assure you.'

Morton was reluctant to leave the subject. 'Are you some kind of agent for the Scottish Tories?'

'Getting closer now, Morton,' Melville smiled. 'In fact, I spent six months working for the Tories down in Galloway at the last election. I'm not and never have been a member, but I was tasked with building up the vote down there. It's a difficult area; a three-way split near enough. My job was very specific. I was to contact all the recent incomers in the area and ensure they voted the right way. I had lists of names… from somewhere. It was believed the nats might take the two seats there, so I was recruited to help prevent that.' He grinned. 'And it worked. In fact, the incomer vote came out solidly for the Tories and they kept both seats.'

'Lists of names?'

'Ah, don't ask. Anyway, it was a job. Someone had to do it. So in that sense, I was a Tory. In another sense, I'm a NBP man, and also, elsewhere I'm working for UKIP and even sometimes for Labour. Do you see the common thread here?'

'I do,' Morton said, wearily. 'So the "large organisation" is generally combatting Scottish nationalists?'

'Got it in one, son! I'm a patriot.'

'A patriot?' Morton mused. 'A British patriot? You have an employer yet they cannot all be one and the same organisation... how could it be? I mean Labour, Tory, UKIP and maybe even Michael Ramage's party if it stands in elections – are going to be fighting against each other?'

'You think?'

'Aren't they?'

'That's for you to find out.'

'Come on, just give me a name.'

'Egbert.'

'What?'

'Donald.'

Morton smiled wryly. 'That's very funny, but I just don't see you as an employee of Egbert... or Donald. Is it a bureau or a private company? Or is it a network of freelance "liaison officers" like you? And who pays? Whose money is behind it? You don't have to tell me, just give me sight of a payslip or something.'

'Really, Mr Morton, I've given you everything you need. I can't have anything appearing in the *Scottish Standard*. Sooner or later, it would get back to me. But I can assure you, we are not breaking any laws or doing anything dodgy. Everything I do is totally, one-hundred percent legal.'

'But who's paying for it? If it's not government money?'

'I didn't say it wasn't. It's not a government department but it works alongside government. That's what I said. But I've said enough. Let's change the subject. Are you for another?' He indicated his empty pint glass.

'Eh, no, my shout. Same again?' Morton waved to the barman. Melville had as good as hinted some of the money was government funding, presumably filtered through some laundry process but maybe some public figure like Carnoway was fronting it? Maybe Lord Carnoway of Froy was the money man? Although he felt Melville was in one sense toying with him, he also felt he was bragging, maybe even enjoying stringing him along. Originally he'd felt a sense of menace from him in the pub, that he and his associates were a physical threat to him. But here in the hotel, he'd been friendly. Even when he discovered Morton was a journalist. He couldn't work him out and therefore had to discount most of what he had been told as not necessarily true. He decided to sit back and wait to see what more Melville would volunteer. There was a story somewhere for him, but he needed actual details, not just supposition, boasting and vagueness. He sipped the froth on the head of the fresh pint and waited. The waiter took their plates away.

Shall we move to more comfortable seats?' he asked, nodding at the sofa near the gas-effect fireplace. A crowd of customers came in, their coats soaking wet.

'Why not?' Melville nodded. 'Bag the best seats before they do.'

Morton stood up and lifted his pint. Melville was mellowing, he felt. He was going to attempt to lull him into giving away more information, ply him with alcohol and try to find out what he knew. It would cost him but would be worth it.

CHAPTER FIFTEEN

There was no sign of Melville the next morning in the bright, white airy breakfasting room, next to the bar. Morton lingered over the guilty pleasures of a full fry-up; eight items, including black pudding slice, mushrooms, several cups of coffee. In the end he hadn't managed to get more information out of him despite investing in several pints and whiskies. He had persuaded him to write down his email address. Which looked real but may turn out to be bogus. Melville had baulked at giving him his mobile number on the grounds of it being a work phone. He still couldn't decide what he felt about the man; was he an idle boaster, or someone who enjoyed pretending to be a man of mystery? He wasn't actually a racist. He'd found that out; his previous racist comments were part of his act as an organiser for the New Britain Party. It *was* an act, though he was undoubtedly a British patriot with out-dated attitudes on subjects like colonialism, empire and feminism and gender diversity. But not a racist *per se*, though these things were subjective. He'd also claimed at one point to be a former pupil at Hutcheson's, which was something Morton could investigate.

Morton pondered the word patriot, a word nowadays more associated with right wing American bigots or an anti-aircraft missile. Like its counter – the word traitor – these were terms associated with another age, with helmets and chainmail, the gibbet, heads on spikes on castle walls. Or the smoke and bombs of the Blitz where patriots kept an eye out for traitors who were usually foreigners or disillusioned fifth columnists and Marxists, educated at Cambridge, spying for the Soviets. These were terms most people now avoided. They were in some way tainted, perhaps overused. What was their meaning, if any, in Scotland in 2010? Morton wondered. He knew the word derived from *patria*, Latin for country, but Scotland was a nation, Britain a state and on your passport nationality was defined as UK which related you to the reign of a monarch! The Prime Minister was always sounding off about Britishness and British values, to the derision of nationalists who claimed he was simply trying to co-opt Tory terrain or persuade English voters he was, although a Scot, a Scot of the decent, thoroughly British, kind.

A minority of people in Scotland, he knew, if given the choice, would define their nationality as British. The majority were Scottish first, British second, and a minority were Scottish only, didn't consider themselves British at all. It was obvious Scotland was re-emerging as a potentially independent state and with it feelings of Britishness would decline but there would always be that special bond, not least because of family ties and the social connectivity of the neighbouring nations. It was, in short, a land of divided allegiances and suspect loyalties. For most ordinary Scots in 2010, the decision was whether to continue to support Labour, the party of the embattled prime minister Gordon Brown, the party that had, albeit reluctantly, legislated for devolution or to flip the coin for the nationalists and the brilliant young first minister in Edinburgh leading the charge for independence. It was an age-old dichotomy. Sir Walter Scott had debated his conflicting allegiances to Scotland and England in his literary works. John Buchan believed 'that every Scotsman should be a Scottish nationalist', Robert Louis Stevenson defined himself through his rebellion against the Anglicising respectability of the genteel classes. A nationalist group in the 1970s proscribed by the SNP for being too extreme, had been chaired by no less than arch-Tory reprobate Sir Nicolas Fairbairn. But if all these icons were tossed up into the air and divided into two piles; Scots and English, there would be no such confusion. The confusion was perhaps caused by the oddball notion of 'Britishness'.

And now Alan Melville. Well, he'd had extensive military service under the union flag; years of God saving the Queen in barracks and parade grounds. And yet his own father had come through all that with his political views secure and strengthened.

Morton drained his third cup of coffee and looked around. He was alone in the breakfasting lounge, no sign of Melville. He went through to the bar. The barman from last night was there, clearing up behind the bar.

'You haven't seen the chap I was with last night?'

'Bar's not open yet,' the barman grinned, drying glasses with a towel.

'True,' Morton said. 'You know him… I mean, he's here a lot?'

'Sometimes he's here. But I don't know him. I just serve out the happy juice.'

'Okay, thanks.'

Morton hesitated in the foyer, casting a glance at the receptionist who was on the phone. He waited till she had ended the call then went over. She was a nice-looking lass. Jennifer it said on her name badge. He was going to try a little of the old Morton charm.

'Excuse me, don't suppose you're able to tell me if my friend

Alan Melville has checked out already? I thought we were to meet at breakfast.'

'Melville? What room number?'

'Sorry, don't know that. I'm Morton, room 234.'

'Melville? Can't find a Melville.'

'What? Man in his fifties, suit, raincoat… ex-military type. Comes here a lot.'

'Sorry. I can't find the name.'

'Really? Baffling. Well, can I pay my bill?'

'Room 234. You've paid accommodation and breakfast.'

'Yes, just dinner and drinks to pay.'

'Right. I've got it.'

As he paid, Morton said: 'I had dinner and drinks with Mr Melville, so he does exist.' He smiled. 'In fact, he put his meal and drinks on his room tab, round about the same time I did.'

'Oooh, naughty!' the receptionist said, smirking, moving the mouse on the desk. 'Oh, I see it. Steak and chips? Mr Munro. Roger Munro.'

Morton exhaled. 'Why would he give me a false name? Do you have his room number?'

'I can't do that. Anyway, he has checked out. Two hours ago.'

'Well thank you,' Morton said. 'This is my real name by the way.'

'Of course. I'm not sure what I can do about it,' she confided. 'He paid his bills in the name of Munro. Maybe he was just trying to kid you on?'

'Ach maybe. Funny guy. He gave me an email address. That's probably fake too.'

'Sorry Mr Morton, I can't possible divulge….'

'You've been a great help, Jennifer, thank you.'

As he left the hotel and descended to the carpark, he found

himself slightly amused. It figured that Melville, or Munro, was a man of many identities. A spook or spy or agent provocateur of some sort. The email would be fake, of course.

Although it was cold, it was dry, for the moment, as Morton drove down Duke Street. He found a parking spot about midway between the Albion pub and the closed-office and walked back. Tam the barman was opening the doors.

'Sorry, not open, son,' he said, seeing Morton. Then he grinned. 'Pies are no hot enough yet!'

Morton laughed and put his hand up to his mouth. 'Once burnt… twice shy…' he cracked. 'Nah, just wondered if you knew when Munro would be in?'

'Munro?'

Tam looked baffled. 'Wha…?'

'Sorry, Melville.'

'That lot? The New Britain crowd frae the office? Doubt they'll be here the day. Maybe the morra.'

'Cheers.'

The shop wasn't open. As he stood at the door pondering, a postman came past him. Morton immediately felt in his coat pocket for keys and began to make a pretence of unlocking the door.

'Having trouble?' the postie asked, letters in his hand.

'Ah, always a bit stiff.'

'There's mail for ye.'

'Thanks. I'll take it.'

As soon as the postie turned his back, Morton stopped the pretence and moved away, pretending to make a call on his mobile. He returned swiftly to the car, feeling the fear and guilt of an amateur thief. Two letters.

The first letter was addressed to 'The Secretary, Glasgow East Branch of the New Britain Party' and was a general circular to all branches and associations of the NBP from Michael Ramage about forthcoming events. Of minor interest. But the second was addressed to Alan Melville and marked Personal. The sender was Julian Hutchison from 'This Island Nation' at an address in Marsham Street, London. Morton knew that was where the Home Office was based and remembered looking up the organisation on the internet a few months back. A pro-union think-tank allegedly privately funded. It was short, an instruction for Melville.

Dear Alan, further to discussions last week, Raymond has confirmed the location of the premises in Wright Crescent, Renfrew, off Paisley Road, just before the sewage works. He intends to carry out the work on 19th and will expect you there early afternoon. Yours, Julian.

Morton reread the letter and looked at the postmark: 15th but today was the 19th. He felt a shiver in his spine. It had taken four days to be delivered. Probably Melville had expected to get it yesterday. Raymond must be Mearns. If he went there, he would see them both together and find out what the hell they were up to. On the other hand, Melville hadn't received it, wouldn't receive it, so he might not be there. He used his Blackberry to phone Rami's desk phone. No answer. He left a message: 'I'm in Glasgow. I think I just might be onto something.'

CHAPTER SIXTEEN

Renfrew is infinitely anonymous, Morton thought as he drove west from the city centre. A sprawling industrial enclave on the northern fringe of the proud burgh of Paisley. Industry had been and gone here, but clung on in places, though its many untidy remnants were more numerous than the signs of viable concerns. He left the M8 at junction 27 as if he was going to the airport, turned off the A741 Renfrew Road into Paisley Road and found that he had overshot. He took a left turn into a road that led to a drop off area in front of a Primary school, turned and came back more carefully. This time he spotted the turnoff into Wright Street which was signed as a dead end. It was built-up but derelict, disused, plenty of rotting brickwork, wooden panels replacing windows, peeling posters on mouldering walls. At the far end, beyond the pavement, there was a line of parked cars. He presumed they belonged to workers at the big factory or mill which was still in operation. He could see a path through the scrubland leading in that direction. About halfway down, beyond the cars, as the road surface increasingly degenerated, the patched and broken strip of tarmac led down towards the river.

It seemed to head down into a low-lying birch wood and wasteland. He could make out the glint of the White Cart Water through the tangled branches of scrubby bushes and stunted trees. At the bottom of the lane there were more ruinous buildings and a large sewage plant that extended under the busy motorway. Over the river, on the far bank, he could see a budget hotel and the evenly spaced lights of the airport perimeter and Abbotsinch Road. Morton knew if he was to drive down towards the sewage plant, he would make himself vulnerable. Better to wait on the road and keep watch. It was just after midday. He would be able to watch them arrive but even as he thought this, he was turning the car and returning to the main road. At the bottom of Wright Street on the junction with Paisley Road, he decided he was too close. He had remembered a very large retail park nearby, on the other side of the motorway. He turned onto Renfrew Road at the lights, heading right down over the top of the M8 to the roundabout for the shopping centre. It was the Abbotsinch Shopping Park, with a large B&Q and a dozen or more large stores, Dunelm, SCS, Sofology and there was a Costa.

A sign advertised more than a thousand car parking spaces; it would be easier to hide. He drove through the busy main car parking area to a smaller parking area where he hoped most of the vehicles belonged to staff. He managed to hide the VW Beetle between two larger vehicles.

He stepped over the small wall and walked round the high concrete perimeter wall at the back of the site. He easily found Turner Drive, a narrow service road at the bottom of a steep slope that snaked under the White Cart Viaduct. In the shadows there, below the M8 he looked across to the sewage treatment plants on the riverbank and dropped down the slope onto a smaller footpath that worked its way north to wasteland. He now had a good unobscured view of the building at the lower end of Wright Crescent where Mearns and Melville would be doing the work, whatever work it was. Mearns would arrive soon. Melville's appearance was less likely. He had the letter in his own pocket. He watched the building. It looked derelict, certainly disused. Up beyond his right shoulder was the bulk of council housing, fenced in, and an estate of private bungalows near the junction of the Renfrew and Paisley Road. He wanted to get nearer, have a look around, see the building close-up. Maybe they were already inside? His stomach was reminding him he had forgotten to buy sandwiches. He looked at his watch. Lunchtime. Not for the first time, he instructed himself to get into the habit of leaving a chocolate bar or two in the car, or an apple, even just a bottle of water. Wright Crescent petered out at the entrance to the sewage works. He could drop down and walk through the wasteground to the two brick buildings. Bits of the roofs had fallen in and nearly all the windows had smashed. What kind of work would be carried out in there, he wondered? He picked his way carefully down the grassy slope to the lower path and from there walked quickly on broken remains of the pavement to the buildings and almost immediately discovered that the red-brick edifice in front of him was one building, not two.

He got in through a collapsed mesh fence and went around the back. He could make out the white shape of his car among the parked cars at the top end of Wright Crescent. No-one in sight. The ground underfoot was marshy and weedy, rotting plastic bags whose unknown contents had bleached white in the sun. Clearly it had become a location for fly-tipping. Yet the building was substantial, must have been a prominent public building at some distant time in the past. He came round to a large concrete carpark at the rear that led to iron double-doors, a sort of loading bay. Suddenly, he saw a man walking on his left and crouched down behind a pile of bricks. After a moment or two he realised there must be a path down there too between bushes and brambles at the riverbank and this was confirmed when he heard the man shouting to a dog. He saw the dog, watched the man emerge between ruined buildings and conjectured that the path met the top end of Wright Street. He slipped down to the gates and examined the padlock. It was rusty but secure. And yet... Morton had a feeling, intuition perhaps, that the door had been in use recently. He knelt down to examine the padlock more closely and saw shiny glinting metal where the key had scraped it. He was right. Someone had been in here. Somebody had used the padlock and scraped a line of rust off in the process.

Morton clambered back up to the carpark and walked the length of the building, close to the walls, noting that some of the windows in the lower end were intact. He turned at the gable end and looked to his right seeing the large pans of the sewage works, simultaneously catching a putrid whiff on the breeze. He hurried round to the front entrance, keeping a wary eye up the Crescent. The doors, boarded up had long since been pushed aside or collapsed of their own accord. He glanced up and saw above the carved red stone lintel, 'Municipal Cleansing Department...' and went inside.

Rami El-Jaffari attended the meeting of the Education Committee at Holyrood, and afterwards had managed to get a brief interview with the Minister on development of the new Curriculum for Excellence programme. She'd walked back in sunshine to the office and on the way, ducked into Greggs for a cheese salad roll. As she stood at the counter, her mobile began to ping. She noticed missed messages from several different friends and they all said the same thing. Neil Shankwell was dead. He'd been found dead at his home in Broxburn. He was fifty-five.

'Your change...' repeated the shop assistant.

'Oh, right.'

Outside the shop, fast walking along South Bridge, she phoned Raj. 'I just saw this. Where did you hear it? I'll ring them, thanks, Raj. Natural causes... That's what they're saying? Okay, Raj, thanks.'

Arriving at the office she went straight in to see Hugh Leadbetter.

'Have you heard? The Deputy Electoral Registration Officer at Glenforgan is dead?'

Leadbetter looked up, frowning. 'Well... you think this is something to do with the missing ballot papers? What is the polis saying?'

'I'm on it.'

Back at her desk, she switched on the laptop and saw there was one message on the landline. She pressed play and heard Willie Morton's message. 'Glasgow?' He probably hadn't heard about Shankwell. She'd drop him a message when she had the wording of the police statement. But she couldn't see a statement on the police website. She phoned Raj back.

'Where did you say you got this from? I mean, who? Lothian and Borders? Comms? At Fettes Avenue? Superintendent Maxwell. OK. Thanks.'

She phoned the main number and asked for C Division. Maxwell was unknown to her, but she got put through to Helen Spence of the Comms team, whom she'd previously spoken to on other matters.

'Hi Helen, I'm hearing you've put out a statement about the death of... yes, Shankwell. Who's handling it? Right, what can you tell me, is there a statement?'

Hugh Leadbetter had come through to find out the news and now perched on the edge of the desk. She was momentarily worried that the desk would break and smiled at the thought.

'What's the story?' he grunted. 'Anything doin?'

'Found dead at his home in Broxburn. No obvious suspicious circumstances but in the light of the furore over the ballot papers issue, they're getting forensics in. He lived alone.'

'Right. So... can we speculate, at this stage?'

'Better not. One for the news team. I'll keep an eye on it, and I'll let Willie know. He's in Glasgow.'

'What's he doin there? Further humiliation about his book? Anyway, keep me informed.'

Rami typed a short message to Willie and then put on her headphones and plugged in her digital voice recorder and began to work up a think-piece on the pros and cons of the Curriculum for Excellence while taking bites of her cheese roll.

The two cars came slowly down the patched potholed road. Morton watched them through broken glass from a wrecked office on the first floor. He couldn't see who was in the cars as they passed the building. He wondered what on earth they were going to do in such a wreck of a place. He'd been through most of the ground floor rooms where he could get access but there was a bit of the building on the ground floor that seemed to be secure, a locked metal door, so he'd come upstairs but there were no signs of recent occupation here.

Crouching, he could see that the cars had stopped further down, nearer to the sewage plant. He took a shot with his Blackberry camera wishing he had a decent long-range lens and proper camera, even just a small digital compact. The number plates would probably be unreadable. As he watched, two men got out of the black Mercedes and another taller younger man came from the estate car. They started walking together back up the hill towards him. No doubt about it.

These were spooks of some kind, ex-military, or ex-police but neither was Alan Melville or Darren Barr. He checked the flash was off and took another snap and felt the first premonitions of anxiety. He was a trespasser but, judging by the state of the place, he wasn't the first. There was something hard and intent about the men. He could hear them now, squeezing in, like he had, through the wonky barricade at the front doors. He went out to the corridor and stood at the top of the stair. They were moving away from him, by the sounds of it, towards the section he hadn't been able to get in to. What were they up to? What kind of work was this? He flipped out his Blackberry again to check the sound was off and saw Rami's message. Bloody hell! Shankwell was *dead*? He found the mute button. Didn't want her phoning him when he was doing surveillance on this team. The stairs were concrete, covered in broken glass and detritus from a hundred vandal's sprees. He slipped down quietly but on the ground floor the surface was even worse in places. You had to concentrate. Lumps of dry plaster would explode like a grenade if you stepped on it. And there was the strong smell of rotting, damp walls. He could hear the men at the far end now, and the scraping sounds of a heavy metal door. He moved as quickly as he could along the corridor, navigating shattered metal shelving systems and broken office fitments to get to the hallway. He looked along; no-one. They'd gone inside. He saw they'd left the metal door open. He could hear voices from inside. There wasn't anywhere to hide now. He cautiously peered around the iron door and saw the interior was a vast open concrete-floored warehouse or dispatch area. He saw three large white panel vans. He heard the men giving instructions to each other but couldn't make out what they were saying. He had conflicting thoughts about what he was doing. Perhaps it was all perfectly legal, but instinctively he knew it was connected to something clandestine. Must be. But how could he find out what? And if it *was* dodgy, how could he prove it? He took out the Blackberry, rechecked the sound was muted, and took a series of pictures of the van, the interior of the warehouse, then put the phone back in his pocket and sidled in through the door.

Ailsa McKinnon learned of the death of Neil Shankwell from an email sent from the GMB communications department in London to all stewards and officers, informing them of the death of a senior GMB steward in local government. No mention of his connection to the by election in Glenforgan. She began to think of Willie Morton's investigation. It was odd there was no mention of Shankwell's recent involvement in the crucial by-election and the missing ballot papers. Maybe Willie was onto something? Instead, the email mentioned his decades of public service in the union and there was no mention of cause of death. All she really knew about Shankwell was that he was a typical old-Labour working-class stalwart of the party, not a fan of women in politics or in the union. He had been on the Scottish Executive Committee she was sure, in the Trade Union and Elected members section for a while but that was years ago, and she also had a feeling that he was one of those who had spoken publicly against the creation of the Scottish Labour Women's Committee. A dinosaur. Had he been on the Local Government Sub-Committee? She tried to remember. Maybe. Anyway. Now he was dead and only months after he had been Deputy Returning Officer in a by-election Labour had won and the ballot papers had been thrown out by accident. Was it an accident? Could there had been some funny business? She fervently hoped not. She couldn't condone that kind of malarkey. She was confident it wasn't the kind of thing her party would ever do. She picked up the desk phone and dialled the switchboard at GMB head office, Mary Turner House, near Euston Station.

'Hi, Jim Cargill in Comms please. Ailsa McKinnon, Edinburgh office.' They put her through.

'Hi Ailsa, what's eating you?'

'You put out a circular just now... The death of Neil Shankwell.'

'That's right. In the news section.'

'He's one of ours. Do you know any more about it?'

'Not much, it came from a news-in-brief from Press Association, I think. What's up?'

'Just wondering if there's a cause of death yet.'

'Cause of death? No... assumed it was just... well he has decades of service...'

'And there was no mention of the fact he was Electoral Returning Officer – well, Deputy ERO – in a hotly-contested by-election where the ballot papers disappeared just weeks later...'

'That's news to me. You think he was under stress, or something? You hinting at a possible motive for suicide?'

'Or something. I just wondered why there was no mention of that. The media are bound to pick it up.'

'Oh, I see. Right. Well, I'll certainly look into it. Thanks for the heads-up, Alison.'

'Ailsa.'

'Sorry. Ailsa. I'll get back to you.'

Two of the men had disappeared into the furthest panel van, including the thin one he imagined to be Raymond Mearns. Morton quickly found a hiding place behind a portacabin near the metal double doors. It was the door whose padlock he had examined from the outside, in the carpark at the rear of the building. He wondered where the third man was. The other two were moving away across the space to the far wall. Could he get a look inside a van? The two men were carrying binbags. He could hear some of what they saying.

'…heavy bastards…'

'…plenty to… come on…'

Then he discovered that the third man was up on the mezzanine level, heard his boots clumping on the metal stair. He saw him entering a shed, a sort of cab, lights coming on in windows up there. The other two were piling binbags at the far end in front of what appeared to be a lift shaft. He took the chance to move from the portacabin to behind the first panel van. He had to be aware of his feet being seen below the van. He crouched down and tried to look under the van but it wasn't possible, not enough clearance space and he didn't want to be lying down in case he had to run away fast. It occurred to him for the first time that they might be armed. A sudden loud noise made him look up. Industrial machinery was starting up above him. But the man was coming back down the stairs.

'Come on,' he heard, or was it: 'It's on?' He went around the side of the van and peered into the small window. Stacked full of shiny binbags. He edged to the next van. The same. All the vans were full of them. He took a picture through the window. Wouldn't look like much. Not without a flash, but he couldn't risk it. He took shots of the registration plates of both vans. Could he risk going to the van they were emptying? He would hear what they were saying.

Crouching behind the cab, he could see they were unloading the binbags and carrying them across the floor. Bin bags bulging full of something. One had burst; the contents looked white like paper. He felt a wave of exultation. Of course! He had to take a risk now while all three had their backs to him and shoot a sequence of pictures, then he ducked back to safety. He'd seen enough for now. He knew what they were doing. He looked back the way he had come. It looked clear. He scampered back behind the portacabin. He heard loud grating noises and instinctively knew the men were throwing the bin bags into an elevator shaft, or a kind of feed hopper, of what he now suspected to be an industrial incinerator on the mezzanine level.

The noise had built up to a roaring crescendo. The men were working quickly, pushing and kicking bundles of bin bags into the chamber of the hopper carrying each load up and dropping it into a chute. They had no idea he was there. They were so busy. He needed to get closer. He looked around and saw behind him an internal stairway beside the double doors. He gauged the distance, around fifty yards. He felt vulnerable now not being able to see what the men were doing, but if they couldn't see them…they couldn't see him either. He ran lightly over and turned up the stairs. It was an internal stair, closed in, like a fire escape. He raced up it and found that it turned right into a corridor with several offices. He walked along, believing he must be crossing above the ground floor dispatch area to the other side of the building. There was a junction with more offices on the other side and he could see the lights of the office where he'd seen the third man.

There were windows there and he could look down on the men moving about. Another door led out onto a short stretch of open steel walkway. He went to the edge. Now he could see the vans but not the men. Right in front was the chute, stuffed with bin bags and their contents. It wasn't a lift shaft, he saw now, it was a mechanical hopper. He peered into a thick-glazed tiny window and was looking into a large incinerator chamber lined with burning gas jets on the point of turning from blue and yellow to an angry dark red. There was a set of controls on a panel. He saw a dial and a metal arrow moving between the numbers 2 and 3 on the dial, which he noticed went up to 10. 950°C. With a loud bang that startled him, the load of binbags – some melting in the heat – and their contents which he now saw were bundles of folded white papers, bundled with elastic bands, began to shunt along the chute and drop into the incinerator. If he had a rake or long-handled tool he could have hooked a bag or some of the contents. He fumbled with his Blackberry, leaning forward as far as he dared towards the sides of the chute, to take a video of the contents of the binbags moving along. The thought of the interior was freaking him out and he felt the heat rising even though the walls of the incinerator were thickly insulated. Out of the corner of his eye, he saw the men below moving, unloading. He angled the camera to take video of that, too. But he would have to move. The heat was uncomfortable, and anyway, perhaps he had enough? He was nervous about dropping the phone, took a lot of care handling it to make it safe in his pocket.

He went back into the office and back to the long corridor and down the stairs to the portacabin, retracing his steps to the metal doors. There was no point in staying any longer. Crouching behind the portacabin hearing the roaring of the incinerator and the grating clanking of the hopper and the sounds of the bags being kicked into a pile, he thought he'd better check the pictures and video he had. He needed to be certain he had something, the men, the registration plates of the vans... he double-checked the mute was on, then checked the pictures... blurred for the most part, dark, obscure but the pictures showed the men, the vans, binbags, bulk of tightly-wadded papers... The video was thirty-four seconds long, the preview picture showed a close-up of the papers. It looked good. He put the phone away, stood up. One of the men was watching him.

'Who the hell are you?'

CHAPTER SEVENTEEN

CID officers from Edinburgh and Lothian Police were rarely called to the territory of F Division – the far reaches of West Lothian – the majority of their inquiries being conducted within the city of Edinburgh, in housing schemes and tenements. Being called out to the small town of Broxburn some twelve miles west, was something of a jaunt. It was a cold day but there had been no further snow and though the sun had put in an appearance it wasn't giving away a single iota of heat.

Detective Sergeant Hilary Brown was driving the requisitioned unmarked police car, a black Subaru Impretza, a flashy-looking vehicle with a curious large spoiler behind the rear window, and silver wheel trims. In the passenger seat, her boss, DI Sid Maxfield was enjoying the novelty of a day out in the country. They'd traversed the Gogar roundabout and were heading out between trees and fields. 'Nice day out,' he said. 'Even if it is just a trip to see a corpse.'

DS Brown nodded. She was mentally going over an argument with her eldest daughter which had been unresolved when she'd dropped her off at the school gates. Claire had been doing well, but lately… 'There must be suspicions about it. Can't just be a heart attack,' she said.

Maxfield sniffed. 'Yeah, well, he was fifty-five, found at home, but it's been flagged up because of that row over the by-election. Some rumours it was fiddled.'

'That's right. I remember. Didn't think much about it... rumours.'

'But that's why it was flagged. Keep going through Newbridge. Broxburn's the next place.'

When they reached the small town of Broxburn, Maxfield waved imperiously. 'Just keep going – along Main Street. Not far now.'

'You've been here before?'

'Once or twice. Nice wee place really. Handy for the motorway – and the bridge. Shankwell worked in Glenforgan, would have had to go over the bridge every day to get to work.'

'He worked in Electoral registration? I mean, he was in charge of the by-election.'

'Something like that. We come over this bridge, over the canal here and now turn right.'

'Pretty canal.'

'Keep right on this till the next junction.'

Their destination was at the end of a cul-de-sac backing onto the trees of a community woodland. There was an ambulance and two police cars outside the two-storey block of flats, two up, two down.

'The local plod are here,' Maxfield said. 'F Division's finest. If you'd kept straight on at the bridge instead of turning right, you'd have come to the local station – West Main Street, opposite the new Tesco.'

'Handy,' Brown approved.

The forensic team had just arrived and were preparing themselves in gowns, gloves and overshoes. After introductions, they were told the body was in the first-floor flat on the left. It was a modern block, built within the last five years by the look of it.

'You'll need to garb up if you're going in there,' they were told. 'And even then it'll have to be a quick shufti – we've to do a complete set here, the full works.'

'It'll ruin my hair,' DS Brown joked.

'Never!' said the pale blue yeti-like scenes-of-crime photographer and winked.

The body of Neil Shankwell in a pair of garish checked pyjamas was lying at an odd angle at the foot of the small set of stairs leading to an ensuite bedroom on the mezzanine level. His head was on the carpet, his bare feet above him. There was no trace of blood or obvious injury.

'Consistent with a fall downstairs,' the forensic officer told them, 'arse over tit, though that wasn't what killed him.' He adjusted his spectacles with blue gloves. 'Heart attack. Must have been massive.'

'That was the medical opinion?' DS Brown asked. 'So you guys are trying to find evidence to contradict natural causes presumably?'

'More or less. Looks open and shut to me.'

'The feet are bare,' Maxfield pointed out. 'Any sign of slippers?'

'They are at the side of the bed. Must have come downstairs without them.'

'Right.' Brown took this in. 'But the kitchen floor is a wood laminate.'

The forensic man nodded. 'Yes. What's your point?'

'Cold. Would have been cold. Me, I'd have worn my slippers.'

'Ah, I see your point.'

'Good point, DS Brown,' Maxfield approved. 'It's slightly odd.' He cleared his throat. 'We've been called because of issues to do with the context, background...'

'Of course, but we'll have a better picture in an hour or so.'

'Right. We'll fill in the time speaking to the doctor or paramedic…'

'Paramedic.'

'…who was first on scene, and the local police. We'll be outside.'

Maxfield and Brown sat in the Subaru and made phone calls. The paramedic gave them the details of her examination and impressions. The local sergeant, a large uniformed officer near retirement age by the name of Eric Wyllie clambered into the back seat with difficulty.

'Racey wee car,' he commented. 'Flashy.'

'Nice to drive,' Brown said.

'Well, aye, there's nae much to tell,' Sergeant Wyllie began. 'Been known tae keep himself tae himself. Been living here about a year. Nane of the neighbours kens much about him. He's been seen once or twice in the Green Tree Tavern and in the Grenadier but he's no a member o the golf club. I am, so ah'd ken. Nae married, nae signs o a woman or family, lives on his own. Neighbours haven't noticed many visitors. Works in Fife…'

'Yes, we know about that,' Maxfield said. 'Anything else?'

'That's about it. We checked – no criminal record.'

'We knew that too,' Brown said, exchanging a wry glance with Maxfield. 'So what about his GP?'

Sergeant Wyllie moved his legs in the confined space of the back seat. 'Small car this,' he grunted. 'GP? We're checking with the local community practice. Obviously, we need all the medical details.'

'Obviously,' Brown agreed. 'Well, I think that's everything. Boss?'

'I think so. Thank you, sergeant.'

'As you saw, he was a big man, no in the best condition, a bit overweight, ah'd say. No fit.'

'Yes, in the zone for heart attacks.'

'Aye, right you are. You're welcome tae come doon tae the station… cup of tea… if you've the time. The medical stuff should be in.'

'We might,' Maxfield said. 'But we'll need to hang on here awhile, sergeant, and speak to the forensic team first. Thanks though.'

Panic took over, Morton barged the man who fell over. He turned and fled, into full view across the concrete, pursued by shouts. But he kept going. When he got to the door, he pulled it behind him and sped along the corridor towards the front entrance. He could hear them behind him but he was nearly clear. He pulled the wooden boards down violently behind him to hinder their pursuit and was out, moving as fast as he could, keeping close to the building, rounding the gable end. They weren't out yet. He would never make it across the open ground to the other path. From the gable he dropped down into the scrub towards the river, keeping low through the bushes and straggly birches. When he reached the path beside the riverbank, he crouched and looked back. He couldn't see them, but he wasn't in the clear. He walked quickly away, towards the looming bulk of the M8 motorway, rounding the high mesh fence of the sewage works. He passed under the motorway and along the endless fence of the sewage works. He imagined the men would give up the chase but trawl the nearby streets to catch him when he emerged. They could possibly know who he was, or why he had been there. How had he been detected? It didn't matter. All he had to do was keep away from them and get back to Edinburgh with the pictures and the video. A hundred yards further on, beyond the end of the sewage plant, he found the familiar narrow path that diverged up towards the retail park. He stood behind a tree and watched carefully. All he'd have to do now was scramble up fifty yards into Turner Drive and climb the small wall into the car park and keep low. Which retail premises would be best seemed the best for hiding in? Maybe there was a café? His stomach rumbled but he sneered at himself. Thinking of his belly at a time like this? He could see the narrow road at the foot of the slope where he had come from. It would take him five minutes or less to get to his car. He was too old for this sort of stuff. He looked at his watch. 2.35pm. How long since he had escaped from the building? Five minutes, no, must be less than that, three, four, maybe?

After several more minutes he felt safe enough to break cover, cross the small road, scale the slope, step over a small aluminium barrier at the top into the tarmacked carpark. It was very busy, reassuringly so. Lots of people were milling about. Now what? Get the hell out and back to home turf. He had no reason to hang about. Or should he get something to eat? He couldn't ignore his need to assuage his hunger much longer. Dunelm Mills usually had cafes, and there was the Costa, but intuition and a sense of self-preservation told him instant flight was the best course of action. He got into the car which started first time and he turned carefully out and up onto the junction and the M8 and headed east to Edinburgh and safety.

Raymond Mearns hadn't seen the intruder, but Mouncey had. He'd seen him up close and Keenan had got several glimpses. It had been Keenan, the younger man who had pursued him outside and seen that he had dropped down to the river. He'd come back then and the three of them conferred.

'What did he look like?' Mearns demanded. 'What age... what was he wearing? Tell me everything you remember.'

Mearns got on his phone, contacting his superiors, alerting them to the security breach and asking for advice. 'In the meantime, you guys carry on,' he ordered. 'Keep that stuff moving. We can't move it again.' He'd estimated it would take them well over an hour to unload the three vans and fully incinerate it all. Who the hell was this intruder? Was he just a random stranger alerted by the noise? No, unlikely. If so, he wouldn't have run off. Had he been tipped off but by whom? And what had happened to Melville?

'Did he have a phone or a camera?' he demanded.

'Not that I saw,' Mouncey shrugged. Could have. 'Could have been anyone. Not a vandal though. Smart-dressed. Maybe somebody from the council?'

'Must have a camera,' Keenan suggested. 'Everyone does.'

'But did he take pictures? That's the point.'

Keenan shrugged. 'Depends how long he had been watching us. Maybe he had just come in. He can't have seen much. We've only been here, what, twenty minutes.'

'Long enough!' Mearns snapped. 'Right, get on with it. Quick as you can. Remember we've got to move the vans once we finish. Especially now. Can't afford to leave them here as we planned.'

Mouncey nodded. 'Sensible.'

Mearns was reluctant to pass the matter on to Trenchard and was relieved when Usman told him Trenchard was in a meeting. He explained what had occurred. Usman passed him on to Collins.

'Let's not panic unduly,' Collins said. 'Could be a random chappie. I'd suggest you don't get distracted. I'll contact some operational chaps in the area. Leave it to them and I'll control them direct while they find him. We will find him. Keep going with your operation and let me know when it's concluded. I'll update you then.'

Mearns felt irritated that he was going to be kept out of the loop. He had no idea who the intruder was but it must be a random, couldn't be anything to do with him. No blame could attach to him, he was in the clear. He wiped the sweat off his forehead and joined the other two. The physical exercise was good. They got into a routine, carrying bins over, tipping them into the mouth of the hopper. They had started on the second van now. In their haste, bags were bursting open and sometimes bundles of papers were falling out. They'd have to do a clear-up. An hour and they'd be well away, there'd be no evidence to find.

In an industrial unit on the periphery of Glasgow airport, a phone was ringing. It was a cluttered nondescript office with an outlook over the runways and terminal buildings half a mile away. Sighing, a man answered the phone. 'Rundgren Security. Timms.' When he heard what the caller had to say, he pressed a buzzer on his desk.

'Right, hold and I'll put you over onto video to brief the team,' he said. He switched the call to the video monitor on the wall. The caller's face appeared, blurry and indistinct on the internal camera on his computer in an office in central London. He waited while the team came up the stairs. 'Come on guys, take a seat,' Timms the controller said. 'We have a code 2, less than a mile away.'

Collins on the screen gave the four-man team an outline of the details that were known about the intruder and his last known location, and the call ended.

'Right,' said Timms, 'two teams, two vehicles. Looks like

he's headed on the path under the M8. How has he accessed the location? By vehicle, presumably, so either from the north side, from Wright Avenue or maybe over the bridge, from Abbotsinch Road? Or did he come from the south? Most likely, he's parked close, somewhere off Wright Street or in the housing off Clydesdale Avenue. 'Les, you and Ali check the bridge and keep an eye on the road junction from that end. 'Lee and Stephan work around from the south on Renfrew Road. It's possible he'll be in the shopping park.' He rubbed at the stubble on his chin. 'Yeah, that's my bet. The shopping centre. He needs to work back to wherever he's left his vehicle. We should easily find him but don't tackle him. We need to follow him and find out who he is. Meanwhile, I'll call in SatScan and compare them with movements over the last two hours to get the registration plate.'

CHAPTER EIGHTEEN

Morton saw the signs for Harthill Services. The fuel tank gauge was low, and his growling stomach craved something to eat. He had made the thirty miles in just under an hour, held up as usual on the sections over the Clyde at Anderston and tailbacks through Charing Cross and Cowcaddens but after that it had been trouble-free. He had put distance between himself and Mearns and his men. It was 3.40pm. He turned off, sat in the car and texted Rami. *Think I have something. Will be at office in an hour.* Then he gratefully opened the door and stretched his legs and stiffly made his way over to the service station which he noted with a smile was now calling itself 'Heart of Scotland'. It had been some years since he'd been in the place. Apart from the new name, it hadn't changed much, a new glass footbridge to the west-bound service station, a new long-distance bus hub, but still only a convenience store, BP Connect and the Wild Bean Café. Better than nothing, he thought. And he was desperate for a coffee. He chose a table overlooking the M8 and took a few sips of coffee. Always tasted better when you had a craving for it. He ordered a double ham and cheese toastie and four choc chip cookies and took out the phone. There was no-one nearby, so he began to flick through the photos in the pictures file. They were disappointing but he hoped when enlarged and cropped there might be some useful detail. The battery was low and he didn't have the cable so he didn't bother trying to view the video. He began to eat the steaming hot toastie using both hands, but it was too flimsy, and some fell onto his ridiculously small napkin. His phone went and he scrambled to put down the sandwich. Text message from Rami. *Okay, will hang on till you arrive.* He looked at the clock. 3.50. Better get a move on. No rest for the wicked.

It was Trenchard who took the callback from Timms. Collins had briefed him on the intruder incident. Timms told him his team at Rundgren had been unable to locate the intruder.

'It isn't usual that we have such difficulty,' he said apologetically. 'And we're sorry to let you down. Given that we were practically on top of the location, it's doubly embarrassing. We had teams surrounding the locus within ten minutes of the alert, but there were some complicating factors.'

'Complicating factors?' Trenchard repeated. 'And these were…?'

'We established very quickly there were three potential areas to search on the SatScan and pulled data for each half hour over the two-hour period before the alert and the half hour after it. The three possibilities for the location of intruder's vehicle were immediately to the north of the premises where there were around fifty vehicles parked. Unfortunately, there was a shift change at a local factory and most of the vehicles there left at around the same time. Only three vehicles did not move and one – a female driver – had moved in the next half-hour check. Two vehicles remained but one may be abandoned and the other has been checked and eliminated. In the housing area to the east of the premises, there were fewer vehicle movements and all checked out as local residents. But the third area was a shopping park with over a thousand vehicle parking spaces. Hundreds of vehicles went in and out in each of the half-hour checks in the time period; impossible to check in fact. We established there were no pedestrians over the bridge in the time, so it is most likely, indeed certain, the intruder used the shopping park.'

'But you have the satellite footage… is it really impossible to check?'

'I'm sorry. We don't have the resources. The shopping park is one of the busiest in the country, situated beside a very busy motorway turnoff for the country's largest airport…'

'We will have to accept it, then,' Trenchard said reluctantly. 'And perhaps it is not so serious. The operatives did not think the intruder saw very much or had been there long. There might be an innocent explanation.'

'Yes, the premises had been heavily vandalised… were not secure.'

'Except that the intruder ran away.'

'Perhaps he was simply looking for something to steal… exploring… and in the circumstances, felt afraid for whatever reason?'

'Okay. Thank you for your report. That's all, I think.'

It was 5.30 by the time Morton got through the traffic in central Edinburgh and found a space to park in Niddry Street. As he walked across the road to the *Standard* office he could see there were some lights on up on the first floor. He keyed the out of hours number into the keypad at the South Bridge entrance, entered the small vestibule and got the lift up. The press room was almost deserted except for Rami and a couple of others.

'I hope it's good, whatever you've got,' Rami said, looking at her watch. 'An hour, you said.'

Morton pulled a sad face. 'Sorry. Thanks for staying.'

'So – what have you got?'

Morton took out his Blackberry and briefly outlined the trip to Glasgow, following up Barr's information, to see the office in Duke Street, his meeting with Melville, his interception of the letter and the strange activities at the disused Renfrew Municipal Waste depot. He waggled the phone. 'I've got some pics and a short video but I'm not sure they're all that useful.'

'Plug the phone in to my laptop,' Rami said, 'Let's download them and look at them.'

There were nine photos and the video. The exterior of the Municipal Cleansing Department; two cars in longshot too distant to read the licence plates; three men walking; three white panel vans in a dim interior space; two men carrying black binbags; shiny binbags inside the rear window of a van; registration plates of two of the vans; a close-up of bulging piles of bin bags and bundled papers; the incinerator window and part of the control dials; the three vans from above.

'You did well,' Rami said, approvingly. 'Nine pictures. It builds into a kind of narrative. I'm sure we can get some of these enlarged.'

Morton was downbeat. 'The quality is so bloody poor. And the video is… could be anything… men unloading a van. Hold the front page.'

'No. The video looks well dodgy,' Rami said. 'I mean, it looks suspicious. Those do look like ballot papers. I mean that's what they look like. The men look furtive.'

Morton snorted. 'That's wishful thinking really.'

'But who are they? The picture of them walking up the road can be enlarged. We might be able to make out their faces. We've got the car licence plates. They can definitely be checked and the van registrations. Best of all, that close-up of the stuff going into the incinerator… brilliant.'

'But very blurred,' Morton murmured. 'The best one is the exterior of the Cleansing Depot because that was the only one taken in full daylight.'

'Willie. You put yourself in danger. I mean what are they doing? Destroying ballot papers? That's what it looks like. This is evidence of a crime. You did brilliantly!'

'Could be,' Morton reluctantly agreed. 'Evidence. But the by-election was in November. Two months ago. The papers might have been 'lost' or as we believe stolen or removed any time after that... so how on earth did they end up in Renfrew?'

'Ask yourself who? Not why?'

Morton frowned at her. '*Who*?'

'This Mearns fella was at the count you said. Now he's in Renfrew destroying the ballot papers, months later. He's the link.'

'Yes, but *is* it him and why now? Why wait all this time?'

'He must have had his reasons. Maybe all this time they've been sitting in the vans in this depot? Or maybe they were only recently moved to the depot for incineration?'

'And anyway,' Morton reasoned, 'maybe it's not ballot papers at all? Maybe it's just... I don't know, financial records of some perfectly innocent business or other. The photograph is impossible to tell. Yes, it *looks* like bound packets of ballot papers, but... can we prove it? I mean, where are the ballot boxes?'

'The ballot boxes were returned by the council after the count, Willie. The papers were stored in binbags. We know that.'

'If only I had a decent camera,' Morton mourned, looking sadly at the phone. 'I mean the camera is only two megapixels. I can't see the photos being enlarged much without them just becoming a pixelated mess.'

Rami was using the laptop's magnifying icon to examine the photos. 'But look, here, in the close-up shot of the folded bundles, you can see a red elastic band around the bundle. The top one looks like it could be a grid, you know, for the names of candidates and parties. And that,' she pointed with the leg of her purple specs, 'that could be a partial electoral registration number. We need to get expert help. And we should make a return trip to the place, see if they've left anything behind.'

Morton sighed. 'To do that we'd need to get a big group together. Don't fancy going back by myself, even though I think they'll be long gone.'

'Okay, Willie, first thing, get these blown up, then show them to someone. A friendly polis? Who do we know…?'

'I know a retired chief inspector… Donald Todd,' Morton said, 'but whether he'd…'

'Oh, I know somebody. Mike Broadfoot – a snapper. A technical genius.'

Morton nodded. 'I've heard of him, never met him. Freelance.'

'I'll give him a shout. Ask him to come in. That close-up is the key. Is it a ballot paper?'

'And the three men. Is one of them Mearns? And who *is* Mearns anyway?'

'Agreed. The two faces are crucial. Those two are the priority. The other pics and the video just back up the story. Can we get someone to run the licence plates through the PNC? I'll ask Hugh about that. He has someone, on the payroll. Or so I believe.'

'So I've heard,' Morton nodded. 'If we could print it out, I could show it to some people to corroborate one of them is Mearns.'

'Who's that then?'

Morton grimaced. 'Well, Ailsa McKinnon knows Mearns by sight and might have an idea about the others.'

'Oh, your girlfriend?' Rami said archly.

'Behave!' Morton snorted.

'Joke! Who are the others?'

'Darren Barr. I know where he lives. The third is Alan Melville or Munro – if I could find him. Which reminds me, I need to check the school roll at Hutcheson's. He said he was a former pupil. That was the only factual detail he mentioned that I can check. Could be untrue of course.'

'Okay. Do you think we could get a sample ballot paper to compare it with the picture?'

'Janet Kirkwood MSP,' Morton said. 'I could show it to her – and see if she can help with a sample paper. But speaking to her... I'd have to swear her to secrecy.' He looked at her. 'Rami, do you think this adds up to a story... maybe to flush them out?'

Rami fidgeted with the chunky silver skull-and-crossbones-ring on her index finger. 'Too early. Keep this to ourselves for now. If we are wrong, it would be disaster. We'll speak to Hugh in the morning. In the meantime, I'll give Mike a shout. Let's sit on it until we speak to Hugh. Not much more we can do now.'

Morton retrieved the VW Beetle and drove by a circuitous route, finding a space to park halfway up Napier Road then walked round the corner to his parents' substantial house in Merchiston Crescent. His father was in the lounge in his threadbare chair, in cardigan and slippers, spectacles perched on his forehead, watching the TV news.

'Ah, the son and heir,' he remarked as Willie came in. 'This chappie Shankwell who died was the Returning Officer at the Glenforgan by-election. Seems suspicious to me.'

'And hello to you too, pater,' Willie smiled. 'Wait till I've got my jacket off. Where's mum?'

'She's out with Libby. Some opera committee or something. Anyway, sit you doon.'

The Shankwell story was the second item on the Scottish news. The police had concluded 'natural causes' but their investigation was ongoing. The political reporter touched upon the fact Shankwell had been Deputy Returning Officer for the 'controversial' Glenforgan by-election where the ballot papers had disappeared.'

'Controversial?' his father repeated.

The Reporter seemed to be suggesting that Shankwell had been under pressure over the missing ballot papers issue though he did not elaborate.

'Oho?' his father said. 'Are they hinting at suicide? A dodgy affair all round. Certainly takes the gilt off the gingerbread for yon Mr Broon.'

'Well, yes. Bit of a coincidence. I met Shankwell. Not a nice chap at all. Practically threatened me. Said he would have me "sorted out".'

Stuart Erskine fixed his intimidating gimlet eye upon his son. 'Oh, *did* he? And where was this?'

'In the council offices at Glenforgan. I'm looking into the whole issue, you see.'

'Are you indeed? Well!'

'That's what I do, dad. Investigations. Shall I make us a cup of tea?'

'Not for me, William. I've a quiche and baked potato in the oven. Are you staying for tea?'

'No, best get home. I'll make myself a cuppa.'

'Flying visit,' his father grumbled. 'Still, at least you came.'

CHAPTER NINETEEN

Mearns had checked and double-checked the building to ensure no trace of their activities remained, except for a skip full of hot ash. After switching off the incinerator and examining the whole length of the feed hopper and the chute, he finally opened the double doors of the dispatch area in the fading westward light. He was still on edge from the incident and alarmed that the intruder had not been traced. But the job was done. He tossed sets of keys to the others, got into the first van and slowly drove up the ramp out to the concrete wasteland and the constellation of lights from the airfield half a mile away. He waited while the other vans followed, jumped out, closed the doors, locked the padlock and led the convoy along the Paisley Road in the evening traffic to the garage four miles away. Once they were secured there, he drove Mouncey and Keenan back in the Range Rover Freelander to collect the two cars. There wasn't much chat on the return journey.

'Job done, boss,' Mouncey said. 'No sweat.'

'You think?' he muttered. He hoped that was right. Keenan as usual kept his thoughts to himself.

'These things happen,' Mouncey said. 'He was a nobody.'

He watched them drive away and soon was heading east along the A741 in the dark under streetlights. In ten minutes he was back at the industrial estate at Meadowside overlooking Dumbarton across the Clyde, driving slowly past the electrical contractors, plumbing supplies unit, wholefoods distributor – he noticed there were lights still on there – and a few cars at the electrical contractors but the plumbers and wholefood distributors were closed for the day. He passed the empty units and stopped at the gate. There was no-one and it was silent except for the noise of aircraft taking off and landing a few miles away. He drove around the building past clumps of weeds sprouting through the tarmac to the rear to the paved courtyard with high brick wall on three sides. He got out of the car and could see the moving lights of traffic across the Clyde on the Glasgow Road.

Mearns entered his living quarters and switched on the TV, changing channels to the news. It had been a busy day. He'd missed the main news stories, and it was now covering sports. He switched channels. Shankwell's death was now being linked to the missing ballot papers. He had expected it. But they had nothing. He shucked off his jacket and sat down to remove his boots and in stocking-soles walked over to switch on the kettle. He opened the freezer and looked at the stack of ready meals, selected one and stripped off the outer packaging, glanced at the frosted label and put it in the microwave. He made coffee and waited for the microwave to ping.

Morton arrived in the office before 8am the next day but found Rami already there, with a stout young man poring over her computer screen.

'You're early Willie,' Rami commended.

'Well so are you!'

'I'm not a freelance. This is Mike Broadfoot – Willie Morton.'

'I've heard of you,' Morton said.

'Yes, I'm a freelance too,' Broadfoot joked, nodding at

Rami. 'I've had a look at your snaps. They are poor quality, no question. I think we might be able to do something with them. I could resample them at a higher DPI, editing them in Photoshop at say, 400%, then save them. Sometimes it works. Can I have your phone?'

Morton handed it over. Broadfoot glanced at it. 'Blackberry Pearl 8120, that figures. Two-mega pixel. Only good for outdoor pics, tends to blur in low light.'

Morton sighed. 'Yes, I know that.'

'And the video quality is piss poor, jerky, about 12 frames a second. Pity you'd not used a decent digital camera. You can't beat good glass. I mean industry standard even for mobile phone cameras now is eight mexapixels.'

Rami laughed. 'Poor Willie!'

'Anyway, if you could take out the microSD card, I'll see what I can do. No promises.'

Leaving Mike to work on the photos, they went through to Hugh Leadbetter's office. Willie had jotted some notes and took the notebook with him.

'Here comes trouble,' the editor rumbled, lifting his feet off the desk.

'You're not wrong,' Willie joked. They quickly brought Hugh up to speed, Leadbetter nodding, pursing his lips. Finally he slapped the tabletop.

'Okay. Well… And Mike's working up the photos? They'll be crucial.'

'I'm thinking of turning everything we've got to the police,' Morton said. 'We need to have them looking into this Mearns character. They look like thugs, honestly Hugh. Up to no good.'

'Sounds good,' Leadbetter agreed, 'but… guys let's not blow it. Is there more we can do to stand up the story without giving any of it away? Give me a note of the vehicles and the reg numbers and I'll have them checked oot. Let's keep our powder dry for now.'

Leadbetter's desk phone rang. He snatched it up. 'Aye? Whit? Now? They're *here*? Okay, send them up.'

He put down the phone and turned to Morton. 'Christ, Willie, they're on the ball! That's the plod coming tae see you.'

Morton felt his face flush. 'Police? What can they want?'

'We'll soon find out.'

'Maybe they're going to do you for trespass?' Rami joked.

'Very funny!'

The two policemen filled the doorframe of the small office; a detective inspector and a female sergeant. The inspector, a large, flabby man in a raincoat like a grey tent cast a jaundiced eye at them. 'Who is William Morton?'

'Me,' he said, standing up.

'Right, is there somewhere private…? I'm DI Maxfield and this is Sergeant Brown.'

'I'm Leadbetter,' said Hugh, 'the editor and I'd like to sit in.'

Rami stood up. 'Okay, I'll leave you guys to it.' She winked at Morton. 'Better confess *everything*.'

'Hah!' Morton said. 'Anyway, fire away.'

'You met a Mr Neil Shankwell two weeks ago? We're investigating a claim of harassment made against you.'

'Harassment!' exclaimed Morton and Leadbetter together. 'He made a claim against me?'

DI Maxfield looked around in vain for a seat. 'He didn't. But a claim was made by a colleague.'

Leadbetter stood up. 'Wait a minute. Shankwell is dead and… Better get some more seats in here, hang on a minute.' He came back with two small stools and Morton saw the malicious gleam in his eye. 'Here you go, if we can fit these in.'

'Small office you have, Leadbetter,' DI Maxfield observed.

'… and small seats,' quipped Sergeant Brown with a grin. She was nice-looking, around forty, neat in a zipped brown leather jacket and black trousers. She wryly watched as her boss positioned himself on the stool, so that he was somewhat lower than the table level.

'Now, we're all comfy,' Leadbetter said sarcastically. 'Harassment, you say? Should we get our solicitor in here?'

'No, no,' Maxfield blustered. 'These are just questions. As you said, Shankwell is dead. This is in the context of a wider investigation of his death.'

'Right. A colleague?' Morton said. 'In the electoral registration department at Glenforgan?'

'We'll come to that, Morton,' Maxfield said. 'First your side of the story.'

Morton told them of his trip to Glenforgan, getting lost in the corridors and finding himself by a mistake in Shankwell's room. 'Hadn't realised speaking to a public servant was going to be construed as harassment,' he said. 'Certainly didn't expect him to be so angry about it, or to threaten me.'

'Threaten you?' Sergeant Brown asked gently. 'What did he say, exactly?'

'Said he would "have me sorted out." And he came at me with the clear intention of punching me.' He mimed the actions of Shankwell intending to throw a punch.

'So,' said Sergeant Brown. 'Quite an altercation occurred?'

'Not really. He didn't actually hit me. He phoned for security. I was only asking questions about the missing ballot papers. Trying to get to the truth of what had happened. He refused to talk about it…'

'The press officer there had given you what appropriate information was publicly available,' Maxfield remonstrated.

'She thought you had left the building. And the inquiry into the matter was being handled by the Scottish Courts Service. Was that not good enough for you?'

Leadbetter laughed. 'Aw jings. We'd better close doon the paper... Look, officers, Willie's my investigations man. He's a specialist at looking intae jiggery-pokery in local government, into findin oot the stuff they dinna want us tae ken. That's what Willie's aw aboot. That's what journalism is!'

'Now, don't you get lippy with me...' Maxfield started. 'This is a police investigation. We're asking the questions. No need for sarcasm. A man's dead.'

Morton noticed a slight smile on Sergeant Brown's lips as she turned away. 'Speaking of which,' he began. 'It was natural causes, wasn't it?'

Brown turned in his direction. 'Probably, but we keep an open mind. We're looking into Shankwell's life over the last few months.'

'Including of course, the connection with the furore over the missing ballot papers?'

'Everything,' Maxfield said, portentously, 'that touches upon his life, and any physical altercation in his office clearly needs to be investigated. Would you say, Morton, that he saw you as an enemy? Or as a threat?'

'A threat?' Leadbetter scowled. 'Are you trying to fit us up?'

'Of course not. No.'

'So there is undoubtedly, in my view anyway,' Morton said, reasonably, 'a direct link between the by-election and his death. There must be. Otherwise, why would you be here, questioning me about... about my questions to him... that provoked such an angry reaction? I think... he was under pressure about something. That's what made him so angry. You know there are rumours about the by-election being rigged? I didn't think it was remotely possible, even when it was revealed the ballot papers had gone missing, but you know what, I'm starting to think there might be something in it. Hugh… should we…?'

Leadbetter scowled. 'Naw… well, maybe….'

'I want to show you something. Confidentially. Some photographs. About a man called Raymond Mearns.'

Morton saw the shared glance between the inspector and the sergeant. Did they know the name? Had they already come across it? 'Mearns is a former Labour official,' he told them, 'and he was at the count, where Shankwell was Deputy Returning Officer. So they must have known each other.'

'Carry on,' said Sergeant Brown. 'If this man has a connection to Shankwell, we want to hear about it.'

'I discovered that Mearns was using premises in Renfrew, the old Municipal Cleansing and Waste depot on Wright Crescent.'

'Renfrew?' queried Brown. 'That's interesting. Carry on.'

'Is it?' Morton frowned. 'Well, it's a disused building, mostly derelict now but there's a part of it that is still locked and secure, the part where the old incinerator is. Mearns was there with two other men and they were stacking black plastic binbags – whose contents were what looked to me like folded bundles of ballot papers.'

'Really? Quite a claim,' Inspector Maxfield said. 'Can we see these photographs please?'

'The quality is poor,' Morton said. 'We're having them enlarged. My colleague…'

'Best tae get Mike in here. He's aboot somewhere,' said Leadbetter. 'I'll get him.' He left the room.

They sat in uncomfortable silence until Leadbetter returned with Mike and a laptop.

'This is Mike Broadfoot,' he said. 'DI Maxfield and Sergeant Brown.'

'Hello.'

'Okay,' Mike breezed. 'I've managed to improve the quality of the piccys a wee bit. The video is still poor.' He grinned at the police. 'Two-mega-pixel phone camera, honestly!'

They crowded round the laptop as Mike booted up and inserted the USB stick. 'Willie, you'd best do the honours,' he said.

'First picture is the place where it happened,' Morton said. 'The cleansing depot in Renfrew, just across the river from the airport. These are the cars they arrived in, the three men…'

'Yes,' Mike explained, 'we enlarged the faces a little but it's badly pixellated. You can just make out the features.'

'That one there is Mearns, the skinny guy,' Morton said, leaning in and pointing. 'Then, this is inside the locked area of the building. Three vans, the registration plates are quite clear, and this, inside one of them, shows piles of the binbags.'

'Those do look like binbags,' Sergeant Brown said, with a wry smile.

'Nothing illegal about binbags,' Maxfield said, dismissively. 'Could be anything inside them.'

'This is the incinerator,' Morton continued. 'But here's a close-up of the material they were feeding into the hopper, you can see the bundles of folded paper.'

'I made an enlargement of that,' Broadfoot told them. 'It's faint, but clearly a grid pattern, that *could* be a list of candidates. And there's a partial number that might be an elector number. That could be checked.'

'Yes,' Brown said. 'We can look into that.'

'Thanks for your help, Mike,' Leadbetter said.

'I'm just outside if you need anything.'

'Yup, thanks.'

'The video shows three men emptying the vans and piling the bags,' Morton said. 'It's a narrative, see? All adds up. The van loads, the incinerator, destroying the evidence.'

'It's clear what they're doing,' Maxfield said, 'but as it stands I see no evidence of criminality.'

'It looks dodgy,' Leadbetter snorted.

'But only if,' Maxfield said, 'those are ballot papers… otherwise it's perfectly legitimate.'

'But what are they doing in a derelict building?' Morton said. 'That is suspicious. Who gave them permission to use it? Were they authorised to be in there?'

'Were you?' DS Brown asked with a smirk.

'Leave that with us,' Maxfield said. 'Give us a copy of that data stick and we'll take a look into it. Although I'm not convinced that any of this has any direct connection with Mr Shankwell's death.'

'Okay,' said Morton, 'we can do that. But I also need to give you something else.' He produced the letter addressed to Melville from 'This Island Nation'. 'I obtained this.' He coughed onto the back of his hand, hoping they would not ask how he had obtained it. 'I'll give you a copy. It refers to work they were carrying out. This organisation has something to do with it.'

Maxfield read it and handed it to the sergeant. 'Who is this Mr Melville?'

Morton cleared this throat. Where to begin? 'He is an ex-military officer now employed in some unknown London-based group, quite possibly this one – This Island Nation – who admitted to me that he was a kind of agent for various right-wing political groups and the Labour Party…'

'Right-wing?' Brown queried with a smile.

'Unionist groups... Melville is not his real name though, which is Munro.'

'He's some kind of spy, you're suggesting?'

'Yes, we had dinner together in the Premier Inn on Duke Street and he as good as told me that, and clearly he knows or works with Mearns. Well, this letter is the proof of that, and they are all connected to this group.'

'Is Melville or Munro one of the men in that picture?'

'No. He didn't turn up.'

'He didn't?' Maxfield snorted contemptuously.

Morton grimaced. 'Well, I... he may not have seen this letter. Which was sent to him at an office in Duke Street, Glasgow, previously used by the Labour Party now by the New Britain Party.'

'This is becoming a bit of a fairy-tale!' Maxfield snorted. 'Apart from how you managed to acquire it, by theft, I presume... it's all highly speculative and with no connection whatsoever to the death of a man in his own home. I think we've heard enough, although I will take a copy of that letter. We may need you to come in to a police station, Morton, and gives us a statement about your altercations... meetings with Mr Shankwell.'

CHAPTER TWENTY

Once the police had left, Rami came back into the office. 'No-one arrested, I see.'

'Very funny, Rami,' Morton grunted.

'What do we do now then, team?' Leadbetter said. 'Have we a story, for fucksake?'

'Nearly,' Rami said. 'I think. We need to check up on this Melville Munro character,' Rami said. 'Hutcheson's, military lists. There must be way to find out what he's up to. Ditto Mearns. Try all our sources in Labour and at Glenforgan. Also, why Renfrew? What's the connection? Is Mearns from there? And 'This Island Nation'. Who's pulling their strings? Who are their funders.' She smiled sweetly at the others. 'Have I left everything out?'

'Seems comprehensive to me,' Morton murmured.

'*Death of By-Election Official Linked To Missing Ballot Papers*? Leadbetter said, tentatively. 'But only if we can come up with some proof they *are* ballot papers. Not fucking sales dockets or... used sanitary towels! That's the key to this, not these dodgy geezers Melville, Mearns and Munro. Get tae Glenforgan, Willie, and get a copy of the ballot paper so we can compare our picture. Somebody must have one. Speak to the Electoral Returning Officer...'

'Ron Marshall.'

'That's the boy. There must be spare ballot papers floating

around somewhere. One that wisnae used… or a sample… somebody must have one. And check out that number… is it an elector registered to vote? If so find him or her. Did he or she vote or not vote? Come on guys. Let's get to work!'

The next morning, Raymond Mearns was in transit from the unit at Meadowside Industrial Estate, Renfrew and his flat in Kelvinside when his phone buzzed. He reached to the dashboard and put it on speaker. Trenchard. He was just coming off the A8 onto the Shieldhall roundabout.

'No problem, I'm in the car.'

'An update for you, Raymond. An advance warning of sorts. It appears that the Strathclyde police are to visit the premises you used most recently… near Glasgow airport.'

'Oh well. They won't find anything.'

'Yes, keep well clear. I was tipped off by a contact at a high level. Apparently, there are photographs.'

'The intruder?' Mearns drove rapidly down into the Clyde Tunnel, keeping in lane under the artificial lighting. 'He had a camera?'

'Yes, apparently. The police now have copies of these photographs so I'm going to try to find out a bit more about that, but I presume therefore that the intruder has discussed with the police what he saw and shown them the photographs which he took. Are you able to shed any light on how much he might have seen?'

Mearns sighed. Mouncey and Keenan had believed the intruder had not seen much but then neither thought he had had time to take photographs. He thought back to what they had been doing and where the intruder had been.

'He was behind the vans, so about forty or fifty feet away from us. He couldn't have heard much or anything because the incinerator was working. He would have seen binbags, of the kind that is used by millions for lots of things. The papers were bundled tightly with elastic bands but they were hidden inside bin bags.'

'He saw you unload the vans? Could he have seen inside the vans?'

Mearns slowed as he came up to daylight again and the complicated arterial knot of roads and slipways looking for the turnoff onto the Clydeside Expressway. 'Yes. But what he saw was bin bags. It could have been any commercial rubbish. We might have been contractors getting rid of old accounts, old receipts, that kind of thing. Any photographs would be useless, unless…'

'Unless what, Raymond?'

'Well, the worry is, the bin bags bursting open but we took great care to make sure that didn't happen.' He slipped off the Expressway onto the roundabout and continued past Partick rail station into Beith Street heading for Byres Road and Kelvingrove.

'I'm reassured to hear it.'

'And it's all gone up in smoke anyway,' he said. He slowed to a stop at traffic lights. 'We were very careful. We didn't chase the intruder; we finished the task, and we were very thorough in checking the area before we left. They will find nothing there at all. Except maybe a half-tonne of ash.'

'Good. I've asked Timms at Rundgren to keep a discreet eye on the police visit today and when I get an update from my police contact in due course, will give you a further update. What can you tell me about this man Melville. Why was he involved? *Was* he involved?'

'He's not involved,' Mearns declared, passing Hillhead underground station. 'He's a useful contact, a link to some groups in Glasgow. I'll put it into a briefing. My contact with him has been minimal. We've never met in person and contact has been made through a third party.'

'The think tank?'

'Yes. They seem determined to forge links between all kinds of groups on the ground which is ridiculous and I have no truck with it. But… it allows me to have an overview of what's going on, and who's out there.'

'Talent-spotting?'

'Exactly. Though so far, only knuckle-draggers. So I'm keeping him at arm's length and anyway he didn't even turn up. And then we had this intruder. I've been thinking about that. There may be a link between him not turning up and the intruder.'

'Hmn. See what you mean, Raymond. You're right to mention it. I'll make a note of it.'

'I'll be interested to find out who the intruder was.'

'Of course. As soon as I hear… bye.'

Mearns turned right into Great Western Road and shortly after, parked the Range Rover in his resident's space outside the block of flats in Colebrooke Mews. Although he knew the intruder couldn't have seen anything that would merit the word evidence, it irked him to think of him there, spying on them, a man who was out to get him, a man who knew something, even if he couldn't possibly prove it, whatever 'it' was. The more he thought about it, the more convinced he was that Melville had some connection. Or Darren Barr. That idiot. Somebody had said something. Something out of turn.

If Alan Melville was around fifty, he'd have been at school from the mid-sixties to the late 1970s at a rough guess, Morton considered as he began to surf the online pages of Hutcheson's website at the spare desk in the press room, next to Rami's desk. He found himself drawn into the vibrant picture of life at a school in Glasgow that was broadly similar to his own education at George Watson's in Edinburgh. A school, established exactly one hundred years before his own, whose Latin motto was *Veritas* instead of his own school's *Caritas*. It was like looking in the mirror. He had played rugby against them once in his teenage years in the Scottish Schools Cup.

'Anything?' Rami asked over her shoulder.

'Sorry?' Morton shook himself from his daydream of school rugby days. 'No. There's a school magazine but the online version only started this year. The magazines I need will be from the mid to late seventies, assuming Melville stayed till the age of eighteen. I'll need to go to the school, or the local history archive in Glasgow. Won't be digitised. You?'

'Well, look at this… it's a media story about restructuring at Renfrew Council. The closure of the old municipal Cleansing Department. Look…'

Morton swivelled round to look at Rami's screen. 'Yup, that looks like the building.'

'I thought so. And look here… guess who was the Deputy Director of Cleansing and Waste at Renfrew?'

Morton frowned. 'Who?'

'Neil Shankwell.'

'*No?*'

'That was just a year ago. Looks like he moved to Glenforgan about that time, to join their Cleansing Department.'

Morton was reading the screen. 'And then was transferred to the electoral registration office two weeks before the by-election date. More coincidence!'

'Certainly is! But you've got to wonder… we need information about local government salary scales. He was a deputy

Cleansing director in Renfrew then deputy Cleansing director in Glenforgan, okay that seems normal but then a promotion – so-called – to deputy ERO. Would that actually *be* a promotion?'

Morton slapped his thigh. 'I see what you mean! Or a move of convenience? And would he still have the keys to the old Municipal Cleansing Department and incinerator at Renfrew? We suspect he knew Mearns and Barr... now we're getting somewhere!'

Rami pulled absently-mindedly at her braids. 'We need to speak again to Ron Marshall, Willie. What happened to the previous deputy ERO? How did Shankwell move from Cleansing to take up that post? Was that a usual sort of move? Seems odd to me. And right in the middle of a by-election? Forget about Melville just now, let's get over to Glenforgan and see Marshall.'

'Okay Rami,' Morton nodded, 'and we could meet up with Janet Kirkwood, she'll be there doing her constituency surgery, and maybe a local councillor I've already met, Ian Brown, and see if we can get a ballot paper sample, while we're there.'

'Brilliant. We'll have to take your car.'

'Right, okay... why?'

Rami shrugged. 'I don't have one, do I. My husband is using ours. I have a bike, but it'd take too long!'

'Okay.'

'Don't worry, you'll get expenses for petrol.'

CHAPTER TWENTY-ONE

Mearns had no concerns about his own security. In the flat at Colebrook Mews, he was someone else, with a cast-iron legend that had been constructed over several years. If there were straws in the wind about Raymond Mearns, none of that had any connection to the person he was in Kelvinside. Everything was sealed, compartmentalised. Even when he saw reports on the evening news that a newspaper had published a story claiming links between the death of Neil Shankwell and the missing ballot papers, he merely smiled wryly. Now he knew that the intruder worked for the *Scottish Standard*, typical. This was manna to those shit-stirrers. But they had nothing really. Yes, his own photograph had appeared in the story and that had been culled from CCTV no doubt, it had that blurry, pixellated quality. It could be him, but it could be dozens of other men too. Trenchard had been critical of his decision to attend the count in person, given the circumstances, but he had been unable to resist it. He had needed to ensure that the process continued smoothly beyond the verification of the ballots to the actual counting process. It had been essential to be able to provide a definite answer to the question: had it worked? And it had. There could be no unravelling of that fact. As he sat in front of the TV with a glass of beer, he reflected on the straws that floated tantalising beyond reach of the police. The photograph at the count of a man invisible, whose antecedents, parents, upbringing, family… whose entire existence could not be proved. The photographs at the old Cleansing depot taken by the intruder were too poor quality for faces to be recognised even with the digital tools the police now possessed. Mouncey and Keenan were well tucked up in a safe house in London. Their legends were safe. They had all worn rubber gloves. Melville he had not met in person; all they had was his name on a letter written by others to Melville. He had never met Shankwell in person. That they knew each other might be inferred but there was no proof of it. Shankwell's death had been organised professionally. He had had a bad heart; nothing could be proved. Which left Darren Barr. As the image of Barr's face formed in his mind, he found that he was involuntarily clenching his fists. Barr was a lowlife, a clinger and definitely a weak link. Barr had been photographed with him at the count, despite him trying to evade that. He could be identified by Barr. He might have kept notes, emails, although it seemed unlikely. He had some information from the early days. And he was the type that would crack easily, who might even now be talking to the police… Barr was a problem, always pestering him for money. Worst of all, he had not told Trenchard about Barr so he could not now seek assistance. Barr was a loose cannon. And there was only one way to deal with loose cannons.

Shankwell Death Linked To Missing Ballot Papers was the shoutline on newsagents' boards as Morton drove the VW into the main street of Glenforgan. The story, headlined on the front page of the *Scottish Standard* and continuing on pages 2 and 3 had several sidebars: *Missing Labour Official Sought by Police*, and *Burning The Evidence?* and *Was By-Election Rigged?*

'We've certainly made a splash,' Rami approved. 'Which is good. Maybe Marshall be in a more co-operative mood now the police are on the case as well as us.'

'Hope so. I'll park round the back of the library. Kirkwood has her surgeries there.'

'Better do Marshall first though.'

'Of course. The media officer's name is Alison Bridger. She's okay. We'll go to her first.'

Rami's phone was ringing. She scrambled to open it. 'The boss – ' she gestured ' – what's up? What? Oh well, that's their problem. We're about to interview the ERO and the local MSP. Okay.'

Morton parked the car in a tight space. 'What's he saying?'

Rami tutted. 'The police are not happy with our story. "Premature" they say. Tough shit, I say.'

Morton laughed. 'Yeah, well there's nothing factually incorrect in the story. Maybe they're just a little sensitive… or, maybe…'

'Maybe what?'

'I never know who's pulling their strings. A couple of years ago…'

'Let's not go there. Let's assume CID are playing it straight on this one.'

Morton laughed derisorily. 'Well, there's always a chance of that!'

Next day, Morton walked to the Grape & Olive on Broughton Street in soaring winds whipping the branches of trees about and carrying and dropping litter wherever they pleased. The trendy vegan café was busy inside. The tables and chairs on the forecourt had been chained together, the awning rolled in. Ailsa sat by herself in the condensation and heat, sipping a chocolate mocha. It had been several weeks since he'd seen her; a considerable cooling of their nascent relationship, if relationship was the right word.

She looked up and smiled. 'Hello Willie... okay?'

'I'm fine. How's things, union-wise?' He hung his leather satchel on the back of the rickety wooden chair.

'The usual. Up to my eyes in it. Pay claims, balloting of members for strikes. Anyway, thanks for coming. I've been following the story... I can't believe what's happening. How bad is it? Do you really think Shankwell was involved in some kind of rigging?'

Morton exhaled. 'Ailsa – I don't know. That's for the police now.'

'Don't tell me if you don't want to.'

'It's not that. I would... only I don't know. The forensics folk will look into it. I was there yesterday – I mean Glenforgan – but we didn't learn anything new. Do you want a sandwich, or something.'

'I'm fine, Willie, thanks, I've ordered.'

He ordered a coffee and a mixed-bean pasty at the counter and sat down to wait. 'Anyway, I've something to show you,' he said briskly. 'Some photos.'

'Okay.'

He showed her the enlarged picture of the three men that had been printed out onto paper. 'Is that Mearns?'

She peered at it. 'It could be. Maybe, can't say for sure. Don't know the other two. Who are they?'

He put the picture back into his inside pocket. 'I'm hoping the police will tell me. But I watched the three of them putting binbags what looked like bundles of ballot papers into an incinerator. Glenforgan council have admitted the ballot papers were being kept in their premises in binbags.'

'I just can't believe it.' Ailsa shook her head. 'I just can't. And what do the police say?'

'Well, apart from what I saw and a few poor-quality photos I took on this Blackberry, there's no evidence.'

'Why did he do it? What was the point of it? I can't believe real Labour people were involved. I don't even know what his role was... I mean, he was there at the count, he was on our list of counting agents, but how he got on the list I don't know. Somebody must know.'

'Yes, well, Ailsa. It will all come out. Meanwhile the police are looking for Raymond Mearns but not finding him. He's hiding out, which in itself says a lot. No doubt about it, he's involved in dodgy things at the least. Criminal stuff too maybe.'

Ailsa looked searchingly at him. 'And what will all this mean? I mean, if it turns out something illegal went on? Will they have to rerun the bloody thing?'

'I can't answer that. I've no idea. Honestly, I know it might upset lots of people but... well, anyway. Let's change the subject. I was going to speak to you about Neil Shankwell. It seems he transferred to Glenforgan from a job in Renfrew.'

'Renfrew? I wouldn't know, but somehow I think of him as from the West of Scotland somewhere. I remember he was on Labour's SEC – the Scottish Executive Committee – in the trade union and elected members section and, you know... I also remember he spoke against the idea of creating a Women's committee.' She grimaced. 'He was old-school, not the kind of Labour member that I was ever totally friendly with. Which is why I didn't recognise the name when you first mentioned him to me. Anyway, I don't know what he's been up to. You must think he's been involved in electoral fraud, and so must the police otherwise they wouldn't be looking into it.'

'He could be innocent, Ailsa. The death could be just a complete coincidence. Although I thought when I met him, he seemed a bit... as if he had something to hide.' Morton frowned. 'Which is probably why I had McPlod on my doorstep...'

'You were interviewed by the police?' Ailsa murmured. 'But... why? Surely Shankwell died of... heart attack, wasn't it?'

'They said they were looking into everything. Fair enough. But if it was a heart attack, well, that's... I mean...'

'Were they actually saying you were a suspect?' Ailsa suddenly smiled. 'I remember you telling me you didn't like him... what did you call him?'

Morton thought. 'Well, I didn't... just said he was rude and that was suspicious as if he had something to hide.'

'I wonder what the party will make of it? I'm attending an event tomorrow in North Queensferry. The PM will be there, making a speech though it's a fundraising rally. The press were invited and will probably now turn up in droves.' She smiled and put her hand on his wrist. 'You could come as my date.'

Morton laughed. 'As long as I'm not going to be burned at the stake, or pelted with stones.'

'That's a different kind of event. We don't do those much these days.'

'Maybe Rami would want to be there too.'

'Of course. But you don't have to. The media will be there asking questions about Shankwell but only at the start and for the speech of course. They'll not be able to ruin the rest of the event. Or at least, I hope not!'

'I'd better come then.'

'There will be an outdoor barbeque – if it's not raining.'

'How are you getting there?' Morton asked.

'Well, I usually cadge a lift.'
'Ha! I thought I might cadge a lift with you.'
'That'd be difficult. I don't have a car.'
'Oh. Okay. Right.'

'You'll just have to sit tight old chap, and it'll all go away,' said Trenchard. To Mearns, it sounded as if he was in a restaurant somewhere. A busy place. He wondered if it was a Ministry staff canteen in Whitehall, or a private club. 'There can be no evidence or proof,' Trenchard continued, complacently. He did sound smug, Mearns thought. 'Our contacts in the Scottish police authorities are keeping a close eye. Nothing to worry about, then we'll be back to business as usual.'

'I suppose so,' he murmured.

'In the meantime, Raymond, a nice holiday would be an option. Let me know, and I'll get tickets and make all the arrangements at this end. Perhaps somewhere hot. Have you ever been to Africa?'

'*Africa*?' Mearns repeated faintly.

'Kenya, specifically.'

'I have no interest in going there.'

'A pity. Lovely country. I was brought up there, you know. My father was a District Supervisor in the Colonial Police from the Emergency in 1952 to the end of British rule in 1963. It was an idyllic place to live as a child, beautiful country, rather like the Scottish Highlands, you know, Raymond, very similar. Those were happy days.'

'I'm sure,' Mearns muttered, wishing the man would ring off. There was nothing more to say.

'And most of the Kenyans were decent, law-abiding chaps but occasionally there'd be a nationalist flare-up, exciting for us youngsters. Mostly, it was hotheads at the university.' He laughed dryly. 'My father thought they should have kept them out of university in the first place. So they'd get them into custody and keep at it until they cracked or quieted down. Occasionally, my father had to nip things in the bud, but not often and he hardly had to shoot any of them, though some did die in custody.'

'Interesting. Well, I've no intention of going abroad at the moment,' Mearns said. 'Because as you know, there is unfinished business. I think it's best to keep a low profile but some things have to be... tidied up.' Trenchard had agreed and with a final "keep your pecker up, Raymond," had rung off and Mearns had gone into the hall to put his jacket on. He selected his heavy waterproof parka. It might rain and also it had a decent interior pocket where he could put the steel monkey-wrench that he'd double-wrapped in polythene and taped over with duct tape. It fitted neatly and didn't look obvious. He pulled on a black beanie hat and insulated gloves. He collected the keys to the cottage in Fife and with a last look round, switched off the lights and locked the door.

CHAPTER TWENTY-TWO

The next day seemed dry though cold. He'd spoken to Rami, and she offered to drive, planning to borrow her husband's car.

'Great, my old Beetle is a bit tight for three.'

'Three?'

'I've promised Ailsa McKinnon a lift.'

'Oh, did you?'

Morton laughed. 'Now, don't be jealous!'

'As if!'

Ailsa turned up just before noon. He had gone outside to the pavement to wait. She lived in Wester Hailes, just a bit further out. He'd wondered what kind of car it'd be. It turned out to be a shiny blue Peugeot 207 and when it rolled to a stop in front of his block, he thought that it looked brand new.

'Nice car,' he said, climbing in. 'Very clean.'

'Very new, Willie. Asim bought it in December.'

'Very smart,' Morton said. 'I'm selling my car very soon. Has to go. I can't afford it.'

'Oh dear. Pity you can't get a staffer job, Willie. Right, now it's into the New Town? You'll have to direct me.'

'Okay. Get over North Bridge and down Leith Walk. Annandale Street. Not far.'

'So, Willie, have you something to tell me?' Rami asked archly. 'You and Ailsa?'

'Chums,' he said and would say no more. 'I wonder what Brown will say today?'

'Deft change of subject.'

'If you say so.'

When they picked up Ailsa outside her office, Rami began to gently probe her on all subjects, Morton just listened. Rami was a born inquisitor, curious to know all the details of... everything. Soon they were on the Forth Bridge, high over the river, where he could see two ferries docked at Rosyth. He knew that Scotland's only sea link to continental Europe was in trouble and had been suspended, although in a matter of weeks the DFDS subsidiary Norfolkline would resume sailing on the route to Zeebrugge. There had been enough car passengers, but not enough lorries had used the service, preferring to continue to clog up the motorways of England. Rami was questioning Ailsa over what she knew about Shankwell.

'Ron Marshall didn't get on with him,' Rami was saying. 'He didn't say as much, but I got the impression he had been overruled over the appointment. After all, Shankwell's entire career had been in Cleansing and Waste Management. What did he know about elections and being a returning officer? Though maybe that wasn't why he was appointed?'

'You think he was appointed to help rig the election?' Ailsa snorted. 'Whaaat!'

'Well, maybe. We don't know anything for certain at this point.'

'Aye, well, I've no doubt some of the less-responsible hacks will be flinging all kinds of ridiculous allegations at the PM this afternoon – thanks to what you put in your story.'

'So what are you saying, Ailsa?' Morton grinned. 'That we're the responsible media?'

'I read your story. Obviously, some of it was speculation.

Look – if there's been some kind of criminal activity, or a cover-up, it needs to be rooted out. Labour wouldn't get involved in that… we are in government for heaven's sake!'

Morton laughed derisorily. 'Governments – of all stripes – do terrible things to keep power. But we the people, the weary hacks try to find out they're up to, without fear or favour.'

'You'd better keep a close eye on that Salmond. He has chancer written all over him.'

'Oh, we will,' said Rami. 'Now what was the address in North Queensferry?'

* * *

Raymond Mearns had read the story in the *Standard*. He had gone into a newsagent and actually bought, for the very first time, the hated nationalist 'rag'. He grudged giving them the fifty pence. He stood in the kitchen and quickly scanned the story. At least the picture they had used of him was such poor quality that even his own mother wouldn't have recognised him – even if she had wanted to. He had a brief glimpse of his parents sitting in the kitchen at Collessie Street, Craigend, with the bleak view over the backs to the multis of Mossvale. He shuddered. Drab lives. Thank god he had got out of there!

It wasn't going to be necessary to make big changes to his appearance. Maybe a tweed bunnet and plain glass spectacles. The story simply galvanised his need to cut off the loose end. Speed was of the essence. Although Darren Barr didn't know exactly where he lived or the name he used, he did know where his parents lived. Not the exact street, but the council estate. And Barr knew what he looked like. He knew other things. If the police or this annoying journalist Morton got to him, god knows what he might blurt out. He stood at the mirror, adjusting the brim of the bunnet, pulled up his jacket collar, put on the heavy bakelite spectacles and left the flat. He looked like a million Scottish men, classless, anonymous, unnoticeable, undistinguished in every way, an ordinary man on the way to middle age, the kind of man that stands on the terracing in their hundreds of thousands, the kind of man who could be an office worker, a bin man, a football manager, an insurance salesman, a local councillor, businessman – anything.

The event was being held on grass open space beside a community centre at the top of the hill, backed by high banks of thick gorse. Rami had been forced by the number of cars blocking the narrow road, to park at the bottom of the hill and the three of them had walked up the path together. From the top there was a view south of the stanchions of an electricity pylon, the Forth Bridge and the broad river.

The community centre was a modest one-storey concrete-block with a disabled ramp, the tarmac car park's thirty spaces filled to overflowing with double-parked vehicles of the media that had verged up onto the playpark and along both sides of narrow Brock Street. Below the carpark, beyond the building, was an expanse of grass on which a white marquee was erected, and beyond that a jumble of four-storey housing blocks.

'All here,' Morton said, gloomily. 'Sky, PA, Beeb, Reuters, STV – that looks like CNN!'

'Surely not?' Rami exclaimed.

'I count four tabloids. You could write the headlines now: "Embattled Premier Makes Last Stand High on a Windy Hill."'

'Well, we'll see,' Ailsa said petulantly. 'I see the vultures are gathering.'

'They can detect blood in the water from miles away,' he murmured.

'Anyway, look, Rami – thank you for the lift. I'll get myself a lift back with someone later.'

'Sure? Don't want to be seen with us, Ailsa, is that it?' Morton laughed.

'You can understand it,' Rami agreed. 'Anyway, we're only staying for the media part. We've not been invited to the function.'

As Ailsa joined friends and colleagues at the large marquee, Morton and Rami mingled with the media – most of whom they knew – at the side of the building awaiting the arrival of the Prime Minister.

'Is he walking?' Morton asked reporter Geoff Hume from the Press Association.

Hume tugged at his salt and pepper beard. 'Is he heck as like!'

'I thought he might. Only lives five minutes away.'

'He's the Prime bloody Minister. Can't be seen walking.'

And then Brown arrived, driven by his wife Sarah in a small family car and was enveloped in the media scrum. He was in a suit but in deference to the social event, had left off his tie. Morton felt a little sorry for him. Even his weekends were victims of media intrusion. A microphone stand was magicked from somewhere and a Labour press officer in a red tie began to circulate copies of the speech. Morton got a copy to share with Rami. It was short and the first few sentences were of only local interest; the constituency fund-raising effort, then a shorter, slighter version of the usual Brown speech: proud to be British and to share and promote British values… a renewed sense of our national identity, a sense of national destiny… a strong sense of being British that helps unite and unify us…'
He pointed out the next paragraph to Rami and read aloud:

'"Even before America said in its constitution it was the

land of liberty and erected the Statue of liberty, I think Britain can lay claim to the idea of liberty…" *even as we were trying to suppress and kill the American upstarts!*' Morton added. 'Bit of a rewrite of history there? Remind me, Rami, how many other independent nations has Britain colonised, bullied and terrified into submission… in the name of liberty?'

Rami laughed. 'Shush, he's speaking now.'

Morton knew that Brown's detached retina forced him to remember to combat the slightly skewed impression this gave when facing an audience and cameras. He managed to appear relaxed and unfazed by the dozens of media hacks and their rude and jostling behaviour. Morton remembered then that the *Sun* had got hold of the fact that his youngest son had been diagnosed with cystic fibrosis at a very early age, just two years ago and had gleefully splashed the story all over the front pages without mercy. The prime minister had admitted to being reduced to tears by it. Bastards they were! Morton thought. Inhuman beasts.

At the end of the speech, the clamour began. Questions were shouted at him about the by-election enquiry and when he was going to call a general election. He answered a few but the shouts were too many and too frenzied, so he turned away with a smile and a wave to meet up with his people. He started to become charming in his saturnine kind of way, over-smiling and doing that lip-sucking thing, his wife at his side as they sauntered off to meet constituents and party workers.

'Come on, time to go,' Rami said, pulling his sleeve. 'Complete waste of time. This will only make a sidebar story.'

'Forty-three,' Morton said. 'I've just counted. Forty-three Britain, British or Britishness in the speech that lasted, what, six minutes. Yup, Brits 43 Scotland 2.'

Rami snorted. 'Very much a theme with him.'

'Yeah, won't impress the English voters though. As far as they're concerned, he might as well be wearing full highland dress and waving a blood-crusted claymore. He's a jock and he can't change that, no matter how many times he bleats about how proud he is to be British.'

Mearns had been several times to the Glenwood housing scheme, lines of windows facing each other across narrow streets, and knew Barr's house well. It was a real shithole area where a stranger stood out, a source of suspicion tracked secretly from numerous windows. It was an area frequently visited by convoys of police cars, sheriff officers and on occasion, repo men, tally men, loan sharkers' enforcers. There was a vacant house somewhere nearby where you could buy an assortment of drugs through a letterbox at any hour of the day or night.

Mearns knew the best way to approach was from the rear beside the stream. He parked there, several streets away on the edge of the scheme, put on the bunnet and the specs and walked up the hill through the open wasteland. He travelled through a succession of untended gardens and blind gables, drifting up to the rear of Barr's flat entirely unobserved. He stood behind the remains of four conjoined weed-covered brick sheds clustered around a telegraph pole and kept watch on Barr's kitchen window. He couldn't see lights, couldn't see movement. He looked at his watch. Just after three. It was Saturday. Of course! Fitba. He knew Barr spent a lot of time in the Gunners' Arms, a twenty-minute walk away in the town centre. He reproved himself for not checking that out before driving into the scheme. He heard a distant ambulance or police siren then it cut off, then started again, then it got fainter. He couldn't stand here forever, although it was unlikely he would be seen. *Saturday*. Barr would be at the football. Not Ibrox but the next best thing for him, in the pub with his Rangers' chums. Mearns knew the Gunners was the howff of choice for the local bluenose brigade. Lowlifes like Barr couldn't afford subscriptions to Setanta Sports, so the pub would be full. And he'd be there for the duration.

He walked quicklyly back to the car but changed his mind when he got there and walked on the pavement into town. He found that the bunnet was making his head itch and he had to keep demisting the spectacles. It occurred to him that to really disappear into this environment all he needed was a Rangers' scarf.

Rami dropped Morton off on the Slateford Road as she headed home. He strolled into Shandon Place hearing the sudden roar of the crowd at Tynecastle. Hearts were at home to Aberdeen. Leadbetter and his boys would be there. As he approached his door, he saw an unfamiliar vehicle – a black Toyota RAV4 with a roof rack and blacked-out rear windows – parked at the kerb. The doors opened. He recognised DS Brown in her brown leather jacket – how apt – he thought, but not the young DC getting out on the driver's side.

'Mr Morton, how are you, sir?'

'Sergeant Brown. On a Saturday, too?'

'Yup. This is DC Martelli.' She smiled. 'Can we come in?'

'Of course.' He led them upstairs and opened the flat. 'I'll get the coffee on, if you've time?'

'Not for us, Mr Morton, thanks, you go ahead. Just wanted to give you an update…'

'Fine.'

They sat at the breakfast bar in the kitchen while he switched on the filter machine. Sure you don't want…?'

'Thanks, but no,' DS Brown said, having a good look around. Morton wondered if his domestic arrangements would pass muster. He liked the two-tone colour of her hair, blonde and brunette at the same time, tawny colour. He wondered if she was around his age. She smiled at him and he realised he'd been staring. He looked away.

'You probably feel you've been ignored, Mr Morton, but that's not the case. With our colleagues in Strathclyde, we've been following up the information you gave us. We've uncovered Mearn's parents so we know that is his real name, whatever the name he is going by now.'

'His parents?'

'They live in a council house in Craigend, near Garthamlock but they haven't seen or heard from him they say for about five years. They had a phone call from him around then. He told them he was going to work in London. Nothing since then. But we know a lot about him now, his upbringing, his schools, his interests. What we don't know is where he is now, what name he's using or where he works.'

'All that is pretty suspicious, isn't it?'

'Yes... not entirely uncommon. We had the impression from them that he felt he was... embarrassed... would you say, DC Martelli?

Martelli, a slim dark-haired man in a dark green raincoat, nodded. 'Embarrassed by them. That's what they said. Felt he was above them.'

'It wasn't a very affectionate family in my opinion, Morton. He was very critical of their... hated was the word they said he'd used... the council estate and wanted something better for himself.'

'His former school friends said the same,' Martelli said, reading off his small black notebook. 'A snob they called him.

He was good at PE, the head teacher said but never really stood out academically, or in any way really. Anonymous.'

DS Brown laughed. 'Quite! But the thing is we've not been able to locate him. We'll keep a watchful eye and continue to liaise with our colleagues in Strathclyde and elsewhere but until we get a new lead there's not much more we can do.' She shrugged. 'A new lead would be the name he's using now. And of course,' she hesitated. 'There's not actually any evidence of wrong-doing. Which I know you'll disagree with… but until new evidence crops up, we're a bit stuck.'

Morton spooned coffee into the filter in the top of the machine. 'He must be on file somewhere? How can he create a new identity and disappear in this day and age? There's CCTV footage. And why is he so keen to be invisible? What's he got to hide? Who employs him?'

DS Brown stood up. 'We don't have the answers yet, Morton, but we just wanted to keep you updated. We're not ignoring you… but there are limits to what we can do, what we are *authorised* to do.'

'Well, at least you believe me,' Morton said. 'That he's out there, that he's involved in something… that he might have been involved in rigging a by-election.'

Brown tapped his forearm as she turned to leave. 'Well, I'm only a sergeant. What I think doesn't really matter. There are bigger beasts at play… bye, Morton, we'll keep you updated.'

Morton stood looking after her. '*Bigger beasts*? What was she trying to tell him?' He followed them to the door and as he closed it realised he still had the spoon in his hand.

Mearns sauntered into the outskirts of the town centre wearing the tweed bunnet and plain-glass specs. He kept an eye out for CCTV cameras but didn't see many. It was natural to him to look down at the ground, jacket collar up and hat brim covering his face. There were a few charity shops, a down-at-heel furniture store, a small greasy spoon café, a chemist, two pubs that looked quiet, two convenience stores opposite each other, small queues at bus stops, another chemist, a council community housing office, a public toilet and at the far end, the Gunners' pub. He walked past and saw through the open door, a football match in progress on the large TV screen and heard the heckling and sudden roar. It was packed. Barr would be in there with his drinking chums. He looked at his watch. If the match had started at 3pm, it would soon be half-time. He heard a mightier roar inside and outraged shouts. He didn't want Mearns to see him, not yet. He had time to kill so he strolled back to the chemist and went in and bought two packets of 12 Panadol Extra 500mg. He stood at the till. There was no CCTV in here either. The assistant, a pale, middle-aged woman with narrow plastic specs, wearing a white nylon jacket, looked sharply at him.

'Only one packet.'

'Sorry?'

'I am only allowed to sell one packet at a time.'

'Why?'

'Well, in case you…'

Mearns fingered the corner of his specs. 'Ah, I see. Didn't know that. What a silly rule. Okay. Just one packet then.'

He fumed as he left the shop and headed straight across the road to the licenced convenience store, a J-Mart. No CCTV here either. It had very narrow aisles, like being inside a maze. They had packets of 24. He slipped two inside his jacket and took two packets to the counter. The Pakistani-woman in a quilted anorak over her sari, didn't demur, took his money wordlessly, without any question and he was outside.

He went into the café and ordered a coffee. It came in a heavy clay mug. He added milk and sugar and found a table and sat down. There were cakes but he didn't feel hungry. He was thinking what he had to do. He could watch the street from where he sat though he was certain Barr would stay in the pub till after five, maybe much later, unless his money ran out. He had to get him on his own. Find out what he knew. Had he seen the newspaper story? Had he been approached by the police? Had he already told them everything he knew? He didn't know much but it was enough. It was too much. The coffee was too strong. He suspected it was granules not proper coffee. It had a funny bitter aftertaste. So was he going to have to hang around for hours waiting here? No. Check and positively confirm Barr was in the Gunners. Then get back to his flat on the grounds he would have to go home sometime and most likely then he'd be alone. So get into the flat and wait for him? Or better still, turn up close behind him with more drink and pretend to be friends. Turn up with money he owed him. Even though he didn't owe him anything. That was the idea! Barr would be happy to get money and some more beer. And Mearns would know right away with one look what Barr was thinking about him at that moment. Then he could adapt and do what needed to be done, whatever that was, whatever method it involved. Didn't really matter. As long as it was done.

CHAPTER TWENTY-THREE

Morton rarely discussed his work when he was at his parents' house in Merchiston Crescent. It was a large comfortable house and both his parents were keen on gardening, even in the winter. His father pottered about in the green house while his mother went out to cut some fresh herbs from a covered area she referred to as the herbarium, which looked to her son's untrained eye, like an untidy area covered in weeds, then she would settle to cooking the Sunday lunch. He sat with a glass of beer at the kitchen table watching her, the radio on in the background.

'So, this Ailsa…?' Margaret began. 'She's an actual girlfriend?'

'Not really, mum. She's… I like her, but, well, she's…'

'That's a shame. She sounds nice.'

Morton sipped his beer. He knew she was hinting that he invite her for Sunday lunch but that was a big step to take. Anyway, he felt Ailsa had gone off him, due to the story he had written and the possibility that it might lead to the Glenforgan by-election result being overturned. But it wasn't just that, there was something too forced about the relationship. Maybe because it had arisen unexpectedly when he was there to question her, as if he had used her merely as an information source. Don't eat where you shit, as someone had said. There was always going to be this issue of whether they were on the same side. He wasn't on anybody's side; just wanted to get at the truth, even if that was highly subjective. Anyway, the idea of a by-election being rigged was ridiculous. He couldn't begin to understand how it could be done. He heard the front door open and close.

'That'll be Libby now,' his mum said. 'Bang on time.'

'Hi auntie,' he said. He stood up and they hugged and he kissed her cheek. Standing up, she was the same height as he was sitting down, shorter than his mother, her older sister. Despite this, she had a headteacher's authority.

'Mags, how you doing, sis?'

'It's on the way.'

'What is it?'

'Roast beef. Ca ye no smell it?'

'Sinusses!' Libby laughed. 'Bunged up. That's the wee blighters for ye. Who'd be a teacher?'

Later he discussed the weekend's sport with his father on the sofa in the living room. Scotland's Six Nation's results had been poor and there was continuing criticism over team coach Frank Hadden. 'At least they beat England,' his father said, 'but losing to Wales and Ireland, I mean, his record isn't great, only one win in the tournament. We should be doing a great deal better.'

Morton nodded. 'Yes, his record is better than Matt Williams though. At least he's an insider, knows that squad.'

'They should bring back Ian McGeechan. He did two terms remember, eight years in total and had nearly a fifty percent win rate. How are you getting on with your by-election enquiry?'

Morton filled him in on the progress. 'The police have been unable to trace Mearns. He's using a different name.'

'Nasty piece of work,' Morton senior averred. 'Watch yourself. Someone's paying him. And probably paying him more than you get. They'll have his back. If they have rigged an election, there must be a big team behind it. And support at the top level too, no doubt. Better be careful, William.'

'Oh, I will be. I've still got no idea how it would even be possible to do such a thing. When I first heard the suggestion I thought it was insane. I mean you're talking about around thirty thousand voting papers in thirty-four polling boxes across a wide area of countryside. Glenforgan is a semi-rural constituency with lots of villages. How could you do it? And without being detected?'

Stuart Morton gave him a diffident look. 'I wouldn't put anything past them. Whitehall warriors. Perfidy is their middle name. The British officer class is the most devious known to man. If they wanted to do it, they would find a way. No matter in which part of the empire it was.'

A few hours earlier, as the light of dawn began to lighten the curtained windows of the ground floor flat in Glenwood, Raymond Mearns stood at the back door which his leather-gloved hands were holding open a crack, looking out to see if the way was clear. It looked cold and frosty out there. Behind him, sprawled in his chair was the bulk of Darren Barr, belly bulging whitely below the hem of his Rangers shirt, head lolling over the back of the chair. Pink froth was visible at his mouth and had poured down his chin and dried blackly there, staining the teeshirt. His arms hung limply down and beneath him lay empty cans of lager. All around on the floor lay more empty cans and the packets of Panadol that Mearns had sprayed and wiped very carefully and pushed into Barr's fingers, then dropped. The whole process had taken hours. Mearns had plied him with lager, each can laced with powdered Panadol. Hours of drunken insensible conversation, increasingly confused, until Barr, more asleep than awake, had succumbed to unconsciousness.

Mearns looked out at the back greens. He had the sweaty smell of the place in his nostrils. The man lived like an animal. It disgusted him that he had ever spent time with him or confided in him. It had become easier when Barr stopped talking, started burbling, making drunken noises then he had lapsed into a long silence, shifted imperceptibly from being a person to an immobile object. It had taken ages. Mearns had continued the process, using a rolled newspaper funnel, to drip into him more lager laced with powder. By 3 am., he felt that the process inside Barr was irreversible, but he had continued unchecked without any problem until all the lager was gone. He would never wake, he was sure of that. And, as he stood at the back door, feeling the cold fresh air of the dawn on his cheeks, he knew he had had no option. It had been the only way. It was not even as if he was going out on a high. Rangers had dropped points he'd said and only just scraped a draw against Hearts with a last-minute goal. Barr had lingered in the pub with his pals commiserating while he had spent an hour in his car grinding down the Panadol capsules with a penknife blade into a fine powder and pouring it into a small Bank of Scotland polythene bag. It was the kind that could be used for twenty pounds' worth of pound coins or one pound's worth of bronze coins. Useful little bags.

Mearns had watched and waited for long hours in the back green as darkness fell and finally he saw him, watched him stumbling along the street, fumbling the key in his lock at midnight. Then he simply followed him in, tapped on the door before it was barely closed. Barr had looked around in alarm but seeing the six-pack he'd grinned. 'Mearnsie, man!'

'I've got your money. Or some of it.'

'Awright!' He'd peered at him, drunkenly swaying. 'Mearnsie... *you*. No seen you for ages, man. Got ma money, eh? Right. Good man, sit yersel...'

He'd realised that Barr had no suspicions, no fear of him. He hadn't seen the papers or the news. He was well plastered, kept going on about the decisions of the referee that had robbed Rangers of the full three points. He seemed to think he was still in the pub. Mearns who had kept his gloves on, snapped open a can and went into the shithole of a kitchen, opened the can, poured some out and siphoned the Panadol powder into it, swigged it from side to side then returned to the main room and handed to Barr who took it and greedily swallowed, then he went back and did the same with another. After that it was easy.

'So Darren... what were you saying about your uncle in Glasgow? You never mentioned you had an uncle in Glasgow.'

'He says I should go to the polis, but ah tellt him...'

'What did you tell him?'

'Ah tellt him... no, ah tellt him... nothing. Ah didnae tell him, Mearnsie... aboot the... drivers... the vans.... Ah tellt him nuthin.'

There was talk, rambling talk about the drivers but Mearns didn't believe that Barr had ever known their names, their surnames. He'd met them, seen them, could point them out in an identity parade, if one was ever set up. There was an element of doubt. He had to be certain.

Barr's death was in keeping with the way he had lived. There would be few to mourn. He looked at his watch. It was nearly 7am. Time to go. He had gone over everything thoroughly, anything he had touched had been wiped or was in the carrier bag he had taken. Barr's body wouldn't be found for days. Time to go. He slipped out quietly and pulled the sheet of paper free so that the backdoor latched behind him. Then he was away, jinking down the frosted grass to the brick sheds, the telegraph pole, the gable of the end house, to the next gable and down the waste ground, wet on his shoes and trousers, to the path by the street. No-one about, no early dog walkers to his car at the end of the lane. The windows were obscured with condensation or a thin layer of frost. He took off the bunnet and the specs and his gloves. He had things to do, vital business to take care of.

Rami's story was on Monday's *Standard*, page five: *Labour Tight-Lipped Over Missing By-Election Agents*. Morton read it while drinking coffee at the spare desk next to hers, waiting for the editorial meeting downstairs to end. It was based on a brief email from Labour Central office denying 'impropriety' and stating that all by-election matters should be dealt with initially by the returning officer or by the electoral commission. Most of the email repeated the information about the Scottish Affairs Committee Bill passed at Westminster and the conclusion reached there that the missing ballot papers had been lost due to administrative error. Rami had a second story on page eight about the Prime Minister's visit. He chuckled to see she had used the words "embattled premier's last stand" which had been his suggestion.

He heard them coming back from the meeting. Rami beckoned him from the doorway. 'Come into Hugh's office a moment Willie.' She looked triumphant.

He stood up and went through just as Leadbetter appeared, carrying a stack of files on his chest. 'Make way…' he boomed, kicking the office door open and dumping the files on his desk.

'Right team, take a pew. We've been having a discussion,

Willie, and Rami's got a wee theory we need tae test oot.' He rolled his eyes. 'Brainstormin, blue sky thinkin…'

'It's really not complicated,' Rami said. 'Rigging an election wouldn't be easy, perhaps impossible even, but… but if they had always planned for the ballot papers to go missing… if in fact, they had always planned to steal them… rigging the result would be *much* easier. For one very simple reason.' She grinned.

'Okay,' Willie said. 'One very simple reason?'

'Every voter has an elector number on his or her ballot paper that identifies them. Yes?'

'We know that.'

'But the system is in two parts: each ballot paper is verified to be that of an actual elector, by the electoral number and that's done at the polling stations. When an elector hands over his or her voting card or gives their name to the polling station staff, they tear off the ballot paper from the counterfoils book which has this electoral number on the back. These are known as the CCNLs,' she laughed… 'that's completed corresponding number lists. Well, he or she goes and votes and puts the paper in the ballot box. The staff draw a line through the voter's name and elector number on the electoral roll and in the counterfoils book only the stub of the ballot paper remains, which has the elector number on it. So that's the process in the polling stations.'

Morton nodded. Leadbetter sat back, pulling at his beard.

'But… and here's the thing… the procedure of verifying elector number and elector name for each particular ballot paper is *not* repeated at the count. Because once the ballot papers are in the ballot box, that's taken as read and no-one does that again at the count, as part of the counting process. For one simple reason.'

'Which is?' Morton asked, frowning.

'Because the ballot papers have now been *used*. Each has a vote on it, a cross made by an elector. So staff would be able to see which way an elector, or to be more precise an electoral registration number, had voted. You could thus identify who had voted for an individual candidate thereby breaking the confidentiality of the Representation of the People Act and the law! So at the count, because this process of verification has been done in the polling stations, the only verification that takes place is to check each paper has on the back a valid elector number. And that of course is when the political parties' volunteers try to count the votes for each candidate by glimpsing the ballot papers as they are turned over for this process, in full view. Which is not easy of course.'

'So... where does this get us?' Morton said.

'Well, simply, if you are confident you can remove all the ballot papers before the result is ever questioned, or if you are going to steal them at some point after the result is declared, all you need to do is supply the correct number of completed ballot papers in each ballot box from every polling station to the count, and as long as each has a valid registration number – any number will do – on the back, they will be counted as valid votes. And the result will proceed from there.' She smiled and lifted her palms uppermost. 'Long live British democracy!'

Morton and Leadbetter looked at each other and said nothing. Morton shrugged. 'It's not clear to me...'

Rami exhaled. 'You're not understanding it, Willie? Here's my theory, right. You have a small team and well in advance of the election, you get an identical set of ballot papers printed, with elector numbers on the back, the candidates listed on the front. In every way identical to the real thing. Probably even ordered from the same printer. Perhaps you have had the assistance of someone on the Electoral Registration Office team?'

'Shankwell?' Morton said.

'Makes sense,' Leadbetter grunted.

'Maybe,' Rami said. 'Let's leave that for now... you order the number of ballot boxes you need, perhaps from the very same supplier that supplied Glenforgan Council, identical in every way. We know there were thirty-four polling stations, and a total of seventy-two ballot boxes. You mark the boxes up with their polling district and station names so they're identical to the set the council are going to use. Your team fill in the thirty-thousand-odd ballot papers over a period of days using pencils, pens, as if they are the voters, but you do it to ensure it will guarantee a certain result, with variations in certain districts. Again political assistance will help here. The voting slips are folded and chucked in the appropriate ballot box. The boxes are stacked in the rear of three panel vans ready for polling day. A few days before the election, the vans are taken to a secure and secret location, possibly an old garage or warehouse close to the counting hall. Each of these vans has a rear door and a sliding side door. That's crucial and the two compartments in each van have a wooden partition between them. So that when you look into the side door, you only see the boxes that were put in from that door. When you open the rear door, you see the ones in there only. See,' Rami grinned with a flourish of her fingers that rattled the rings, 'it's magic. Magic vans. Meanwhile as real voters do their business on polling day, you have polling agents passing on the turnout percentages in each box to the men in the van teams by mobile phone. Why? Because they have a method of adjusting the number of ballot papers inside each box to match the actual turnout...'

'Jesus H Christ!' exploded Leadbetter. 'How the hell could they do that?'

'Easy, very easy,' Rami said quickly, warming to her theme. 'You're talking about only twenty-four ballot boxes in each of the three vans. These have been pre-filled to match a certain turnout, maybe the previous turnout in each of the districts, but they have little bags of prepared ballot papers marked maybe ten per cent, five percent, two percent, one percent… for each district so they just add the extra that's needed. The topping up process would probably start about eight pm, so they'd have two hours to do that – plenty of time – and then seal each box. Then they're done. They collect the sealed ballot boxes from the staff at each of the polling stations, load them into the side doors, lock that door, drive to the count and unload the fake boxes to the counting hall from the rear door. They'd have around an hour and a half to do that. Plenty of time to make fine adjustments inside the rear compartment of the van. After they've dropped off the boxes at the count, they swiftly drive the real boxes away somewhere to a hiding place and at some point, destroy them. Done!'

Morton whistled through his teeth. 'Jeez! And with the support of the person on the Electoral Registration team, they would have been hired to collect the real ballot boxes from the polling stations in runs,' Morton suggested. 'Officially. So they'd have identification, signed by the Returning Officer…'

Leadbetter was looking glum. 'Disgusting… if this is true. Official?'

'Absolutely, boss,' Rami said. 'Completely official. That kind of job is sub-contracted. Sheriff Officers have long been complaining that they are not set-up to do the work. They want to transfer the authority to the returning officers as is already the case for EU and Local Government elections. And of course, councils haven't the staff these days to do it. So, your team gets appointed to do it. No questions asked.'

Light from the anglepoise lamp reflected off her chunky rings as Rami grinned. 'Yes, and nobody is remotely bothered about the CCNLs – the counterfoils or even the marked-up registers – as long as the final turnout corresponds with the number of ballot papers. It never exactly tallies of course, and the teams in the vans are bound to be a percentage here or there out... that's the difficult part for them, making the numbers inside each of the seventy-two boxes match the turnout but they must have had a sophisticated method...'

'Aye, but...' Leadbetter said, banging his fist on the table. 'That's all very well, but now ye're tellin me there's goin tae be twa sets o voting papers knocking aboot... so has yer man, Mearns burnt the lot... both sets?'

CHAPTER TWENTY-FOUR

The sun fought its way through an early morning haze as Raymond Mearns drove east around the outskirts of Glenforgan. He had pulled the sunshield down as he headed towards the coast. He was thinking about the long night and what he had done to Barr, not regrets exactly, his sense of justification overwhelmed that, but a weariness of spirit. And he was also thinking ahead to what he would say to Oliver Trenchard. He would have to ask Trenchard for a favour. It would be a black mark against him because he had not taken advice earlier. Trenchard may even accuse him of having given the impression that everything was done and complete and tidied up when it wasn't. He turned onto a quiet country back road that twisted and turned through fields and woods. And all because he had wrecked a perfect scheme, the meticulous workings of the team had been thrown in jeopardy by his last-minute whim to be there, at the count, in person. But he had had to see the success of it at first hand. Couldn't keep away. It was like a death-wish. And because of that, his name had appeared on the Labour counting agents list, not his real name but... and Barr had been involved again, a loose cannon, and CCTV pictures had appeared of him and Barr, and that had proved the Achilles heel. But Barr was gone. The intruder was still at large, but he couldn't have seen much and anyway, could have no proof of anything. The evidence was incinerated, well, half of it was. He felt the sudden chill in his fingers. Half of it. He had to make that call now. He pulled into a layby, beside two tall trees, on a downward slope with a view to the sea and the small coastal villages. He watched the ripple of the Firth of Forth and could see the faint smudge of the East Lothian coast beyond, North Berwick, the Bass Rock, which he knew was about twelve miles away and, the sands of Aberlady or Gullane Bay – he wasn't sure which. Further to the west he could make out the wink of lights at the power station at Cockenzie. He took out his mobile phone and rang Trenchard. It was early but he'd be there.

'It's Raymond Mearns...' he explained and waited. He watched a small fishing boat far out, little more than a red dot heading towards the Isle of May. He could make out the undulating line of white water at her bows.

'Good morning, Raymond. I didn't expect your call. Everything all right?'

Mearns could hear the tension in Trenchard's voice. 'I need a bit of help,' he told him. 'I have a problem.'

'I see.' There was an awkward pause. Mearns imagined Trenchard frowning. 'Raymond... I'm not sure I want to hear this. Please explain.'

'Only one set has been destroyed.'

'Raymond... I'm very disappointed. You informed me that...'

'The other set,' Mearns intervened, 'collected in the vans on the night, still in their ballot boxes, were dumped at a property not many miles from the count. It wasn't sensible for the vans to be seen moving about because of the risk, the sheer number of possible witnesses... on polling day. The place was crawling with media, and large crowds of political activists, so I had them taken to a good safe hiding place about three miles away.'

'I see.' Mearns was aware of the icy calm of his superior,

so he hurried on explaining. He wanted to convince himself he had done the right thing. 'I didn't mention this, you know, because I had intended to remove them to Renfrew... with the others but in the circumstances thought it best wait to sit out the big row over the... when the papers were announced to be missing... but the two sets could not be seen to be in the same place. That would have been disaster.'

'I'm not sure I follow, Raymond,' Trenchard said. 'If I comprehend you... you mean the original set, let us call it, from the night of the election have remained in a location near... all this time?'

'Yes,' Mearns grimaced, staring out at the stately trees lining the side of the road down to the coast. 'When we collected the bin bags from council premises as arranged just before Christmas, we drove them straight to Renfrew. They've been destroyed. But we couldn't risk making a detour to collect the other set by using the same vehicles in case anyone was watching. The heat was on. The story was all over the news.'

'But why didn't you return to collect them once the first set was destroyed? When you had Mouncey and Keenan with you. That was what I understood to be the plan?'

'Because of the intruder – Morton. I didn't know what he knew, or how much. We couldn't risk going back there again, *and* as you know the police were going to search the premises. We had to abort.'

'Raymond, you've had nearly three months to dispose of both sets. But that said, the intruder was unexpected, not your fault. Although it seems to me you've brought all this upon yourself by appearing in public at the election count. Anyway, criticism and a clear analysis can wait. We're in fire-fighting mode now, so... what do you need?'

'I need a driver and a large vehicle, probably a flatbed truck.'

'Usman,' said Trenchard briskly. 'He's in Scotland, in Glasgow. I can have him mobile in half an hour. Give me the address and postcode. What kind of location?'

'That's the problem,' Mearns said. 'It's in a place that's difficult to find. It's a cottage on the cliffs at the end of an unmade track, a mile from a main road. The kind of place where a large vehicle would look odd, but we'll have to do it. There's only a couple of other cottages nearby, old people, and one holiday rental which is probably not in use just now. I'll send you exact co-ordinates once I get there. If Usman simply backs down the last fifty yards – he'll see where to turn – then he and I can load the bexes and get out in half an hour or so and get clear. And this time, we'll bring it well clear, south of the border, preferably and that's the second thing I need. A secure incinerator.'

'Well, that's no problem. I can pass on the locations to Usman. And once you get there, I suggest you get a train from there to London and take yourself out of the picture, stay put. Is there anything else you've not done or not told me?'

Mearns almost told him then, and the name of Darren Barr hovered on his lips for a fraction of a second, but instead he said. 'No, that's it. Finally.'

'Okay, go to the location now, send me the co-ordinates, and keep it secure until Usman is with you. Then our problem is solved.'

Willie Morton was halfway across the Forth Bridge when he heard his Blackberry ringing. He glanced at the passenger's seat where it sat poking out of the top pocket of his folded leather jacket. It kept ringing, annoyingly. But there was nothing he could do. The white Beetle rumbled over the bridge in two lanes of heavy traffic heading for the M90. He hoped it wasn't Councillor Brown saying he couldn't make the meeting, in which case this would be a wasted journey. It was only when he came to the Halbeath junction and was able to turn off the M90 onto the A92 and find a layby that he could stop to look at his phone. It was Rami and she had left a text message: phone me asap. He phoned.

She answered immediately. 'What's up?'

'Marshall's emailed me the list of Labour polling agents. Forty names, all the usual but Darren Barr is on it. His address is in Glenwood...'

'Yes, Rami, I've been there, remember.'

'So you have. I'll get the police to go there now. There's no Raymond Mearns on the list, but there is a Raymond... Menzies. And his address is given as MacDuff cottage, MacDuff Lane, East Wemyss.'

'Bloody hell, Rami! That must be him. Menzies – Mearns, too much of a coincidence.'

'Yes, Willie, but don't even think of going there on your own. According to the map, it's about four miles from the centre of Glenforgan. I'll pass the address on to the police too. They'll look into it.'

'Of course,' Willie agreed. 'I'm nearly at Glenforgan now. I'll ask Councillor Brown about the list if you send it to me.'

'Will do, Willie. And remember...'

He cut her off. 'Oh dear, Rami,' he said to himself. 'Such poor reception!' He consulted the map in the secret pocket behind the passenger seat and saw that he could continue on the A92 to the north of Kirkcaldy and from there it was less than two miles to East Wemyss. He started the engine. Councillor Brown would have to wait.

Mearns parked in the large public space on High Road, opposite the playground of the primary school. As he got out and locked the car, he realised he had forgotten to arrange for a driver to remove it. He clicked his tongue in annoyance but realised he could pass the information on to Trenchard with the co-ordinates of the cottage and it would be arranged. He went into School Wynd and down to Back Dykes onto the foreshore and continued along the shore path northwards, passing the last of the houses at Weavers' Court when the path skirted the entrance of the first of the famous caves, this one of red sandstone with a metal grille to protect it. He knew that the grille was there not just to protect children from injuring themselves but also to protect the caves and their Pictish markings from vandals who had on one occasion at least driven old cars inside and set them on fire. The path wound along the shoreline between bushes and the entrances of several other caves. He came to the treed gorge that rose to the ruined castle about a hundred yards from a small, tarmacked road that led east to the town of Buckhaven. He knew above him was the large modern cemetery that sprawled across the top of the plateau. The cottage was a hundred yards further round, unobtrusive, set back a little from the coastal path and protected from it by a drystone dyke. Behind it was a ploughed field and, just in view, a larger house. MacDuff cottage was derelict of course and locked up to discourage vandals or druggies. He stood at the wooden door whose green paint had blistered in the sun and looked left and right along the coastal path. No-one. The door was padlocked. He didn't have a key – didn't need one – he knew the interior was ruined. What he was interested in was in the shed behind it. It was a solid concrete block and he wondered if it had been used as a defensive structure in the second world war. He remembered the difficulties they had had that night in November bringing the vans down the track, one by one and the frenzied business of offloading the boxes into the shed. It had been very risky in the dark. It retrospect it had been a poor choice for location, but on the map it had not looked so difficult. On the map it had looked remote, private, far from prying eyes. He had not reckoned on the narrowness of the path, the slope, the lack of turning at the cottage and the nearby house at the top of the slope. He had not bothered to check it out prior to the operation, something he could not possibly admit to Trenchard.

After a quick look around, he unlocked the squeaky aluminium up-and-over door and saw that everything was in order. The entire space was filled with black plastic boxes. Seventy-two. Most still had the white polling district numbers and polling station names on them, their seals intact. Although he was tense, and anxious – he found himself smiling at the sight. They looked so neat. But if anyone should see them, the game would be up. It was obvious what they were. He quickly rolled down the door and locked it. He looked at his watch. It might be two hours yet. He would have to sit and wait and keep himself hidden, not draw attention to the cottage. Everything depended on Usman's skill in getting smoothly down the track without alerting suspicion. There would still be some daylight left, with luck. He decided to walk away from the cottage, towards Buckhaven just like a birdwatcher or tourist and sit somewhere on the rocks where he could keep the cottage in view, and text Trenchard the co-ordinates to pass to Usman.

* * *

The police car entered the Glenwood estate and meandered slowly between the deserted blocks to come to a halt halfway along the street. There were no signs of human life though a cat watched them warily from the pavement. The police constables got out, two tall, skinny young men and began knocking on the door of a ground-floor flat. A few curtains twitched along the street and a woman in the house opposite briefly looked out of the window then went away.

'This is the right address?' one of the constables asked the other, lifting off his cap and rummaging in his ginger hair.

'Yup. No-one home. Let's look in the windows just to check. Sometimes folk are a bit mutton. You go round the back.'

A few minutes later, they had a discussion. 'He's in, but not answering. We'll better boot the front door in. He looks dead to the world.'

'Na, the back door is easier… it's just a latch.' He grinned. 'C'mon, Dennis, you know this, burglars always hit the backdoors.'

It didn't take them long to discover the occupant was dead, or seriously ill.

'Don't touch him, Dennis. Let's get back outside and call for back-up, and an ambulance.' He reached for his radio. 'Tango Oscar Charlie…

'What's gone on here, then?' Dennis said as they got back to the front door. 'Bloke drank himself to death? Looks like a Gers fan.'

'Aye, well, Ross, they scraped a home draw against the Hearts. Andrew Little scored a minute after the full ninety, his first goal for them and that saved the day. Walter Smith was no best pleased. But you don't think…? Naw, suicide's a bit extreme even for a diehard Gers fan. It's no like they lost all three points.'

'Maybes aye, mebbes naw, Dennis, we've done our bit. Let's sit in the car and wait.'

CHAPTER TWENTY-FIVE

Rami joined the press lobby in the gallery at Holyrood, looking forward to the weekly joust of FMQs. Salmond, looking even more pleased with himself than usual, was already in situ, while the Minister for Enterprise, Energy and Tourism, Jim Mather, expanded on his Homecoming Scotland Bill. Rami remembered Salmond's claim that it would bring an extra £40 million to the nation in tourist revenues, by reaching out and attracting the huge Scottish diaspora in the 250th anniversary year of the birth of Robert Burns. He was probably right, Rami thought. The hugely wistful advert featuring Dougie MacLean's song 'Caledonia' had struck a chord worldwide.

Her mobile vibrated. A text message was coming through from Colin on the newsdesk. *Barr dead at home suspect alcohol poisoning, police investigating.* She re-read it but the presiding officer, a former farmer of the shires was announcing FMQ, Salmond was on his feet, battlelines were drawn, a rustle of papers and expectation fluttered through the airy vaults of the steel, glass and red cedar debating chamber. She pulled up her notebook.

Morton had not previously been in East Wemyss, a small town of nearly two thousand people, and had no idea of the layout. All he knew about it was that it had famous sea caves with early Pictish drawings on the walls that had to be protected and that it was, had been, a big coal mining area. He drove slowly along the main street and avoided turning off into a narrower street. He passed the large carpark opposite the school, continued to the far end of the town, saw the road to Buckhaven, but turned in a space in front of a convenience store and came slowly back. Wasn't much to it. He saw a narrow road heading down to the shore just before a large cemetery and the top of a red sandstone ruin protruding from a clump of trees: MacDuff's Castle? He reasoned that the cottage and MacDuff's Lane would be close by. He parked on the street in front of a terraced house screened by a thick hedge. He looked at his Blackberry. A text message from the newsdesk. Barr was dead. Jeez! Morton smiled grimly. Suicide? He didn't think so. Nor was Shankwell's death natural causes. He just had a feeling about it. It was all adding up to something. Someone, or some people, were remorselessly covering their tracks, eliminating loose ends. And Mearns was involved. But he was closing in. And this time, he had the proper equipment: the dictaphone, the Canon SLR with the 200mm lens, that could take decent video. He stuffed them into the leather satchel, with the battery flash unit, notebook, small bottle of water, two chocolate bars in case he had to do a long stakeout. He got out, swung the satchel over his shoulder and locked the car. He pushed the keys under the rear fender and set them on the tyre. The Beetle's rear fenders curved out over the top of the tyres, unlike the cut-away front ones which revealed the entire wheel. It was a handy place to hide the keys. He wondered if all V-dub owners did that. It wasn't an original 1960s Beetle, of course, it was a 1980s version manufactured in Mexico.

He waited for several cars to pass and crossed the road and started down the unmade track. Halfway down on the left side, was a cottage with a profuse garden and roses climbing on arches and trellises. The front wall was supplemented by a large poster board with a hand-painted saltire and legend: *Independence for Scotland* with entwining thistles around the lettering. It made him smile. He could imagine his father's delight. The old man would undoubtedly stop to speak to the man in the garden. He was on his knees, a jolly old man, battered straw hat on his white head and heavily bearded, weeding. Two of a kind, Morton thought, except this man was a bit younger, maybe in his late sixties.

'Hello,' Morton said, smiling. 'My dad would like that,' he pointed at the board. 'He's one of you lot.'

'Of course.' The man grinned. 'And you're not? Or not yet?' He stood up and stretched his back. He was wearing a padded shirt and baggy jeans.

Morton shrugged. 'Something like that. Is this MacDuff Lane?' Morton asked.

'Aye. It is.'

'And that must be MacDuff's cottage, down there?' He nodded at the shoreline.

'Aye. Derelict now. Folks died. I've no idea who has it now.'

'A fellow called Menzies, apparently,' Morton told him.

'You know more than me.' He lifted his straw hat to scratch his head. 'Mind, I had trouble there a few months back. Some white vans tried to park. Maybe that was the owner's doing. I never met the man. They came and went. Funny business. In the dark too. I suppose it might get knocked down, but I think someone's using the shed as storage, so maybe that's the boy, Menzies.'

'Well, better get on. Nice talking to you,' Morton said. He needed to get a look at the place. But had to be careful. Mearns might be in the vicinity. He remembered Rami's warning not to go on his own. Too late for that now. He returned to the street and entered the cemetery gates. He was going to walk over into the trees to see if he could get a better look along the shoreline.

Mearns had got nervous, sitting on a rock a few hundred yards from the cottage. Every few minutes, he was jumping up and walking around. But now he decided to slowly saunter back on the path to the front of the cottage. There was a seat there cemented into the flat worn surface of a rock. Inevitably, the seat had been vandalised, graffitied, even set on fire, its plastic surface warped and blackened in places. He perched uncomfortably on the edge, reached into his jacket pocket and found several unused packets of Panadol. He had a headache. He felt deeper into his pockets. Where was the small polythene sachet, the mixed-coin bag that he'd used to hold the powdered capsules? He knew with blinding sudden clarity that he had left it by the sink in Barr's kitchen. He searched again, both pockets, in vain. Yes. That was where he had left it. *Shit!* But he now remembered he had had gloves on, his prints wouldn't, couldn't, be on it. In fact, maybe it strengthened the case that Barr had committed suicide, maybe it showed premeditation? As long as his prints were not on it. But were Barr's prints on it? No, they couldn't be. They were on the packets of pills, yes, but... not on the sachet! Well, nothing to be done about it now. He pushed out two capsules and took them one by one, swallowing them with saliva, a useful trick he had always had. He looked at his watch. Usman was late. But he knew it had been little more than a hour since he spoke to Trenchard so Usman could be another hour. He wanted to get it over before it got dark. Already in the west the sky was darkening, from a navy-purple to a wintry red, the sun was a thin orange line half-hidden between gravestones in the cemetery. He saw movement against it; a man walking there. But the man disappeared into the trees. It was too far away to make out any detail but… Alarmed, he stood up, looked left and right and dashed to the back of the cottage at the edge of the field to get a better view. The man was gazing up at MacDuff's Castle. He caught the glint of something. A camera. A tourist? Here? It seemed unlikely. But something about the man irked him. A stranger, walking in a cemetery at this time of the afternoon, in late January? On his own? Cameras were dangerous. He didn't want any pictures of Usman and the truck. He wished he had his binoculars with him. The man had gone, presumably walking down to Back Dykes and the foreshore further on. He realised it would be possible to check him out. That would give him something to do until Usman arrived. Better safe than sorry. He had left two torches and a head torch by the shed door and he retrieved one of them, stuck it in his pocket.

Mearns slipped down to the coastal path and hurried along under the cliffs and trees to the caves and the end of the tarmac road at Weavers' Court. He was directly underneath the steep gorge below the castle ruin where he had last seen the man. He began to ascend using his hands, stopped halfway up. He had the absolute conviction that the man was there, above him, on the upper path. He scrambled back down and waited. If necessary, he could duck behind the entrance to Well Cave. He heard trickling earth, a few pebbles came down, footsteps. He went into the cave entrance and hid behind the freestanding red sandstone pillar. The man was coming down. He looked carefully round. It was Morton.

He descended onto the gravel path and looked over the incoming tide on the shore. To the east, he could see the bay and the shoreline where the man had told him MacDuff's cottage was. From the cemetery he had spotted what looked like a ruin at the end of the track, MacDuff's Lane. He couldn't see it now, because of the cliffs but that must be it. He was going to get into position and keep watch and this shoreline was the best vantage point for that. He glanced casually at the cliffs, bushes and the caves and moved out a little onto the shingle. There was plenty of washed-up sea coal and the usual debris bobbing on the dirty white foam at his feet. He saw the lights across the Forth. He turned back to the track just as a man walked along, heading south. It took him several seconds to realise who it was.

Mearns strolled casually along the track hoping that Morton had seen him, listening intently to the waves on the shingle, the sound of traffic up on the main road, listening for footsteps coming closer. He daren't look round yet. He wanted to look furtive, to draw Morton away from the cottage. He cleared Weavers' Court and came onto the lower section of Back Dykes. If he could get Morton away from the town, away from any observers or passersby, he could do something. The coastal path twisted and turned along the shore but soon it would be dark and then there might be other possibilities. He took out the torch. It was a good military grade, heavy, encased in thick rubber. He was pretty sure Morton had followed him but was keeping his distance. As soon as he got around the next corner, he would take a look, but he had to give Morton the impression that he was unaware of being followed. Morton would be curious what he was doing here. He must know about the cottage, there was no other explanation. So he would feel he was ahead of the game, that he had by a stroke of luck found Mearns' lair. To Morton, it would seem that he had the advantage, that he was in control.

Morton hung back but had stayed close enough to see that furtive glance. He was pretty sure Mearns didn't know he was there. It was the look of a man up to something dodgy. Morton was euphoric and wanted to text Rami but didn't want to lose him; the evening shadows were lengthening. Where was he going? Why was he going so far from the cottage? There must be a reason. Perhaps he was leading him to a hiding place or perhaps that derelict cottage was a blind and he lived somewhere else nearby? But it was difficult to keep him in sight. He had speeded up. The path was ascending between overhung cliffs into thick grass wilderness laced with bramble bushes. He came cautiously up to the top and couldn't see him. He hurried forward. Mearns had disappeared. Where had he gone? He could see the pale light on the track further round the shoreline, but Mearns wasn't there.

Mearns had remembered coming across the subsidence halfway up the brae just around the next corner. It was almost invisible in the high grass and gorse bushes. He knew it was the former cave entrance that had somehow got connected to an airshaft of the Michael coal mine. The largest coal-producing mine in Scotland had been closed after the disaster in 1967 when nine miners died, of whom three bodies were never recovered, but this entrance had been found by kids and subsequently sealed up to prevent access. Since then, wild animals, probably badgers, had made a large hole and you could get inside. It occurred to him if he could hide, hopefully Morton would continue for miles and get lost.

He would have to be quick. He scrambled off the path and down, shone his torch, saw the hole and got in legs first and slithered inside. He shone the torch ahead of him. It was narrow and not deep. He switched the torch off and waited for

Morton to go past. He looked at his watch and waited for the luminescence to display the time.

Morton had been running to keep up and had seen the torch flash on and move round and then off. Ah? So that was it? He'd gone to ground. He would be looking out, watching him, so he continued along the track, past the point where he'd seen the light, then doubled back and walked over the mound above where he thought Mearns was. He thought: Does Mearns know he's being followed? Or had he always planned to come here? What was in there? Was it a substantial cave? Maybe... just maybe that was where the ballot boxes were stashed. Surely not? Yes, it was private, out of the way, but inaccessible except by the coastal walking path which was walked perhaps by dozens every day. No good as a hiding place. On the other hand, perhaps they were buried underground? Paper would rot quickly in the wet soil and sea air. Was that it? Was this the place? Unfortunately, the light was almost completely gone, meaning he couldn't take pictures. He waited. Mearns was not coming out. He inched forward and got to his knees, looking down at the lip of the hole where he had seen the torchlight. Suddenly, there was a flash of light from inside. He *was* in there!

Mearns had listened for and heard the movements of his pursuer on the mound above him. He couldn't stay here. Usman would be arriving back at the cottage. He had to provoke an encounter but Morton was bulkier and fitter than he was. But he had the torch. If he could bring him down into the dark... So he slithered further into the cave and switched the torch on.

CHAPTER TWENTY-SIX

DI Sid Maxfield and DS Hilary Brown were in the main CID office at Fettes HQ, bending over the computer reading a lengthy autopsy report on Neil Shankwell's death.

'Hedging his bets a little?' she suggested. 'Over-cautious.'

'Nowt nor summat,' he pronounced. 'Seems to me though there's more that is suspicious than not.'

'I agree. The least we can do is keep an open mind. He fits the profile for cardiac infarction but… no mention of the slippers.'

'Yes,' Maxfield murmured, stroking his chin. 'Or why he was going downstairs in the middle of the night. His bedroom is ensuite Maybe it'll come out in the Fatal Accident Inquiry in a fortnight. And taken with this, now, Mr Barr's death. I mean he fits the profile of total loser, alcoholic, definite markers for suicide but the fact that they both knew each other… They were both together at the by-election count. It's deeply suspicious. I'd put money on both being murder. Barr's certainly.'

Brown stood up and massaged her neck. 'Hmn. And if so, what was the motive? Was it the same perp?'

Maxfield shook his head and looked at her from under his thick eyebrows. 'That's just the thing, DS Brown. Shankwell's death if it *was* a murder… was meticulous. I mean we can't say for certain that… but Barr's was messy. The sachet of powdered painkillers on the sink. I mean. Why? If you're going to take a lot of painkillers and you're drinking beer, why not just pop them in one at a time, swig em down? Why waste time grinding them to powder and putting them in your beer? And where did he grind them down? There's no trace of powder anywhere else. Nah! Someone's been there. Left the wee bag behind. That was a mistake. But forensics will be all over the place like a rash.'

'Horrible death,' Brown shuddered. 'Must have taken him ages to die. Perhaps he was so out of it, he wasn't in any pain?'

Maxfield exhaled. 'Look on the bright side. But I'm afraid… well, I've seen these before, they say a fatal dose is anything upwards of twenty but it's highly painful and it doesn't just carry you off to sleep and you die while asleep. That's a complete myth. No, anything but, your stomach, specifically the liver is overwhelmed and starts producing toxins which attack the body. It can take up to a month to die but it's irreversible. In a way, Barr was lucky. His liver was already well-shot. He died relatively quick.'

Morton carefully manoeuvred himself down the little mud slope. It was almost fully dark. He looked down. The light in the interior was very faint as if Mearns was moving away. He wondered if he could get pictures without the flash unit, using the lowlight setting. He crouched and saw the faintest trace of torchlight. What was this place? A series of caves? A hiding place of sorts, of course. He hitched up the buckle of his satchel. There was just enough light for him to get in. He wished he had a torch but if he kept close to Mearns, he could see what was going on. He levered his feet in and slid down about five feet, feeling the spoil give way beneath him. He was in a small narrow cave, the light ahead descending and diminishing. The floor was beaten earth. Mearns was moving inside, ahead of him. Why? Where was he going? He had to lower himself to get through the doorway and found he was in what appeared to be a room. There was graffiti on the walls, beer cans, the stink of human urine. Was this another coastal defensive position from the Second World War? Stepping carefully to avoid kicking the beer cans, he ducked to get through a low door and saw it led to a vast chamber lower down with several tunnel entrances. In front of him was a pile of stones and spoil but at the far side, lower down than he was, he saw the torchlight moving into one of the tunnels. It was a secret realm. Should he get back out. Mearns was trapped. Or did he know another way out? Most of all, what the hell was he doing? Was he aware he had been followed? No, he couldn't be, could he?

Morton saw that the cave or wartime lookout post had joined an old mine shaft. He saw a succession of light fittings on the ceiling connected by metal pipes gleaming in the flash of Mearns' torch. He could have shouted to him. An old mine shaft. To the left he saw similar tunnel entrances. He felt slight misgivings. Easy to get lost here, but the growing darkness frightened him, and he hurried forward. Why had he not brought a torch? Idiot!

Hugh Leadbetter was putting on his coat ready to go home when his mobile buzzed. It was Rami El-Jaffari.

'Uh?' he grunted into it, looking out at the dark night sky and the pattern of lights of the high buildings at the rear of Chambers Street. He was under time pressure. He had to do shopping at the Gyle and get back in time to take his laddie to football training which was not a thing he could ask his wife to do. 'I'm heading out,' he protested. 'What's up?'

'Willie's not answering his phone. I think he's gone to East Wemyss.'

'East Wemyss? *Whit*?'

'The cottage that we think was used by Mearns,' she explained. 'I told him not to go there on his own, but it's been two hours and no word.'

'Willie will be alright,' Leadbetter snorted. 'He's a big boy now. Was there anything else? Are the polis going there?'

'I haven't heard anything. I did pass the address on to them. To DS Brown.'

'I mind the lassie. Well, I'm sure Willie will do… whit Willie does…keep me informed and don't worry.' He charged down the stairs and pushed through the doors out onto Southbridge, crossed the street between two lines of stationery traffic, heading for his permit space in Niddry Street.

* * *

Mearns had at one time considered the old mine workings as a potential repository for the ballot boxes. It had the advantage of being near to Glenforgan, being private and likely to remain so for many years, if not forever, as a gravesite, but he had decided that the many disadvantages, particularly the problem of van access, ruled it out. However, he had made a study of the old mine workings. He knew quite a lot about the shafts, the seams, the vents, the location of the pumping houses, stairways, lift cages. It fascinated him in a funny sort of way. So he knew he was in some old tunnels quite close to the surface. He was aware of that because he knew that the first coal face was more than half a mile down, and he had hardly descended at all since coming in the cave. This was probably the old workings of Mine Shaft No 1, disused for nearly a century and, supposedly, filled in completely. But this bit hadn't been. You could tell its period by the old-fashioned light fittings, the lack of steel beams or concrete linings. This was just an abandoned nineteenth century tunnel that probably didn't connect anywhere to the shafts that had been worked when the mine was closed in 1967. He waited, listening to Morton's feet behind him. Had the man no suspicion that it was a wild goose chase? He looked at the bright screen of his phone. Usman would be at the cottage. It was time to go. There was no mobile phone reception. He moved on and saw the narrow ventilation shaft on the left. Sloping down into blackness and not lined in any way, the sides had partially crumbled inwards. He shone the torch down. It looked deep. This was the place. There was a junction directly opposite.

He stood in the junction tunnel and flashed the torch on the rickety handrail then switched it off and waited. In the dark, Morton was coming. He could hear his movements on the earth. Morton would believe he had turned into the junction and would be hurrying to catch up. He waited, torch clenched in his fist. He listened intently until he imagined he heard the noise of breathing. In here, sound was magnified. He lashed-out horizontally with the torch at shoulder level, felt the solid, jarring connection with bone, heard Morton falling away and then heard no sounds. His hand and wrist tingling, he switched on the torch. A lucky blow. Morton was out, sprawled on the earth. He laid down the torch and with hands and feet rolled him into the ventilation shaft, hearing the body sliding and slithering away and out of sight. Time to go!

Graham McInnes was in his kitchen, with his 'birds of the British isles' apron on, wrestling with a new malt loaf in the bread-maker when he heard, and felt, the vibrations outside his cottage. He had eased the load out of the pan and was trying to free it from the plastic paddle without ripping too much of the warm dough away.

'Good grief! What now?' he exclaimed and put the loaf down and went straight out of the door. A flatbed truck with covered sides was backing down the narrow track in the dark, lights on, its reversing alarm whining. It blocked out the streetlight from the main street but he could make out a man in the cab, intent on steering, eyes on his mirror.

'Hey!' MacInnes shouted. 'Watch my gate!' He went out into the narrow space between the truck and his gate and slapped its front fender. The driver looked down, white face barely visible above the wing-mirror, holding his foot on the brake.

'That bloody thing is too big for this lane!' MacInnes shouted. 'It's no meant for things that size, man. Where are ye going anyway, at this time of night?'

The window wound down. 'MacDuff Cottage,' the man said, gesticulating with his thumb. 'Just down there.'

'Well, it is,' MacInnes conceded. 'But you'll have some job getting it down. That cottage is empty, derelict…'

'Ah, we're clearing it out, mate,' the driver said. 'For the new owners.'

'At this hour? In the dark?'

'I was meant to be here earlier. Anyway, won't take long, an hour tops. Don't worry about your gate, I'll make sure I don't touch it. I have driven this before you know.' He laughed. 'Nice apron by the way,' and began reversing again.

MacInnes watched him and wondered. *MacDuff Cottage is popular today.* He remembered his conversation with the young man with the leather satchel. What was going on? It seemed unlikely that any new owner of the cottage would do anything other than demolish it, so maybe a clearance was in order, but it was a heck of a size of truck for a small place. And he knew there was nothing inside it anyway. He had often peered in the windows. He went back into his house and jotted down the registration number of the truck. Just in case, he told himself. Funny goings-on. Then he remembered the cooling bread and went back into the kitchen. The main evening news was just coming on and he wanted to see what bad news about Scotland the BBC had come up with today.

Mearns rapidly retraced his steps. It was easy, nothing to it, when you had a torch. Morton didn't. Shame! There were enough twists and turns to make it interesting but whether Morton would remember them when he woke up, *if* he woke up. It had been a solid blow on the skull. He'd been poleaxed.

He reached the three-way junction and flickered his torch around. Which tunnel led to the exit? He went in the wrong one at first. The eyes deceive you in torchlight, he thought. He scrambled out into the big cave with the piles of spoil, then out into the cold fresh night air and the loud noise of the sea and a constellation of streetlights across the firth. There was a partial moon and it helped him to find some flat stones which he placed to conceal the hole. He wiped his hands on grass already wet with early frost. Using the torch, he raced along the path back to town, along in front of the curtained houses at Weavers' Court, passed the caves and, looking up, saw moonlight glinting on the covered sides of the truck. It was sitting on a downward slope at the end of the lane beside the cottage. He charged forward, keen to get on with the task, stumbled into the narrow track through the grass and up to the cottage's front door.

'Usman? It's me,' he called softly. There was a rustle from nearby.

'Where were you?' Usman said. 'I couldn't find the bloody key. I've been sat here half an hour. And I had a problem with the neighbour.'

Mearns shone the torch. 'It's okay. I had a problem to deal with. Here's the key. What problem with the neighbour?'

Usman grabbed the key. 'Nothing to worry about. An old git complaining. He wasn't happy.' He bent down to the shed lock. 'Shine the light... I gave him a story about clearing out the cottage for new owners.'

Mearns lifted up the squealing aluminium door in the dancing light of the torch. 'Right. You did well. I know who you mean. He complained about the vans in November.'

'I wasn't here then. Anyway, he went back inside once I'd got past his house. He was just a moaner. He won't contact the police – I think.'

'I agree. Even if they did – they wouldn't bother about it. Why would they? Right, let's get this lot loaded and get the hell out!'

The aluminium door made a louder screech as it was pushed fully horizontal. But the time for caution was gone. Now was the time for speed. They began to work hard and fast, throwing boxes up onto the deck of the truck. They had to hope no-one would come to find out what the noise was. It would take them half an hour, he thought, including taking a careful look round afterwards to make sure none of the paper bundles had slipped out, or labels come off the boxes. As he straightened up, he was surprised by the sudden roar of the incoming tide as it pushed up the shoreline towards the path and the wrecked seat in the moonlight.

CHAPTER TWENTY-SEVEN

The council terrace in Glenwood was blocked by police vehicles, an ambulance and several unmarked cars used by the officers of the forensic team. On the scrubby front garden of the house where Darren Barr had lived, a blue forensic marquee had been set up and moving lights inside it indicated ongoing activity. Lights blazed from the uncurtained windows and revealed officers in white hazmat suits moving about. Flashbulbs popped continuously as the scenes of crime photographer compiled a comprehensive gallery of pictures of the scene and the corpse. A few local residents watched the activity from their windows, partially silhouetted against large colour TVs where a football match was in progress. Two police officers were going door-to-door and for once the local residents were co-operative. Death is exciting, always attracts a crowd. Few residents had known Darren Barr, even fewer had talked to him but many knew he was a Rangers supporter. No-one had seen anything on the night in question. No-one admitted to having been in The Gunners on Saturday. There was a limit to how much co-operation they were prepared to give. Few residents were in the police fan club. None got a Christmas card from the Chief Constable. In the darkness there was activity as the ambulance moved position to park opposite the front gate. The body of Darren Barr, covered with a white sheet and fastened to a stretcher, was carried out for the trip to the morgue and a date with the pathologist. As it drove away, more forensics officers arrived, the evening police shift replaced the dayshift and the residents sank back onto their sofas to catch the end of the match and await the omnibus edition of their favourite soap opera.

There were bright lights, stars, constellations whirling and flashing. But it couldn't be a party, because of the absolute and utter silence. There was an aching pain behind it. The earth smelled dry, ancient with a hint of mould, decay, abandonment. The eyes opened but could see nothing, dazzled by flashing lights. He was lying on his face and his legs were up the slope behind him, hands deep in dry soil. His head was crashingly painful but he was aware, and aware that it *was* pain. Aware that he, Willie Morton, was in pain. Had he fallen or hit his head? Some time passed as the pain and the lights diminished and anxiety and concern and awareness flooded into his brain switching on the lights and machinery inside. Mearns. Something solid. Mearns had whacked him. There was no light. It was all in his head. He instinctively knew then that Mearns had gone, was not near. He was lucky to be alive. He moved his right hand through the loose earth and with difficulty raised it to his temple and felt for the pain. It felt damp, maybe there was some blood? He moved the left hand and had to work it free from under the satchel strap. Where was he, exactly? Over an indetermined period he had half-rolled, twisted and pulled himself into a sitting position. He felt that he was on a steep slope. It was complete blackness except for the play of lights in his eye sockets. Closing his eyes helped. Well… he was alive. He fumbled for the satchel and pulled it round into his lap. Feeling inside it, his fingers enumerated the contents. He fumbled for the bottle of water and took a mouthful. Water had never tasted so good. Something you take for granted every day, fresh water. He carefully capped it and returned it to the bag. What he was sitting on was loose and dry; he felt under and around him. He had the sudden irrelevant picture of his father appraising it as good potting soil. He felt in his inside pocket for the Blackberry and as he brought it in front of him the screen came on from sleep mode, bright in the darkness, the screensaver of a coral reef, the water impossibly blue, dazzling him but casting shadows about him. He held it up and saw beneath him the spoil falling away, steeply downwards, far below. He felt a wave of panic. Christ! An air shaft of some kind that had partly collapsed. He carefully half-turned and saw that he was about twenty or thirty feet below the rectangular entrance of the main tunnel. He touched the damp area on his head and brought his fingers to his eyes. It was bleeding. He put the phone away and in darkness began to scrabble carefully upwards on all fours in the slipping soft soil.

The phone call from DS Hilary Brown of Lothian Police to the Contact Centre of Fife Police HQ had been received around 2.30 pm and passed on to the CID office on the top floor of the spacious and modern buildings at Chicago Place on the southern outskirts of Glenforgan. It was a small department of one DI, two DSs and four DCs, and all were out on enquiries. A civilian worker had glanced at the printed memo and stuck it on a nail on DS Grieve's desk, knowing he would see it when he came on shift at 5pm. It didn't look hugely urgent, and it might be downgraded and rerouted to the local uniforms, but she couldn't take such a decision.

When the shift changed, Grieve was keen to continue some work on another case and it wasn't until just after 6pm that he glanced again at it.

'Sheila?' he called over the top of the screen. 'This note from Lothian CID. When did it come in.'

Sheila looked up in annoyance. 'What does it say on the note?'

'Well, I know the time it arrived, but it has the name Menzies and the name Mearns...'

'Mearns is on the wanted list, Menzies is an alias,' Sheila shouted. 'Anything else you need to know? Why don't you just read it?'

'Thanks, Sheila,' he said, muttering under his breath, '*grumpy sod.*' He stood up. 'Who's free? Alasdair? Up for a wee jaunt?' The DC at the window desk looked round. 'Could do. This can wait. What's up, boss?'

'Check out this address at East Wemyss for a wanted man. Raymond Mearns.'

'The killer?'

'Hud on, son, we don't know that,' Grieve snorted as he heaved on his thick coat and buttoned it up. 'We'll just go take a wee nosy.'

The soil was so loose it was difficult to get traction and took him a long time to get back onto the beaten earth of the main tunnel and safety. He pulled himself onto it and sat, took out the bottle and sipped a mouthful of water. Even these simple actions were re-establishing his control over his predicament. He was going to get out of this. He remembered the SLR camera in the satchel. It had a small pop-up flash, but then he had the detachable flash unit too. That was a powerful thing. He drew it out, fumbled for the tiny metal pin that fired it and pressed. It was like a flash of lightning in the confined space of the tunnel, illuminating for a second the hard packed earth of the walls a long way back. Or was it red sandstone? The flashlight dazzled him, but it was better if he held it at full arms-length directed away from him and didn't look at it. He set off the way he had come, firing the light every few seconds. He was pretty sure it was the right way because he had been coming along and then was hit on his right temple by Mearns standing across from him in the entrance of the junction tunnel. The bastard had pushed him down the shaft, obviously expecting him to fall much further. But he hadn't and he was in good shape, all things considered.

Firing the flash unit every few seconds, he made good progress back to the bend and then the sharp turn upwards and came to a three-way junction. That was a problem. He didn't remember it. Which tunnel had he come from? He knelt down to examine the floor of each, no signs of footprints. It was not obvious. He had been so intent on pursuing Mearns that he had not paid much attention. He shone the flash unit into each one. They looked identical but he thought the middle one was probably right. He'd have to take a chance. He felt in his pocket and found a ten pence coin and placed it on the floor, then he set off in the middle tunnel which started to turn sharply, and he knew that was wrong, so he went back to the coin. He next tried the tunnel on his right and it was straight for nearly ten minutes but going downwards and then it ended; blocked by an impenetrable pile of rubble and soil. This one was wrong too. He hurried back to the coin. But the coin wasn't there! How could this be? But there was only one alternative tunnel facing him. He mustn't panic, he told himself, must be a simple explanation. It wasn't the right junction, that was clear. He shone the flash both ways and concluded this other entrance was just a side tunnel that he must have missed as he hurried along. He had been firing the flash every ten seconds or so, time enough to have completely missed the entrance. No need to panic. He continued on the main tunnel and a few minutes later to his immense relief came to the coin, which was very bright and obvious in the flashlight. So... it was the left one that was the correct one, was it? He took out a five pence coin and placed it at the start of the middle tunnel, that was the bending one. And placed a two-pence piece on the right-hand tunnel, that was the blocked one. So the left one must be correct. He hurried along it but it didn't go far, in less than a minute it was completely blocked ahead. *What?* Had Mearns blocked it? He couldn't have; too risky, he might have trapped himself. No, he had to go back. He stood at the junction looking at the three coins. Was he going mad? It must be the middle one, despite his earlier misgivings that it was wrong. He hurried along it, came to the bend and carried on round and saw that it was dropping down. It felt wrong but then he recognised the vast irregular outer chamber with its piles of spoil and rock and high up on one side a narrow doorway. That was it. He'd made it. He flashed the light against the walls. It was more of a cave really, he thought, feeling a wave of satisfaction come over him: he was going to get out. He scrambled up the sides past the pile of rocks he had hidden behind when he first saw Mearns moving into the tunnel. What doesn't kill you makes you stronger he thought as he clambered into the small square chamber and flashed the light around to see the narrow hole that would take him out into the world. But it wasn't obvious. Then he saw the deep marks of feet and recognised the earth slope he had scrambled down. He crawled up and saw in the light clear evidence that Mearns had made some efforts to plug the hole from outside on his way out, the bastard! He laughed aloud. 'Not going to stop me now!' He dislodged rocks and dodged stones falling in on him and then he could see sky, moonlight, stars, and hear the almighty roar of the sea and was scrabbling towards it. Yes!

CHAPTER TWENTY-EIGHT

Morton emerged from the coastal path onto Back Dykes, grateful for tarmac under his feet, and streetlights. He wasn't going to risk stumbling along the path in the dark after all he'd been through. Not with the chance that Mearns might still be about. The more he thought about it the more he was convinced that it had been a decoy. And he'd fallen for it. Mearns had been aware of him following and had deliberately led him into the mine. To kill him or to get him out of the way, but why? And why was Mearns here? Did he live here? Was this his hideaway? What did he have to hide? He was relieved to get back to the bright lights of the town, lights from houses, streetlights, light flaring from pub doorways. He looked down at himself. He was covered in mud! His knees were shiny with it. He certainly couldn't go into a pub, much as he craved a pint of beer and maybe a hot mince pie to go with it. Even Tam's in the *Albion Arms* in Duke Street! He got into Main Road and continued past the playground gates of the school. A man walking a dog looked at him: 'You awright, son?'

'Yes, I had a bit of a fall but I'm alright. Thank you for asking.'

'Bad cut on yer heid, son, better get it seen tae.'

'I will, thanks.'

His car was parked across the road: a comforting sight, representing safety, normality, his ordinary familiar life. He was strongly tempted to get in and drive away, but there was unfinished business. He stood at the top of MacDuff Lane and saw lights in the window of the cottage of the cheery old chap he had spoken to earlier in the day. He observed in the streetlight deep rutted mud tracks at the start of the lane. Those hadn't been there earlier. He looked down towards the Firth of Forth which he could hear but not see. A burst of accordion music inside the cottage hit him like a waft of homesickness. Saturday nights, Radio Scotland, the Doric tones of Robbie Shepherd, another world of an older Scottish identity. He walked in the gate under the trellis and knocked. The music stopped.

The door opened. The cheerful, white-bearded man stood on the doorstep.

'Hello,' Morton said, 'sorry to bother you…'

'It's satchel-man,' the old chap said. 'We spoke earlier.'

'We did.'

He looked Morton up and down. 'What have ye been doing, man? Ye're covered in sharn! And is that a cut on your heid?'

'It's a long story.'

'Well, I've got plenty of time for a long story. Ye'd better come in. I'm Graham, by the way.'

'My name is Willie Morton.'

Morton was ushered into a cosy living room that was warm and bright and tidy. 'I'll just move my squeezebox and ye'll get a seat. Wait a minute though – are ye as clarty at the back as ye are at the front? Hang on, don't move! I'll fetch a sheet before ye sit down.'

Morton sat on the sheet on the sofa and instantly felt sleepy as the tension and stress of the last few hours hit him.

'What you need, my friend, is a good dram. And I'll join you.'

The whisky was a good single malt. Morton sniffed it. 'Speyside?'

'Aha! Ye ken your whisky. It's an Ardmore twelve-year-auld.'

'Lovely.'

'You were asking after the cottage down bye, MacDuff?'

'I was.'

'I've a tale to tell about that. But your tale first.'

Morton told him about the wanted man, Raymond Mearns and the investigations into the potential rigging of the Glenforgan by-election. MacInnes was astonished.

'I can't believe it, this what you're telling me. I was there masel, at the count. I'm an activist. And this man Menzies…?'

'He may be involved in a murder too,' Morton told him. 'But you said you had a tale about the cottage?'

MacInnes put down his shot glass. 'Aye, well my friend, about six o'clock this large flatbed truck wi covered sides turns up and backs down the lane. Near took my gateposts with it. Backs all the way down to MacDuff cottage. I spoke to the fella. I mean it was pitch black. He said he was supposed to have been there earlier – he'd been delayed – and they were clearing out the cottage for new owners?'

'Right. And is he still there?'

'No, they're away. About half an hour ago.'

'He said *they* were clearing…?'

'There was only one of them that I could see, but he did say *they* were clearing it out. Anyway, I took the number just in case. And he was right about the timing, it took him – or them – less than an hour. I timed it.'

Morton laughed. 'You should be in Neighbourhood Watch.'

MacInnes snorted. 'I am Neighbourhood Watch!' He

sipped the whisky. 'But you haven't told me what happened to you. How the hell did ye get so clarty?'

'Well…' Morton began, 'I saw the man, Mearns, just down there on the path, just below the castle ruin. Walked right past me and of course I recognised him. Well, that's another story… but I followed him because I thought he was looking furtive. I thought he might lead to his hiding place. But I wasn't as clever as I thought. He'd made me – knew I was following – and was decoying me away.'

MacInnes sat up. 'Hold on. Decoying you? Decoying you away from the cottage? Ah… wait a minute.'

'Of course. And the man arrives with the truck. You said six pm? So that was it. That was the idea. They were loading the truck, putting the… I'd better phone the polis.'

Graham handed him the cordless landline.

'Any idea of the number?' Morton asked.

'Hang on, I'll get it for you.'

There was a loud knock on the door. 'Bloody hell, it's a busy day,' said Graham. 'Hold on, hold on.'

'Hello, I'm DS Grieve,' said the man on the doorstep. 'Fife CID.'

'Jings. That was bloody quick,' MacInnes said. 'We've no even phoned you yet! Come in.'

Morton was in the act of dialling the number on the keypad.

'Hold on, Willie, the polis are here.'

'Bloody hell! That has to be fastest response time in police history,' Morton joked.

The detective constable looked down. 'What happened to you?'

'It's a long story,' Morton said, 'but the important thing is, Raymond Mearns was here. He attacked me and he and his accomplice are making off in a truck with what I believe will turn out to be the original ballot papers from the Glenforgan by-election. They left here only about half an hour ago. And this good man' – he pointed to MacInnes – 'had the good sense to write down the truck registration plate number.'

Morton didn't know until much later how he had got back to his flat that night. He had related the whole story to DS Grieve, with backup already called and a police team with dogs and torches on the way. They had searched the coastal path for several miles in both directions while a forensic team set up and began to search MacDuff Cottage. But Morton was aware of none of this; his jovial host, Graham MacInnes had poured him a second dram and, in the warmth, and delayed shock of the moment, he had passed out after one sip. With the police using MacInnes' place as a temporary base for updates on tracking the truck and Raymond Mearns and his accomplice, and the comings and goings of the forensic team to MacDuff Cottage, he slept on the sofa until Rami and her husband, Dr Asim El-Jeffari, a hospital registrar, arrived around eleven pm. Asim had given him a check-over and cleaned and bandaged his head-wound although he was still comatose. They loaded him into their car and drove back down the A92, across the Forth Bridge, to his flat in Shandon Place. Morton was groggy by the time they arrived there and put him into his own bed. Rami and Asim spent the next few hours on the sofa in the living room, waiting to do checks on his vision and competency when Morton finally awoke, Asim being concerned about concussion.

It was possibly the smell of bacon that awoke him suddenly just after eight am. He sat up, gasping, imagining there was a fire.

'Morning Willie,' Rami said, looking down at him.

He blinked. 'What are you doing here?'

Dr El-Jeffari appeared behind her, a tall, slim man with a chin beard and worried eyes behind steel spectacles. 'This is my partner, Asim,' she said. 'Do you not remember us bringing you home?'

'Bringing me home?'

'From East Wemyss? From Mr MacInnes' cottage?'

Morton tried to get out of bed but felt weak. There was a pain on the right side of his head. He felt upwards and touched the bandage. He looked at them wildly. 'East Wemyss…? What are you talking about?'

'This is what I was worried about,' Asim said, looking at Rami. 'He should have been taken to hospital last night as I said.'

'Hospital?' Morton said. 'Is there a fire?'

'Aw jeez! The bacon…'

Over the next two or three days, Willie Morton regained his strength and his recall of the events at East Wemyss. On the Thursday he felt well enough to go for a walk. He dressed warmly and put on his coat and scarf. It was a glorious if cold late January day as he walked, the sky wide and open and blue, the brittle sun with no warmth in it, shining, the still bare boughs and branches in Bruntsfield Links and the Meadows. He was feeling pleased with himself, grateful that his adventure, or misadventure, had not resulted in lasting injury, or worse. Rami had been phoning regularly to keep him updated. The police had failed to find Mearns and his accomplice or the flatbed truck and its cargo. There had been an early ANPR hit on the Kincardine Bridge but then it had apparently disappeared. The helicopter had searched for more than an hour after that, north and south of the bridge and all possible routes, initially using thermal imaging cameras, but due to the cost and lack of any further ANPR indications, had been stood down. The FAI on Neil Shankwell was due in a few days and the *Standard* would send someone else if he didn't feel up to going. Although it was still winter there was already a spring feeling in the air. Snowdrops peeked between half-buried roots of the chestnuts in Harrison Park and on the footpath along the Union canal. He was out of condition, a bit weak but full of resolutions to recommence his early morning runs to the Galleon sports centre.

CHAPTER TWENTY-NINE

It was like the return of the prodigal when he walked into the press room the next day. Absence makes the heart grow fonder, even though it had only been three days. Leadbetter came out of his office to look at the bandage on his head. Rami and other hacks left their desks and came over.

'No, I'm fine,' he heard himself saying. 'A little weak still, but...'

'Grand tae see ye back, Wullie,' Leadbetter gruffed. 'Back intae harness, yes?'

Morton laughed. 'I need to reclaim my story. See if there's anything more to add to it.'

Rami had put the last few day's issues of the *Standard* on the spare desk next to hers. 'I'm phoning DI Maxfield shortly, for an update,' she told him. 'And Holyrood... I think there's a statement coming out from Salmond. So we're still busy.'

'Nothing more on Mearns?' he said, sitting at the desk, leafing through the papers. 'He must be somewhere.'

'He must have been tipped off,' Rami said. 'That's obvious. I mean, look, they avoided the Forth Road Bridge and went by Kincardine, an extra thirty-five miles out of the way, I mean, assuming they were heading south. Why? Maybe they thought there were no cameras there? But having made that odd diversion, within a short space of time of the ANPR hit, they go to ground. Either they are still in that area, and that was their destination, or they had made arrangements of some kind, to come off the road and hide – a secure place – because they were aware of the search and the helicopter. What was in the truck, do you think? Was it the original set of ballot papers?'

'I think so,' Morton nodded. 'Yes. According to Mr Mac-Innes, the three white vans turned up in the lane on the night of the by-election. He saw them leaving when he got home from the count in Glenforgan, around three am. He was pretty sure they were dumping their loads at the cottage but when he went to look the next day, there was no sign of anything in the cottage, which is derelict, so it must have been put inside the concrete shed there, which has a locked aluminium door. So these must be the original set, the actual voting papers used at the by-election. The set they delivered to the count that night were the fakes, and that was what they were incinerating in Renfrew. Bit of a sloppy operation really. They should have taken them well away, even maybe to Renfrew and then brought the fake set there later when they removed them from the council offices, but they must have had a reason not to do that at the time.'

'MacDuff Cottage, right by the busy coastal path, bit of a strange location for hiding the papers?' Rami conjectured, frowning. 'I mean it doesn't seem that secure.'

'Maybe it was to be only temporary – and on the map it looks ideal, very private – they weren't to know there was a nosy neighbour. I get the impression that Mearns turning up at the count was a last-minute idea; he wanted to be there to see his conspiracy wasn't rumbled. So he would need a local address to get onto the Labour list of counting agents, and pulled a few strings to get one of the spare spaces. Ian Brown told me parties can have as many counting agents as they want, and he was able to get onto the list somehow. He probably had the connivance or the help of Neil Shankwell. That's what we don't know. What was Shankwell's role? He must have been heavily involved in this kind of scam.'

Rami tentatively fingered the beads in her hair. 'We'll put this to the CID when they arrive. The FAI is on Tuesday by the way. We have to try to bring it all together, assemble the network and work out how everybody fitted into it: Barr, Mearns, Shankwell, the think tank, maybe Melville, and others. There are bound to be others, I mean more than the three van drivers and the truck driver at East Wemyss.'

'Mearns has a lot of connections,' Morton said grimly. 'This is not just one random actor. There's a lot of people behind it, a big organisation with a strong back-up service.'

'Yeah, must be.' Rami was smiling at him. 'Willie, why don't you want the story about the cave and tunnels to be put out? I think you should. Because that is clearly assault, perhaps even attempted murder. That is something they can charge him with, when they catch him. And it's a good story.'

'We'd never make that stick. No witnesses… anyway. I have my own reasons.'

'What are they?'

Morton cleared his throat. 'Well,' he began… 'I was stupid. I should have known Mearns was aware of me. Instead, I let him lead me away from the cottage on a complete decoy. If I had just waited and watched, I would have seen his accomplice, would have been in a prime position to see what they were doing. And caught them in the act. Instead, I was an idiot. That's why I don't want it in the story. The police know about it of course, so if he is arrested, he will be charged.'

'I see,' Rami said. 'Well, it's your call. Must have been a truly terrifying experience. Claustrophobic.'

'Yes. I suppose I might have rolled all the way down the airshaft, god knows how far down I might have gone. I've seen old drawings of the mines there, some tunnels are a thousand metres down, you know? It's like a Swiss cheese and most of it is under the sea. Anyway, talking about loose ends? Any word on Melville?'

'No trace of him at Hutcheson's. Under Melville or Munro. He spun you a yarn, Willie.'

'I'm surprised. He seemed the type, I mean private school.'

'Takes one to know one, I suppose,' Rami suggested with a laugh.

Morton grinned ruefully. 'True. And the think tank?'

'This Island Nation simply denied all knowledge of the letter. Said it was a "deep fake" and claimed not to know Melville or Mearns. The office in Duke Street, Glasgow, was originally leased to the Labour Party but since then, it has been leased on a short-term basis to the NBP. It's listed for demolition in the spring.'

Morton sighed. 'Okay, so despite the stories, these... all we have is circumstantial. And my bump on the head.'

Rami ran her chunky rings through the beads in her braids, making a tinkling noise and looked at him incredulously. 'And two bodies!'

'Maybe the police have got something from the forensics?' Morton ruminated. 'We need some solid proof that anything happened here.'

Morton had been feeling guilty about the way he had left things with Ailsa McKinnon. It had been a rather awkward journey to the event at North Queensferry and he hadn't been able to speak privately as Rami was there too. He texted her. He wasn't sure what she was thinking, or whether she was aware of the trouble he'd had with Mearns or seen the stories in the *Standard*. Several hours later, he had a brief reply from her. Not exactly enthusiastic but he felt it was the right thing to do. He'd asked her out in the first place, after all.

He pulled on his raincoat at half-past three and walked out into the early-dark wintry evening. Wreaths of freezing fog swirled around the streetlights and waited around corners like dead man's breath. He marched along the wet pavements of South Bridge and threaded through the mass of pedestrians on Princes Street into St Andrew's Street and down the hill to the Scottish National Portrait Gallery. Everything was sombre, soggy, nacreous – like being inside a Rembrandt canvas. He was glad to get inside the familiar neo-Gothic building, through the entrance on Queen Street guarded by Wallace and Robert Bruce, reflecting wryly that all the Scots were here, 'baith big and sma, that e'er the braith o life did draw' as Hugh MacDiarmid had it. He moved through to Café Portrait and spotted Ailsa with her back to him sitting on her own at one of the square pine tables under the large arched glass window looking out at the night sky and the lights. It moved him, seeing her there, solitary, looking isolated, vulnerable. He was confused, didn't know what he wanted from the meeting, to apologise to her or to ask her out again or for her to forgive him. Mainly, he didn't want to hurt her feelings.

She turned, hearing him approach.

'Ailsa, hi.'

'Hello again.'

'What can I get you?'

'I've a hot chocolate coming, wasn't sure whether to have a cake.'

'Go on. There's a cherry and vanilla thing and a wonderful caramel and pistachio…'

'Okay, get both and we can share.'

When he was sitting down, he looked around. 'While since I'd been in here. It's impressive, isn't it? I'd forgotten.'

'Yes,' Ailsa said, 'but still not nearly enough women. Of eight hundred and fifty portraits in here, nearly all of them are men.'

'Well, but that's getting better, isn't it? You can't change history overnight.'

Ailsa grinned. 'Is that a bit of sarcasm I hear?'

'Me? No. Wouldn't dare. Your great hero is here of course. There's a couple of pictures of him. I suppose you've been up to see?'

'Naw. I knew there would be. But this place closes at five, so no time today.'

'How are things going?'

'All hands on deck. I think we're on for a landslide.'

'Really?' He frowned. 'In Scotland, maybe…'

'Willie, even in England people are seeing Cameron for what he is, a pink, shiny upper-class twit.'

'But he's the new Blair, Ailsa. He's consciously copied Blair's style. You might well win every single seat up here, but it'll not help keep Brown at number ten because down there the Tories will sweep you away.'

Morton realised from the look on her face that he'd gone too far. Politics was between them. She cared too much about it to be able to take any dig against Labour. Curiously, that partisanship, that feisty campaigning spirit was what had first attracted him to her. But he was much more laid back on the subject. He was a journalist. He had his personal views, was generally on the left and hoped Scots would eventually see the benefits of independence but until that happened, there was no point in wrecking your life or cutting people off because of their views. And he was most strongly drawn to the concept of finding out the truth of everything, of what was really going on. That was what really motivated him. He wasn't willing to keep schtum and suppress the truth for the sake of being a member of one tribe or another, but she was and ever would be. The thought saddened him.

'So, what have you been up to?' she finally asked, stirring the thick layer of melting marshmallows on the hot chocolate. 'Did you find Raymond Mearns?'

'You obviously don't read the *Standard*.'

'No, Willie, nothing personal, but I don't. I saw in the *Record* that Darren Barr was dead, suicide they think, alcoholic poisoning.'

'Well, they did that story on Tuesday. We did it on Monday and we don't think it was suicide. I tracked Mearns down to a cottage in East Wemyss, but he got away. Possibly with a truck load of ballot papers from the Glenforgan by-election. Police are looking for him.'

Ailsa squinted at him. 'You really, really, think he rigged the by-election?'

'I can't prove it.'

'Labour HQ have strongly denied that he was ever a member of the party. That was in the *Record*. Was that in the *Standard* too?'

'Yes,' he deflected her rising but controlled anger with a smile. 'Rami did mention that in her piece. I was in my bed. Mearns walloped me over the head.' He fingered the faint bruise at the temple. 'Not sure if you can see the…'

She peered at his head. 'There's a little mark. Did you have a fight or something?'

'It's a long story.'

'Well,' she said, 'I hope the police arrest him and get to the bottom of it. But I'm sure it's nothing to do with us, nor is the death of Neil Shankwell, though the media love to put these things together and claim it was Gordon that did it!'

'No-one's saying that, Ailsa, really! Anyway, I'm going to be at the FAI for Shankwell.' He cut the cherry and vanilla slice neatly in two and passed half over onto her plate. 'In fact, I believe Mearns is part of a network or organisation that does this kind of thing. I don't think it's the work of a political party.'

'Well, thank goodness for that. Anyway, I need to get home soon, there's a campaign meeting tonight.'

'Oh right. Brownies night?' he said, but the joke fell flat. Not a flicker of a smile.

'The place closes soon anyway.' She glanced up at the clock. 'It's four-thirty, last orders.'

'Nice cake, that caramel and pistachio,' he said, trying to change the subject. 'Think I preferred it to the other one. Less gooey. I'm not really a cake person. Look, I just thought we should meet up so that I could explain...'

She put her hand on his wrist. 'Willie, there's really no need. I like you but... for me, my work comes first. If ever you need an opinion from the Labour side, you can always text me, or phone me. You know where I am.'

'Okay, well, thanks.'

'Now, I'll have to dash. Speak to you soon.' She stood up, pulled on her coat and was off with a little sidelong wave, leaving him there with half a cherry and vanilla slice and mixed feelings of relief and regret.

CHAPTER THIRTY

On the Monday, the day before the Fatal Accident Inquiry, Morton discussed with Rami and Hugh Leadbetter possible storylines. He was going to attend the event, at Kirkcaldy Sheriff Court but didn't expect much to come from it other than confirmation of death from natural causes, due perhaps to stress, or poor lifestyle or congenital issues, and that nothing could have been done to prevent it. There was a very outside chance of the forensic investigation turning up anything suspicious.

'Certainly, he looked like pretty stressed and angry to me,' Morton reminded them, grinning. 'Least I'm not being accused of doing him in.'

'There is that, Willie,' Rami said. 'Meanwhile I've been thinking over the whole thing again looking for loose ends. Remember your Mr Ptarmigan, the original informant, in Glasgow?'

'How could I forget?'

'I can't understand why he would go to the bother of giving you the information and then... walk away. What was his angle? What did he do it for? And why you? Did he impart his theories to other hacks? And where is he now?'

'I've thought and thought about it, Rami. Assuming we are right and the by-election was rigged and Mearns did it on behalf of an organisation or network presently unknown, then anyone in that organisation could be the snitch and that could be hundreds of people. We can rule out Mearns, Barr, Shankwell and the three van drivers. Mearns is the prime instigator. Barr knew *something* and he was there on the night and I feel he was a potential informant – if there was money in it for him – but maybe he didn't know the method or details of the election rigging. The van drivers were too involved to be snitches. That leaves Shankwell. And I've been thinking about Shankwell. Not about his death, exactly, though god knows that's suspicious. But look at the facts. A year after he moved to Glenforgan Cleansing Department and just weeks after the discovery of the missing ballot papers, he's dead.'

Leadbetter looked up from his screen. 'Moved?'

'Aye, he transferred from being Deputy Director of Cleansing & Waste at Renfrew Council to a similar post at Glenforgan.'

'Did you tell me this already?'

'Yup. We did.'

'Bit a switch? Dealing with rubbish to dealing with voters? Two weeks before. And what date was that?'

'The by-election was 26th November, so he moved department in mid-November, not long after the writ was moved.'

'I hope the police are going to investigate Shankwell's link to the Renfrew Cleansing incinerator. That's a little too much of a coincidence.'

'Yes,' Rami said. 'Difficult to prove now though. Willie, remind me when did you get tapped up by this rare bird in Glasgow?'

Morton considered. 'Um, that was Monday 11th January. Two days before the breaking news of the ballot papers being lost, or missing.'

'And just two months after the by-election. And Shankwell died on Monday 18th.'

'Yes. Three days after speaking to me in his office.'

'Bloody hell, Willie! I'm surprised you've not been arrested yet!'

Morton grimaced. 'That's just not funny!'

The Fatal Accident Inquiry opened in Kirkcaldy Sheriff Court on Tuesday 2nd February with a statement from John Goodall, the withery dry-faced Sheriff presiding. that as there had been no criminal prosecutions and the police had determined that the death of Neil Shankwell was on balance likely to have been by natural causes, it was felt that a Preliminary Hearing was not needed. Goodall said that in the circumstances, an FAI itself may not have been required, but that due to 'various statements in the press' – a line wryly delivered with maximum uplift of his white profuse eyebrows – inferring a link with political controversy and a recent by-election, it was felt necessary to offer an opportunity to clear the air. He gave the impression that it was an irritant and a hindrance to good justice. Goodall added that statements had been requested from various groups as well as the family and the police and forensic specialists to address all possible concerns around the sudden death of Mr Shankwell.

Morton had arrived early by train and walked up from the station to join other media colleagues who sat at the back on the media bench. He squirmed in his seat, feeling himself on show, even though he was at the back of the room. It was to his newspaper stories that the Sheriff was alluding, and everyone knew it. From where he sat, he could see the backs of the heads of the family members four rows ahead. He could see various policemen, including DS Brown and others whom he took to be specialists of one sort or another. There was no sign of Ron Marshall or Alison Bridger the media officer from Glenforgan Council. The wooden bench was unyielding and quite soon he felt uncomfortable.

The proceedings began with tortuous and verbose statements by the police officer who was called to Shankwell's address ("I was perambulating in a clockwise direction in the neighbourhood of the deceased's accommodation in the vicinity of Balgonie View upon the day in question when I received a telegraphic communication from my superior officer...") after his non-appearance at work and after family members couldn't contact him on the telephone. Morton jotted down the details: Shankwell was found at the bottom of the stairs as if he had fallen from the first floor to the hallway. The paramedic who had attended the body concluded from various observations that he had suffered a massive fatal infarction either before or after he fell, around four hours before he was found. A police pathologist who performed the autopsy considered the heart attack the reason for the fall and thus the cause of death although the neck was broken in two places. The discussion went back and forth upon these issues for some time, with questions being put to the two medical specialists then Sheriff Goodall dryly announced a lunch break of one hour. Roger Bishop a freelancer for the *Sun*, sitting next to him, snorted. 'Nothing for me. Don't think I'll be back, Willie. I'll leave you to it. There's a double stabbing down the road at Dunfermline Sheriff Court. Juicier.'

Morton nodded. It was boring. As he stood and waited for family members to file past him on the way out, he saw someone he seemed to recognise. The face of a man he vaguely knew. Elderly, stooped, in a grey raincoat and gloves. It wasn't until he got outside onto the steps of the Court, that he remembered who it was. His informant in Glasgow. Mr Ptarmigan!

He pushed his way outside and saw the man moving away from him, in a huddle with several family members. He hurried over and clutched his sleeve.

'Excuse me. I need to talk to you.'

The man looked at him and paled. 'Ah… I wondered…but not here… Excuse me, Jean,' he said to the others, 'I'll see you back in the Court. I need to speak to this man.'

'Follow me,' he said quietly to Morton. 'But don't make it look like we're together.'

Morton stood with his back to the Court entrance. He didn't want to get drawn into conversation with anyone, and he'd noticed DS Brown heading his way. Watching from the corner of his eye the informant walking away across the square in the direction of the High Street and aware of DS Brown behind him he set off at a quick pace, behind the man who was now daundering along, slightly stooped, hands behind his back looking like a tourist peering in windows as he passed. It occurred to Morton he was trying to blend in, be inconspicuous, something that drew attention to him, rather than the reverse, which made him smile. Ptarmigan was not ideal spy-material. He tried to remember the conversation in Starbucks, on Sauchiehall Street, three weeks ago. It was an unexpected opportunity to get the chance to question him again and get actual provable information out of him, starting with his name. It was the opportunity to resolve the entire mystery. He was clearly a family member of the dead man.

The man in the raincoat had stopped outside a busy bakery, amid a lunchtime queue of customers, mostly schoolboys in uniform, and glanced back at Morton. He went between customers and disappeared from view. Morton momentarily felt a frisson of alarm, but he could see him standing beyond the people outside the bakery and understood. The man was going into the tiny café next door. He hurried to catch up. It was called Luigi's, a sort of sweetie shop that also sold ice cream. It was very small, the doorway with an old-fashioned metal bell that jangled when he went inside. The dim wood-panelled interior was filled to the ceiling with shelves of sweetie jars, the counter with every species of chocolate bar and the place smelled of confectionery, strong coffee and frying bacon. There were half a dozen wooden booths along one wall, each wide enough for one seat on each side, and a few rickety wooden chairs alongside. Ptarmigan was manoeuvring himself into the empty booth at the end, so he would be facing away from the door, in front of a plastic bead curtain leading to the kitchen. It was quaint or very old-fashioned. An elderly man with long wavy grey hair, who looked Italian – possibly Luigi himself, Morton thought – was standing behind the counter, smiling, serving some youths. There were two elderly couples and a pair of teenagers sitting facing each other in the booths. The place was tight, crammed in, surprisingly noisy. There was only one door, one way in and out, Morton saw with satisfaction as he folded himself into the seat in the booth, across the yellow formica-topped tabletop facing Ptarmigan, who looked nervous and had his elbows on the table, one hand covering his face.

'No-one saw you?' he asked softly.

Morton frowned. 'Of course not. Now, what do I call you? Up to now, you've been Mr Ptarmigan…'

The man looked at him in confusion. 'What?'

'You're a rare bird,' Morton prompted. 'Three weeks ago, you wouldn't give me your name.'

His informant looked horrified and whispered. 'Joseph… Joe…McLuckie!'

Morton took out his notebook and wrote it down, to the horror of McLuckie, who seemed terrified. 'Calm yourself,' Morton whispered. 'Relax. Nothing to worry about.'

'I actually meant the other one, the other bird…'

'Sorry?'

'The rare bird… capercaillie.'

'Oh, right. Well, they are rare.'

The waiter or café owner appeared, and Morton saw that he had a long white apron over his suit trousers, formally dressed in shirt, tie and woollen cardigan. He was thin, almost emaciated, and very old. His voice was whispery but friendly and as expected had traces of an Italian accent. He took their order, making small noises with his lips and disappeared behind the plastic bead curtain.

'We can talk,' Morton said, indicating the animated conversations going on in the café. 'No-one is listening. You are related to…?' He didn't want to say "the deceased" so he simply waved his fingers. 'How?'

'Uncle,' McLuckie said. 'His father was my brother.'

'Well, I'm sorry for your loss, but you gave me information about the…' he paused… 'the public event… and gave me two names but you didn't give me enough to do anything about it. Perhaps if you had given me more, who knows, things might have turned out differently.'

McLuckie spoke through his palm. 'But I couldn't say more. I shouldn't have said anything. I didn't know any more. All I know was that he had told me not to speak to anyone. I didn't. Not even to Edna, my wife.'

'Did you have regular contact with your nephew?'

'That's the thing. No. We didn't see each other, rarely more than once a year. He contacted me. He was worried.'

'When was this?'

'Early November last year. He phoned me at home. He was phoning from a call box.'

Morton frowned. 'A call box? Didn't think there were many of them still around.'

'Yes. He was in a garage or somewhere and they'd let him use their phone or something. I think he was getting his car fixed. You could hear noises, engines... he sounded really worried.'

'What did he say?'

'He was being put under pressure at work.'

Luigi emerged from the plastic bead curtain with their coffees and Morton's bacon roll.

'That was quick. Not eating anything, Joe?' Morton said. The waiter looked at him expectantly, but McLuckie shook his head. 'I'm fine,' he quavered.

'Biscotti, or a wee slice of cake,' the waiter coaxed. 'Goes awfy well with a coffee, no?'

McLuckie gave in. 'Okay, a piece of cake, thanks.'

The waiter smiled. 'Howabouta fly-cemetery?'

'Perfect, yes, one of those.'

'Plenty sugar. Is good for you.'

Morton watched the plastic beads swinging behind Luigi. He was sure it *was* Luigi in person. He smiled wryly. 'Fly cemetery. Is it only us Scots that call it that? Maybe in England it'd just be a fruit slice or a spiced currant traybake? Who knows. Where were we? Under pressure?'

'Didn't say who from. But they wanted him to move to a different department, to work on the elections. He was used to being in Cleansing, liked it. He'd been there a year, at Glenforgan I mean. Settled in well, he said. A good team, he said. That was the previous time I'd seen him. He was happy then. But he was being pressured to move. Forced. And forced to do things he didn't want to do… That was how he put it.'

'So what did you say?'

'What could I say? I asked questions but he didn't go into details. He said it was not safe to talk on his home phone or his mobile. That worried me. "What have you got into" I said. I wasn't very helpful I'm afraid, or sympathetic. We were just about to sit down and eat our tea.'

'And how did the name Roger Carnoway come into it? I'm assuming it did?'

'No. Not then. I phoned him at his work. We spoke one time more. I asked him who was pressuring him… he was very reluctant. He said from inside the government, that's what he said and he mentioned Carnoway. I thought he said Galloway at first.'

'You know who he is, don't you? I mean Lord Carnoway of Froy?'

'Neil did mention him then, the second time…'

The doorbell jangled and Morton looked over to see a tall, well-built man in a suit and dark coat coming in. He's a suave bugger, Morton thought, brutal looking. For certain he wasn't a shampoo salesman or a poodle manicurist. He was the military-type. He stood there for only a second or two as if coming in. But he didn't. He stopped and looked at the booths, seemed to see Morton and backed out of the door, as if he had made a mistake of some sort. Morton's spine was tingling, and all his alarm bells were ringing. There was no doubt in his mind that the man had been looking for him, or McLuckie, or both.

CHAPTER THIRTY-ONE

And what was even more sinister was that the man was waiting outside. Morton could see his faint silhouette through a stretched white lace screen that obscured the front window display and kept the sun off the sweets counter. He thought back to the faces attending the FAI. Had the man been there? He didn't think so. Then what was he doing here? Who had called him? He drained his coffee. He had to act calmly, didn't want to spook McLuckie. He waved Luigi over.

'Everything alright?'

'Is there a toilet? Men's room?'

Luigi nodded and pointed behind the plastic bead screen. Morton stood up and went through. There was a small stone-flagged corridor and two doors. The toilet was tiny. He looked in. Tried the other door. It led to the kitchen and to the outside. He saw a back green and bins at the rear of the tenement. Perfect. He reappeared in the bead screen, flipped out a ten-pound note and placed it on the table, put a finger to his lips and grasped McLuckie's shoulder. 'Come with me,' he hissed.

McLuckie didn't understand.

'Don't ask questions. Come on!' He pulled him out of the seat. We have to go.'

Luigi came forward. 'Whatsamatter?'

Morton pointed to the tenner. 'Look, thanks, man. We have to go.'

Then they were in the corridor, then on the backstep beside a row of steel bins. Morton found a way across fallen brickwork to the small patch of untidy grass to the rear of the tenement across the far side and found there was an open alleyway to the street. They went through it, Morton practically dragging McLuckie with him, and found themselves on a different street.

'What's this all about?' McLuckie was saying.

'Tell you later. Come on.'

They stood in a back lane in the shade of sandstone tenements, around the corner from the High Street but much less busy. He saw a Museum and down the hill, saw the railway line behind a fence. The station wasn't far away. But that would be the first place they'd look. McLuckie was out of breath, doubled-over, clutching his sides. 'You go on,' he said. 'I can't.'

'Don't be silly. I can't leave you.' But as he said this, he was thinking maybe that was a good idea. Split up. He spotted a bench in a little grass area behind the museum. 'Over here, there's a seat.'

It was quite unobtrusive, secured on two sides by walls and from the third by the building. There was a bush to their side that obscured them from the side street. He let McLuckie catch his breath. But now what? He found his Blackberry and rang Rami.

'How's it going at the FAI?' she asked.

'It isn't,' he told her tersely. 'I'm with Ptarmigan... we had to leave.' He briefly explained to her what had occurred.

'Are you sure? You think this is one of Mearns's gang?'

'Who knows. But it was just the look he gave me, you know. Spooked me completely. He could be after Joe... McLuckie, that's Ptarmigan's real name. Or me. He's probably still looking for me, or him.'

'Willie... best thing get the police. Or go back to the Sheriff Court. They can't do anything there.'

'DS Brown was at the FAI. I could ring her, get her advice. She knows what's been going on.'

'Have you got her number?'

'I think, wait a minute...' he fumbled in his coat. 'No, try wallet, ah here it is. I have it. I'll ring her. Call you back.

'Yes. ASAP. I need to know you're okay.'

DS Brown answered the phone on the second ring. He explained the circumstances. It sounded silly of course.

'A man...? Are you sure?'

Well, he wasn't certain, but... 'It's hard to explain,' he told her. 'I have previous experience in such things.'

'Well, where are you now?'

Morton hesitated. He had to trust her. 'Um, just at the Museum, I didn't get the street name, sorry.'

'Right, sit tight. I'll come by in the car.'

'The police are on their way,' he told McLuckie. 'We'll be safe now.'

'Is it you they're after? Or me? McLuckie quailed. 'What do they want. Neil is dead.'

Morton was thinking quickly about the coincidence of the man turning up at the FAI, which to all intents and purposes was going to conclude Shankwell's death was natural causes. If it was Mearn's gang, maybe they knew Shankwell had confided in his uncle. And they had probably learned that he, Morton, had been tipped off by an informant. Someone had put two and two together and realised that McLuckie and he would both be at the FAI: that it was their best chance of establishing if there was a link between Shankwell's uncle and him. What the man had seen in Luigi's was proof positive. McLuckie talking privately to Morton. But what did McLuckie really know? That Shankwell had been under pressure but hadn't been told from who. But then Mearns' gang wouldn't know that. They would assume the worst: that McLuckie knew *everything* and that now he, Morton, did too.

'You sit tight,' he told McLuckie. 'I'll keep an eye on the street. Don't move till I come back.'

McLuckie's craven look reassured Morton he would be too terrified to come out. He was way beyond his comfort zone. Morton wondered how old he was, maybe early seventies? He went to the front of the museum and saw a few cars moving in the street. It was quiet. A silver Toyota was pulling up. He recognised DS Brown. But she was on her own. No backup. He felt misgivings. Brown parked the car beside him at the pavement opposite the front entrance. There was no-one in the street, somewhere in the distance, a siren, ambulance probably.

Brown opened the car door and gestured to him. She was smiling. Morton was reassured. He made a sign and returned to fetch McLuckie.

'Come on, our transport awaits.'

They walked round the side of the building, him in front, McLuckie behind. And then everything happened very fast. Brown moved towards them, her face grimacing, crouching down. McLuckie shrieked and fell forward. Morton dived under the front fender of the Toyota. The shooter was across the street. The man in the navy-blue coat. Something metal spanked off the fender inches from his face. The man was using a silenced pistol. Brown was crawling towards him. McLuckie was dead, a black hole in the centre of his forehead. Execution, Morton thought. He kept down. A bullet took out the windscreen and a shower of fabulous glass jewellery came over him. DS Brown pulled him down and got around him.

He heard her gasp then a police siren became loud, and he heard shouts and running boots. He had blood on his hands and saw it was coming from Brown. Her jacket was stained. 'Jesus! Are you…?'

A policeman leaned in on him. He was dressed entirely in black, a Kevlar helmet and carried a matt black assault rifle. 'You alright, sir? DS Brown, let's see… flesh wound. I'll get someone… Over here! Medic!'

The next few minutes seemed interminable. A crowd of ghouls had gathered, oohing and aahing. Comings and goings of police, armed police, medics, paramedics. DS Brown was going to be okay. She was in shock, sitting up against the Toyota, a bullet wound in her right arm.

'She saved me,' Morton heard himself saying. 'Who was that man?'

'We'll get him,' someone said.

'Who is this man?' said the officer in charge, bending over McLuckie. Morton felt sick, retched a few times. Finally, he was able to get words out: 'Joseph McLuckie. Neil Shankwell's uncle. His family are here, at the Sheriff Court… the FAI.'

'He's out of it I'm afraid,' said the man in the Kevlar helmet. 'What relationship is he to you?'

'None, at least, it's a long story. DI Maxfield knows…'

'Okay. We'll speak to him.'

He was examined in the ambulance, but he was uninjured except that a tiny fragment of glass had cut the back of his hand. The paramedic stuck an Elastoplast on it. He felt a fraud coming out of the ambulance and seeing poor Joseph McLuckie being loaded onto a stretcher. Suddenly he came to and visualised a story headline: He took out his Blackberry and phoned Rami and told her what had happened.

'She'll be alright? I was so worried.'

'She will. Look,' he said, 'write this down: *Kirkcaldy Shooting Linked to Shankwell FAI*. Yeah? I'll do an outline on the train. I don't know what happened at the FAI after lunch.'

'I do, Willie. It's been postponed. The police worked out the connection with the shooting. Can you believe? In broad daylight?'

'I don't think they'll get that man,' Morton said. 'He looked professional.'

'What if they try again?'

'Jeez, Rami, don't go there. I'll worry about that tonight.'

CHAPTER THIRTY-TWO

A few days later, I was feeling much better, less anxious. I'd been assured by the police that my safety was their concern and that there was no chance of the shooter trying again, although we're all living on borrowed time. Apparently, he had walked about Kirkcaldy and there wasn't a single CCTV picture of him! The *Standard* ran a comprehensive piece based on what we knew so far or could conjecture. It was syndicated, copied or stolen by every newspaper in the land, and some international titles too. Hugh Leadbetter was over the moon, even 'Bow-tie' Bailey was seen to smile though it could have been indigestion. I did several interviews on radio and local TV, a boost to my income, and perhaps rashly decided to abandon the idea of subbing for the moment. I was almost back to myself. On the Friday, I left the team at South Bridge where business had got back to normal, at five pm., and drifted down the High Street. An early evening sea mist had descended and swirled about the streets and wynds and the cobbles were moist, though the February rain was fine, imperceptible. I was thinking about Ailsa; I'd not spoken to her since our rendezvous at the SNPG and hoped there were no hard feelings. I knew she was heavily involved in candidate selection and pre-election campaigning work though there was no confirmation of a date when Brown and Cameron would lock heads and ruck for the keys of the kingdom. I passed Deacon Brodie's on the way and thought about having a pint but carried on and waited to cross to at the junction with George IV Street but before I knew what I was doing, I had recrossed the High Street and was at the top of the Vault Steps and descending those wet stone treads in that narrow chasm in the monochrome light. The pub has two grimy windows of opaque glass at hip height as you descend, and then the distinctly unpretentious swinging wooden door. It is possibly the scruffiest bar in Edinburgh. The place was uncharacteristically empty inside, the quiet hour between late afternoon and early evening, but who should I find sitting there... Archie MacDonald, leaning against the wall reading the *Standard*.

'Caught you! And reading that dreadful rag?'

Archie looked up and laughed. 'First offence, honest! Didn't buy it of course. Pinched it from the seat.'

'That's what we like to hear. Beg, steal or borrow... pay for it only if you have to.'

'Reading all about yourself, actually, old chap. Been in the wars again. But nae deid, as I see.' He shook his head solemnly.

'I'll get a pint. Refill?'

'Ah, um, perhaps. Yes, well, okay, go for it.'

Morton laughed. 'The difficult negotiation with oneself?'

'Something like that. Hard day of litigation. Can barely think straight.'

When Morton sat down opposite, he took a sip. 'So, in the courts today?'

'As ever. Today, morning session only. Meetings after lunch.'

'This is the second time I've seen you here in just over a month. Of all the pubs... this... well.'

Archie nodded solemnly. 'As previously explained, it is near to the courts. None of the advocates would dream of being seen in such a lowdown miscreant's shebeen. A good hiding place. So, Willie, you've earned yourself another bang on the heid if not a bullet in the brain? At least in my profession that doesn't happen. Or not often.'

'That's about it. A *bang on the heid and nane the wiser, MacDonald*!'

'Are you pursuing an action? Taking legal recourse?'

'Well, how? You don't know the half of it, Archie.'

'No.' He gestured to the folded paper. 'Facts are a bit scarce. Newspapers tend to avoid them these days. It did say the first assault occurred in East Wemyss. The aforementioned bang on the heid. And then the attempted assassination in Kirkcaldy – of all places. Fairly seeing the world, and at little expense, are you not?'

'Actually, the first took place inside a coal mine.'

'Good grief. Coal mine? There are still coal mines?

'Long since closed-down. I was enticed inside.'

MacDonald gave a short abrupt knowing laugh. 'One can easily see how that might happen. Coal mines, especially disused ones must be very enticing. Especially if they can advertise the possibility of a free bang on the heid once inside!'

'Very funny, Archie. Anyway, how is Halbron, Finlay & MacDonald.'

'Dead, nearly dead and brain-dead, in that order.'

'A strange kind of firm?'

'Suits many of the clients for they too, are...'

'...dead, nearly dead and brain dead?'

'Absolutely. We do have some clients from the other side, ie not Legal Aid.'

'And a lot of your work is on behalf of the deceased.'

'Death is one of our main employers.'

'Joking apart, Archie, it's been a difficult month. Although there are these people still out there – and I never got to the bottom of the involvement of Lord Carnoway...'

'Ooh, avoid… I seem to recall giving you a warning on that score. Seriously, if you value your health, your sanity…'

'Well, I had no engagement with him. The name was merely mentioned by one man to another who was then shot.'

'Yes, that happens. I know we are joking, Willie, but I cannot stress enough…'

'I hear you. Anyway, the shooter has successfully fled the scene, Mearns disappeared into the woodwork, Melville seems never to have existed at all, even though I had dinner with him in a hotel, and the whole issue of the rigging of a by-election is a completely unproven myth though it obviously occurred. There's no proof, no evidence. Photographs of Barr and Mearns at the count, the photographs I took of them destroying van loads of something that looked like – could have been – ballot papers are not detailed enough. Barr might have committed suicide, Shankwell might have had a perfectly natural heart attack, or it might have been caused by pressure and harassment. The only witness to any theory of that sort is now dead, poor Joseph McLuckie. The only actual proof we have is the bump on the head I got, the bullet Sergeant Brown stopped with her arm, that might have gone into my head. Then I shouldn't have been in the mine anyway. It was supposed to have been securely sealed-off. Misadventure, the police called it. I didn't think they believed me at all, but they did go there – give them their due – and searched and they gave me back my seventeen pence.'

MacDonald did a double take. 'The police gave you back your seventeen pence? Was that an intended bribe? If so, in my opinion it falls rather short of the normal fee scale…'

'Huh, no. It's a long story. When I was trying to find my way out of those ghastly tunnels, I put coins down at each entrance so that I didn't take a wrong turning. It did work. Obviously, or I wouldn't be here now.'

'And your original informant was shot dead?'

'Poor innocent, terrified Joseph McLuckie or Mr Ptarmigan as I like to call him. If he had had real information, he could have sent it to me, emailed, phoned, handed it to the police. Instead, he gave me partial information anonymously – and paid the price. It made them think he knew more than he did – actually, he knew very little.'

'And you've no idea who the shooter was or where this Mearns character is?'

'None. I've got nothing at all. It is possible there will be forensics at Barr's house or at East Wemyss that links to Mearns, but for now the story is going nowhere. Although Shankwell's role looks very suspicious and his death must be, I mean… we've got nothing. It's inconclusive. Unprovable. Like that legal verdict you have, not proven.'

'"That bastard verdict," as Walter Scott called it,' Archie smirked. 'There are moves afoot to remove it from statute. Not before time, Willie, pleases no-one. People think the accused gets away with it and the accused can't entirely establish his innocence.'

'It's a verdict for the times, perhaps. Nothing is as it seems. We live in a fog of ambivalence, ambiguity. People look like patriots but turn out to be traitors, everyone's loyalties are suspect. Scotland is divided between Brown and Salmond, and England wants Cameron.'

MacDonald pursed his lips. 'Very fine summing up, if I may say.'

'Brown is doomed, I believe, Archie. Doomed like a musk ox caught in the yellow eyes of the wolf pack moving in the snow around him.'

'That's very poetic, Willie.'

'Ready to be culled. The law of the wild.'

'That's democracy Willie,' MacDonald said. 'though it doesn't usually involve natural selection or guns. Or at least not yet.'

'Except in my world,' Morton added grimly looking into the dregs of his pint. 'Time for another?'

MORE WILLIE MORTON INVESTIGATIONS

Deadly Secrecy

Willie Morton investigates the death of anti-nuclear activist Angus McBain in the Highlands and begins to suspect he was murdered to stop him revealing what he knew. Is the British Government implicated in the murder of McBain and the movement of illegal radioactive convoys heading for Dounreay?

Scotched Nation

Five months after Scotland's Independence Referendum, Willie Morton's uncanny resemblance to a man let off a drink driving charge on Home Office orders allows him to get inside a secret Whitehall plot by members of MI5, politicians and senior civil servants. But just how far will they go to frustrate democracy?

Oblivion's Ghost

Morton tries to locate Luke Sangster, a hacker on the run from Britain's secret police and is drawn to Assynt, Glasgow and across the North Sea to Denmark and Sweden. But Sangster is not what he seems, and Morton suspects he's being entangled in an entrapment exercise to spread suspicion and distrust amongst the independence movement.

Sovereign Cause

Morton unravels a thirty-year old conspiracy over the 1985 death of Treasury mandarin Matthew McConnacher and the Cameron government's strange reluctance to declassify his report which claimed an independent Scotland would be viable. It leads him to Barcelona where his intern Ysabet Santanac has been arrested as deadly forces unleashed by London and Madrid converge to bury an inconvenient truth.

COMING SOON... *Inconvenient Truth*

All paperbacks £9.99 / Kindle eBooks £1.99

Scotched Nation *also Audible Audiobook*
(Narrated by David Sillars) £12.99

Milton Keynes UK
Ingram Content Group UK Ltd.
UKHW010820220424
441551UK00005B/367